NUMBERS GAME

to Athena -
keep fighting!
Rebecca Rode

Printed in the United States of America

First Printing, 2015

ISBN 978-0-9961532-0-1

Diamond Patch Press

www.AuthorRebeccaRode.com

NUMBERS GAME

Rebecca Rode

Also by Rebecca Rode

How to Have Peace When You're Falling to Pieces

For my husband, Francis, who will always be my Number One;
and for my daughter, whose beauty and spirit transcends numbers altogether.

PART ONE

TREENA

The biggest event of my life was minutes away—thirty-nine minutes, to be exact—and my two best friends couldn't stop fighting.

Dresden rode his custom-made, sleek, silver bicycle to my left. His clean white uniform was tailored tightly to his firm shoulders, and he moved with a certain ease, a confidence that seemed to draw the eyes of every student around us. Fates, he was beautiful. I still couldn't believe he'd chosen me for his girlfriend. He glanced over his shoulder at me. "Come on, Treena. Pick up the pace."

Tali, pedaling her dull black bike to my right, snickered. "Such a gentleman."

We usually headed for work at the broadcasting center after school, but that was over now. Today the yellow lanes were clogged with Level Three graduates, all headed in the same direction—the city center. We would enter as kids and emerge officially Rated adults. My stomach twisted at the thought. I'd looked forward to this my entire life, and now that it was here I just wanted to be left alone. I checked my techband again. Thirty-eight minutes.

A wide-set guy with a black bike pedaled hard in front of me, taking up half the lane by himself. Traffic was especially bad today, but only in the yellow lane where we traveled. The green lanes were clear as could be.

"Look at that line," Dresden said with a chuckle. "It's disgusting how desperate people get." I followed his gaze to the Appearance Sector. A long line of desperate, last-minute customers in purple watched us pass with closed expressions. Advertisements for plastic surgery—"Get Your Rating-Preferred Nose Here!"—vision correction, advanced-formula nutrition pills, and eye tattoos battled for attention on the storefronts and ad boards above their heads. Tomorrow was Rating Day for them. As graduates, we got our numbers a day before everyone else. Lucky us.

The traffic light flashed, and we dragged to a stop. Dresden loved this section of town, where the skyscrapers loomed high above us. The tallest one, a shiny copper edifice, stood at the corner to my right. I pointedly ignored it.

Dres shaded his eyes with one hand. "It doesn't look eighty-two floors high from here, does it?"

"I'm sure it looks higher from the top," Tali said.

It did, but I didn't say so. That meant admitting I'd been up there. The tower housed the Olympus Credit Office, but it was better known for what happened there the night of Rating Day each year. The building's guards would conveniently disappear, and some of the newest reds and yellows—the year's "loser crop," as Dresden called them—would climb the stairs to the top and jump. The morning road-cleaning crew swept up their broken bodies along with the dirt and trash.

The noblest decision they could have made, my stepdad often said.

"Some of the guys are coming to watch tonight," Dresden said. "There were six jumpers last year and four the year before that. Maybe tonight there will be even more."

I fought a sudden nausea and looked away. The light stopped blinking, and Dresden pushed off. He was halfway through the intersection before I managed to follow.

"I don't get why you like him," Tali said next to me. "Are you okay, Treen? You look pale."

"I'm fine. Give Dresden a break, Tali. He's a good guy. There's a lot more to him than you think."

"There better be." She gave a loud sigh as we caught up to Dresden. "Fates, I can't wait for the ceremony to be over. Then everyone will be halfway normal again, and we can just live our lives in peace for another year."

"And that is exactly your problem," Dresden said, glancing at us. "You don't live *in spite* of your number but *because* of it. Ratings are the whole point. At least for those of us living in reality. Peak was a genius when he came up with the system."

Tali rolled her eyes. "That's stupid. The numbers shape themselves to fit us, not the other way around. Ratings are supposed to make order of chaos, make it easier to live our lives. Not *become* our lives."

"Taliyah," I warned. After my big speech about Dresden's qualities, she had to bring up the one subject he wouldn't back down on.

"You don't get it," Dresden said. "And you never will. It's people like you who become yellows and reds. Treena, I can't believe you call her your friend. I hope associating with her didn't pull your score down."

"If you dorks don't stop fighting," I said, "I'm throwing you both off the tower."

Tali chuckled and leaned toward me. "Don't worry about him, Treen. He doesn't often surround himself with us lesser folk. When it comes to himself or others, he'll always choose himself." Her voice rose as if to make sure he could hear. "In fact, if you were lying in the street dying, he wouldn't give you a second thought. Unless you were a green, of course. Not even that—no, you'd have to be a higher green, and he'd make sure everyone was watching before he helped."

"Taliyah," I broke in, my voice flat. "That's enough."

Her mouth snapped closed, but her cheeks flushed pink. Dresden glared at his bike handles, his knuckles white. For him to reply would only add truth to her words. Tali would just have to get used to this. Dresden had been in my life for months now, and if we scored within a hundred points of each other, he would be a major part of it. Forever. She'd have to keep her angry rants to herself.

"Taking the shortcut," Tali grumbled as we approached Harbor Road. "See you there."

"Wait!" I called after her and gave Dresden an apologetic look. "Let's go with her. It'll be faster."

He exhaled hard, but his desire to get there quickly must have overridden his disdain for my friend, because he turned to follow. I felt like a mother juggling two toddlers, trying to keep them both within reach, trying not to choose one over the other. I guess I kept hoping they'd grow up instead of forcing me to make that choice.

Tali was already down the block, pedaling hard in the empty lane. We'd get there faster this way, but we also had to pass the Red District, which was one good reason we usually avoided this route.

"You could at least pretend to be nice to her," I told him as we followed. She was riding faster now, probably because her attempt to escape Dresden hadn't worked. "I'm nice to your friends, you know."

"My friends come from high families, Treena. Tali lives in a different world than we do. You're above her in every way. You'll see that soon enough." He gave me a sideways glance. "That's the beauty of the numbers—it puts everyone where they're supposed to be."

"Shh. Not so loud."

The road was rougher here, and so were the people. They filled the sidewalks, their red numbers glowing on their foreheads like blood. Beggars in worn uniforms lined the filthy street, watching us carefully, as if trying to decide if we carried nutrition pills. I didn't, but I wouldn't have been surprised if they approached us to find out. An image of a mob attacking us as we rode past flashed through my mind. I shuddered and pedaled harder.

It felt like forever, but we finally emerged from the Red District and cut across an empty park. At first glance the city center looked like any other old-fashioned government building, little more than a six-story box with white marble and stately Roman columns. Transports were lined up in front, delivering important people like a giant anaconda giving birth to various shades of purple uniforms. These were the city's elite, people like my stepdad. The side entrance was full of students in white clamoring to make their way inside.

Tali had already parked her bike. Well, thrown it to the ground, more like. She strode toward the doors like a determined soldier going to war. I could only hope she wasn't too mad to save me a seat. We parked our bikes.

Dresden started toward the building, but I held back. "You ready for this?"

He chuckled. "Of course. I've been preparing for this my whole life. You have too, remember?"

"Yeah, but I can't help thinking that there's something I've missed—some little score I haven't earned yet."

He snapped his fingers. "I know! You forgot to organize your shoes by color and style this morning."

"Very funny."

"Look, I've never seen anyone align their life to the Standards as closely as you. You're almost obsessive, Treena. If anyone *doesn't* have cause to worry, it's you. Now, what's really going on?"

I sighed. "I don't know. Have you ever wondered if you really want this? The Rating, the implant, everything?"

He cocked his head and examined me like a scientist would study a bug. "You're joking, right? That doesn't sound like the kick-butt Treena I know. Come here." He grabbed my hand and pulled me toward a tree. A fir tree, I guessed by the needles, although it was plastic. Real trees hadn't existed in NORA for decades.

When we were out of sight, I rested my head against his chest, feeling him exhale in a contented sigh. It was easy to pretend that nothing would ever change when we were together like this. It almost felt like tomorrow was just another school day. Like our first official steps into adulthood were years away instead of minutes.

"You're just nervous," he whispered. "Let me help you forget." My pulse quickened as he lowered his head to mine, and I lifted my face willingly. Our lips met. He was a great kisser— passionate and hungry—and he didn't hold back. I melted into his chest as the heat between us intensified. But all too soon he pulled away, gasping for breath. I groaned, and a goofy smile spread across his face. "And now, it's time to go." He released me and threw his arms wide. "Our destiny awaits!"

I threaded my fingers through his. Dres was right. We'd prepared for this since we could crawl. It was a celebration, not a sentence. I checked my techband. Twenty-two minutes. "Together, right?"

"Absolutely. No matter what."

VANCE

I glared at the concrete sidewalk. The late afternoon shadows inched their way toward the street, taunting us, reminding us that we'd awaited orders for over two hours. Apparently our superiors thought twelve guys had nothing better to do than stand around in the heat. We could sit in the transports, but for me, sore feet were preferable to slow-baked internal organs.

I looked for shade without success. Even in a smaller city like Olympus, everything was hard—the sidewalk, the road where thousands of bicyclists had passed within the last hour, the tall buildings surrounding us like an ugly concrete forest. It was ironic. The only real colors in sight were the Ratings people wore on their foreheads.

"Vance?"

The voice blended with the hum of bike traffic, and it didn't quite register. Then a hand grabbed my shoulder. I moved instinctively, twisting to pin the offender's arms, a quick leg sweep, right fist cocked and poised for the next strike. I didn't realize who my opponent was until he had already hit the ground. Neb, the new boy, was spread flat on the concrete, staring at me in stunned surprise.

"Fates!" he said, his voice catching. "S-sorry, I didn't mean to freak you out. A little jumpy today, aren't you, Vance?"

I groaned and pulled him up from the sidewalk. The kid barely weighed anything. He shook himself loosely, as if to show that he'd meant to end up on the ground all along. But then he reached up to rub the shoulder I'd nearly yanked out of its socket.

"You need something?" I didn't try to keep the irritation out of my voice. If Neb could creep up on me, anyone could. That would never have happened two years ago.

"Poly has an update for you," he muttered, taking a small step backward.

I wiped my sweaty forehead for the trillionth time. Why they made us wear black uniforms in a blasted desert, I'd never know. "Coming."

Poly stood with one leg in the first transport, his dark arms resting on the top, sleeves rolled up to expose dark biceps larger than most men's thighs. He stood upright as I approached, and the metal vehicle groaned in protest. The yellow numbers on his forehead, more orange in the bright sunlight, glowed a bright 501—the lowest Rating possible before becoming a red. One of the biggest insults a NORA citizen could receive.

I resisted the urge to brush my fingers over my own Rating. Not that I cared about the number, of course, but the implanted device made me feel branded. Like the cattle my father and I used to—

Stop. Thoughts of my father were pointless, and I had no time for that now. I accepted the water pouch Poly offered and took a big gulp, swallowing quickly. The nasty aftertaste of NORA's water was something I'd never get used to. "So the Demander finally decided to tell us what we're supposed to be doing?"

Poly sighed, more a deep rumble of air than an exhalation. He hated my nickname for Commander Denoux. "Backup at the city center for the Rating Ceremony. There's word of an unusual Rating being awarded or something."

"Better than chasing smugglers, I guess." At least it was indoors. We'd caught five smugglers today, two of them kids. Hopefully that was enough to convince the Demander that Olympus was subdued enough for us to go back to the capital city. I dreaded another night of uncomfortable surveillance in a transport. Besides, being so close to the integration camp brought memories to the surface that I preferred to forget.

Traitor.

The thought came frequently these days, though not as often as it had at first. The first year had been pretty bad. The second year I'd learned how to dam the guilt inside like the frozen, hardened soldier NORA wanted. What would the third year bring?

How many more years could I take?

"We're to report in twenty minutes. But before we go," he said in his deep voice, "there's something I've been meaning to talk to you about."

I looked away with a grunt. He was nice enough, a good team leader, but his dark eyes reminded me too much of my dad's.

"It's coming up soon, right? The anniversary."

I shrugged. "Let's just go."

"You've been with us almost two years."

I didn't answer.

He paused, then plunged on. "If you're choosing the work-camp route, I need to know soon. I'll need to train someone to replace you."

"I'll let you know," I said. "We shouldn't waste time." I stalked to the end of the transport line where my team waited and gave them the update, feeling Poly's eyes on my back.

As always, the guys stuffed themselves into the backseats, fighting over the edges with the most legroom. They stayed away from the passenger seat. That was mine. I climbed in and slammed the door a little too hard.

The anniversary, Poly had called it. Anniversaries

were for happy married couples, for men who rode in transports to their assignments and came home clean, unstained by blood and guilt. Anniversaries were definitely not for people like me—someone who'd fought for his life around the twisted bodies of his neighbors and friends, their charred remains still smoking in the early morning light.

I tried to think of something else, but the sounds echoed in my brain as sharply as they had that awful night almost two years ago—people shouting, children screaming as their parents collapsed. The sound of gunfire, the rifles held by my clan members, and the chilling accuracy of NORA's strange, silent weapons. Dad's order to take our family to safety.

It was the last thing I'd ever hear him say.

I shoved that thought away and focused on Poly's words. If I decided to extend my military service, it would always be like this. One assignment to another, then another. More lives destroyed. If I chose the work camps, at least that part would end. But so would my freedom.

Not true. I didn't know what freedom was anymore.

Poly wanted my decision. So far, my decision was to not decide at all. "City center," I told the driver and sat back for the ride.

3

W elcome to the class of 2094's Rating Ceremony."
The official over Level Three education,
Professor Bold, ran his hand over his head as if
making sure his hairpiece was in place. Or maybe he
was making sure we could see the green number on
his forehead: 883.

The students and parents in the audience gave an
excited cheer. My stomach felt tingly, but one glance
at Dresden soothed my fears. He sat with his khel
team on the boys' side, relaxed as always. I turned and
looked for my mom, Lanah, in the parents' section. I
caught a glimpse of her near the back, staring at the
floor. Her husband wasn't with her. Good.

I caught a glimpse of Tali's mother as well. She
owned a stonecutting shop and was a bit eccentric,
but I liked her. Last time I'd visited, she'd gone on
and on about how the posterity of NORA's founder,
Richard Peak, were all named after stones and how

rocks had life cycles just like people did.

"Watch and see if I'm right," Taliyah whispered into my ear. Luckily, her anger at me seemed to have dissipated. She was focused on her latest conspiracy theory—something about the government purposefully creating more yellows and reds than in years past. "It's like the foundation of a pyramid," she had explained. "You need more people at the bottom to support the few on top."

Tali refused to believe the truth. People earned the Ratings they got, and that was that. I shrugged. "Sure."

She gave me a sharp look. "Don't 'sure' me, Treena. I'm right." When I didn't answer, she turned away, crossing her legs in complete confidence. Her face faded into the darkness as the lights dimmed. The room quieted and we settled back in our seats.

Suddenly the auditorium doors slammed open. Dozens of blond-headed monitors in silver uniforms streamed in and lined up along the walls and down each aisle. The audience murmured. There was usually high security at an event like this, but there had to be over a hundred of them. Were they looking for someone?

"Wow," Tali breathed. "Check him out, Treen."

A dark-haired guy with broad shoulders had just taken his place at the end of our row and now scanned the audience with his stunner raised. I blinked. He wore black, not silver. Military, maybe? But I caught my breath at the sight of his Rating. Bright red.

A red soldier? I didn't know that was possible.

"Fates," Tali said. "Look at his shoulders. I'd love to uncover those rippling biceps."

"Tali!" I hissed.

His dark eyes narrowed. "Keep talking, ladies, so I can arrest you. Didn't want to stand here for two hours anyway."

"Anything for you, baby," Tali muttered.

"My friend says she's very sorry," I told him. "She prefers to look at you rather than Professor Bold, for some reason."

Our gazes locked. The hardened mask slipped for a split second, and there was a hint of amusement. My face grew hot, but I couldn't look away. He watched me for a moment more before breaking eye contact.

Fate's sake, Treena. You have a boyfriend. I focused on the stage.

The shuffling noises died down and the auditorium went still. Professor Bold looked uneasy, but none of the monitors approached him. He cleared his throat.

"Here we go," Tali whispered. "My favorite history lesson again."

That got a half smile from me. Professor Bold was known to ramble on about NORA's proud past. He'd done it at every school event since we had entered Level Three. I almost had it memorized. Taliyah did. She began mouthing the words as he spoke.

"The New Order Republic of America, or NORA, has a ninety-year history—one that began after the old America broke apart, when Richard Peak stepped forward with the Rating system." Professor Bold glanced at the monitors and ran his hand over his head again. "While previous civilizations—and even the outlands today—have continually fought for order and peace, it is only we who have succeeded."

He paused, and the audience applauded politely. It was the same every year. If we didn't read his cues, the speech would become unbearably long.

"Peak's Rating system solved the ultimate human problem: greed. As long as human beings think first of themselves as individuals, their society will fail every time. When we see ourselves as a thread in the tapestry of a nation, we find happiness as citizens and individuals. It is only through aligning ourselves to our ideals and striving for the very best that is within us that a society like ours can thrive. And thrive, we do."

More applause.

"Right, like the Rating system took away greed," Tali grumbled.

"Shh," I whispered.

Bold continued. "Today we enjoy a society of peace, filled with citizens who contribute to the well-being of society cheerfully, peacefully, and productively; citizens who strive diligently for the Ratings that truly encompass them, their passions, and their potential. Citizens who follow the Standards of Excellence." He paused as if about to recite the

Standards, but he continued. "Today, as in past years, I certainly hope to see many strong greens created. And now we will watch as our graduating students receive their hard-earned and well-deserved Ratings."

The audience applauded. Taliyah and I looked at each other in relief. This speech was shorter than usual. A favorite topic of Bold's was how it was the individual's responsibility to earn their place in the family and society, how we weren't worth the nutrition pills we consumed unless we contributed more than we took. It always reminded me of my stepdad, Konnor— addition and subtraction, contributions and mistakes.

Professor Bold lifted his hand to touch his hair again but stopped in midair and thrust it into his pocket instead. "What do you say, students? Are you ready?"

Louder applause. A twinge of nervousness fluttered in my stomach. Since our nation's leader, the empress, was female, the guys would go first. Tradition and all. I just wanted to get my Rating and be done with it. Luckily, Dresden had already turned seventeen, making him one of the oldest, so he'd be close to the beginning of the list. My heart raced in my chest.

"Let us begin." Professor Bold reached for the first card.

Taliyah suddenly glanced at me with a knowing smile, and I realized that I was gripping her leg. "Sorry."

"No worries." She leaned over. "You have nothing

to stress about, you know. There's no way you guys won't come within a hundred points of one another. You're"—she batted her eyelashes and swatted a dainty hand dramatically—"*made* for each other."

I bit back a smile. She couldn't stand Dresden, but she knew exactly how to cheer me up.

"Shh!" someone behind us whispered, and I noticed that the auditorium had become deathly silent.

"Lile Demenger."

Lile stood and joined the professor, blinking in the spotlight. By the looks of his rust-colored hair, he'd tried to dye his black hair the appropriate shade of blond. Cheap dye, most likely. I fingered my own hair. I'd been dying it for so long I couldn't even remember what my true color was.

"Your score is ..." Professor Bold read the card. "739. Congratulations."

Lile's head bobbed as he accepted his card and stepped back. His parents stood in the crowd and applauded wildly. His score was probably higher than either of theirs.

"Chan Norwell."

Chan hesitated before standing. When he joined the professor, he stared at the floor. He'd been in several of my classes, but I'd never heard the guy speak before.

"Your score is ..." Bold paused. "636. Congratulations."

The crowd gently applauded. 636 was high-yellow

range. Chan accepted his card and stepped back, head down. No one stood to cheer for him.

"Poor guy," Tali whispered, and I knew what she meant. Kids who scored less than their parents were what adults called "at-risk," or the type to jump off the tower. I'd never quite understood their motivation, but today it made a little more sense. What could be worse than becoming a yellow, branded as mediocre, for everyone to see?

Jumping off the tower. That was definitely worse.

"Dresden Wynn."

My breath caught. He stood and strode to the front, his lanky frame seeming shorter from this far away. A silly grin was pasted on his face. I could tell it wasn't entirely natural. The rustling movements in the audience stopped as every ear perked up.

A figure behind the guys' side leaned forward in anticipation. Dresden's dad, tall and regal, just like his son. The Wynns wore some of the highest Ratings in the city, and they lived in the most expensive corner of Olympus.

"Your score is … uh …"

Professor Bold looked at his assistant and showed her the card. Her eyes widened, and she glanced at Dresden, shrugging her shoulders.

My teeth began to grind. Tali put a gentle hand on my shoulder.

"Your score is … 942."

There was a collective gasp from the audience.

My stomach fell to the floor. *What?*

Everyone around me exploded to their feet, screaming and jumping in their excitement. The applause was deafening. Someone grabbed my shoulders and yelled something in my ear. I just sat, staring numbly at the back of the student in front of me. The number echoed in my head.

942.

Professor Bold's desperate voice came over the speakers. "Students, please. Give me your attention."

"Dresden! Woohoo!" someone yelled behind me. A girl.

The chant started to rise over the noise. "Dres-*den*. Dres-*den*."

"Students!"

"Dres-*den*. Dres-*den*."

942. Olympus's previous record was 936, by a near genius. His assignment had been to the Leadership Academy. Some said he was training to become tribune, second only to the empress.

Dresden, what have you done?

One hundred points. My score would have to be at least 842, or the law said we couldn't be together. The numbers ran through my head. Only 5 percent of the NORA's population had scores that high, and I doubted any of them were freshly Rated graduates.

"Dres-*den*. Dres-*den*."

The monitors moved then, turning to face the audience and raising their stunners. The chanting broke down into confused conversation as everyone lowered themselves into their seats. Cheering and standing had never been against the rules in the past. Of course, we'd never had this many monitors in the audience before, either. Maybe they'd anticipated Dresden's score and sent in extra security.

"Students," a younger voice came over the speaker. It was Dresden. Interesting how a number changed things. We were his friends one minute and *students* the next. "Students, thank you for your support, but please listen to Professor Bold. Thank you."

The tall girl in front of me sat down, and I could finally see Dresden's face. Flushed. Triumphant. Very, very happy. He searched the crowd, looking for me. I sank lower in my seat. What was wrong with me? I should have been clapping enthusiastically, like everyone else. No, I should have been *more* excited than everyone else. Instead, I felt sick inside.

Professor Bold took the mic back. "That is an Olympus city record, Dresden. Congratulations. We will watch you with interest."

Dresden's beautiful voice replied, "Thank you, sir. I'm very excited for the future."

Tali turned to me with an enthusiasm I hadn't expected and began to whisper. "That record will last what, fifteen minutes? You've got to be at least ten points above him."

My voice sounded mechanical. "As long as we're within range of each other, it doesn't matter."

The rest of the names blurred together. Before I was ready, it was the girls' turn. Professor Bold seemed calmer now, his voice more confident. "Lorena Conway."

I couldn't tear my eyes away from Dresden. He wore a brilliant smile as he watched the stand.

"Your Rating is … 822. Congratulations."

The next four students received their Ratings, three in the eight hundreds and one in the seven hundreds. Then Professor Bold called Tali's name. She stood slowly, eyes fixed on the stage. When she got to the front, she simply glared at the crowd.

Professor Bold didn't even look at her. He squinted at the card and said in a monotone voice, "Taliyah Fairbanks. Your score is 651. Congratulations."

A gasp ripped from my chest as the audience politely applauded. Yellow. High yellow, yes, but *yellow*. Tali's expression was hard. She turned to the professor, who soberly handed her the card. Anger flashed in her eyes as she uttered a quick thank-you before walking stiffly down to the aisle. There was murmuring in the audience.

"It's a mistake," I muttered. "She should be in the eight hundreds at least!"

The girl to my left, Rena, pursed her lips. "Eight hundreds? Look at her hair. She didn't even try to dye it blonde."

The girl next to Rena shook her head. "It wasn't that. I heard her mom is a yellow, and nobody knows where her dad is. Besides, her uniform is always so … frumpy." She shrugged, a cute, petite gesture, as Tali reached our row. "Seems like she fits the yellow mold pretty well."

The anger welled up inside me like fire. I wanted to slap Rena. She hadn't even tried to lower her voice. Tali stiffly lowered herself into her seat, head held high.

How could Dresden and Tali, my two best friends, have scores so vastly different? How well did the Raters, strangers we'd never met, really know us?

"Ametrine Dowell."

My body stiffened and time seemed to stop. The whisperings in the room came to a halt. Students turned in their seats to stare at me until I felt like everyone in the city was watching me. They probably were.

Somehow my feet knew what to do, and soon I was standing next to Professor Bold. It was the closest I'd ever been to the man. He smelled like sweat and heavy cologne. A genuine smile spread across his face, his teeth bright in the dull light. In his hand was a card. I had a sudden urge to grab it and run away. But I forced my hands to my side and stood tall, facing the silent crowd. The spotlight was too bright to see Lanah, my mom, but I knew she'd be clasping her hands like she always did when she was nervous.

"Ametrine Dowell," he said too slowly. "It gives me great pleasure to tell you that your score is …"

My gaze was fixed on the card as he squinted at it

and then rubbed his eye with one slim finger. Someone coughed, and I nearly jumped. Every muscle and tendon in my body was taut. I found Dresden's still-grinning face in the audience.

Except that this was taking too long. Something was wrong. I tried to lean over and see the card myself, but he turned and held it up to his assistant behind us. She stepped forward and stared at the card, raising an eyebrow. Professor Bold cleared his throat and ran a shaky hand over his sweaty head. The dramatic pause before another record-breaking score? My heart felt like it would leap out of my chest.

"Ametrine," he repeated, his voice somber. "Your score is 440. Uh … congratulations."

My expression must have been one of utter shock, because Professor Bold looked very serious as he handed me the card. There it was, clear and in black:

Ametrine Dowell: 440
Implant Level: Red

The auditorium was deathly silent. The squeaking of chairs and low whispering had stopped, and it seemed as though nobody dared breathe.

I was frozen in place. I stared dumbly at the audience, my neighbors and friends and people who had come to celebrate with us. Someone cleared their throat.

This was a nightmare. It wasn't really happening. Sixteen years of work couldn't end this way. My dreams, my relationship with Dresden, and my future—all shattered by one number. 440. It couldn't be real. No Olympus graduate had ever gotten a Rating below five hundred. Especially not a student who had consistently been at the top of her class. This was dreadfully, horrifyingly wrong.

The audience began to murmur.

A stern-faced female with a tight bun stepped out of the shadows beside me. The woman wore the standard purple NORA uniform, but her right arm had three golden stripes. The Ratings Department. She gestured for Professor Bold to give her the mic and turned to the crowd.

"Students, I am a Ratings official. I ask you to remain quietly seated."

The whispering decreased, but it didn't disappear. A lone figure stood in the back, hands covering her mouth, and I didn't need to see her face to know it was Lanah. She was too shocked to process the official's order. A monitor headed in her direction.

"Young lady, give me the card." The official stood next to me, her hand out expectantly. My eyes burned, but I pushed the emotions back. Maybe it really was a mistake. Perhaps she was about to say so. She'd fix it, and I'd go home and celebrate with my classmates, and everything would go on as planned. 440? It was nearly impossible to be that useless. I quickly handed her the card, as if it were smoldering.

"Students, let me explain something to you." The

official paused. "Your parents already know this, but it's important that you understand something. The Rating Department regulates the data that determines your score through a massive interconnected network. The data is sent and stored from the moment you're born. The Raters know more about you than you could possibly imagine. The Raters analyze the data, assign your scores, and finalize the numbers by printing these cards and affixing their signatures." She finally turned, but she looked past me. "Young lady, will you tell us what is written in the bottom right-hand corner?"

I stared at it, numb. There it was, scribbled in ink: **RMR**

"Out loud, please." She held the mic up to my lips.

I tried to speak, but I knew I'd lose control if I did. I just shook my head.

"It's a signature," the official said, her voice hardening. "That makes it a valid Rating. NORA doesn't make mistakes. Enjoy the rest of the ceremony." She handed the mic to Professor Bold, who stared at it, red-faced.

The audience was quiet. I looked out at the faces of students I knew well and professors I'd studied under. Their collective shock and confusion slowly dissipated but was replaced by something else. Disgust. I could see it in their downturned mouths and sour expressions. They assumed I had done something horrible to deserve this. And why not? That's what I would have thought.

I caught a glimpse of the soldier in black. He stood at attention like the others, but instead of watching the audience, his gaze was locked on me. He frowned, eyebrows creased in something that looked a lot like concern, maybe even pity.

I pulled myself together. I didn't need the pity of a red, because this was all a terrible mistake.

A hand touched my back, and a square-faced monitor eased me gently toward the steps. "Come. I've been instructed to stay by your side until implantation."

I just nodded. Of course. They were afraid I'd run away. Too bad I hadn't thought about it before now. When I started back toward my seat, he shook his head and pointed to the exit. "For your protection," he whispered.

Protection? From whom? The words swirled in my mind, fading in and out like everything else. I felt thousands of eyes on my back as I shuffled down the aisle toward the doors. But the image that would haunt me forever was the expression on Dresden's face. His eyes were dark, his mouth set into a hard line, his jaw tight. He leaned forward in his seat as if he wanted to leap up and run. I had a million questions, but only one mattered as I left the auditorium.

Did Dresden want to run to me—or away from me?

4

I t was as if I'd stepped right into my nightmares. A bonfire, hot and crackling, threw shadows across the town square. Except this time the people surrounding it weren't running in panic but dancing. And the soldiers who stood about weren't destroying but protecting. Watching. There was a big difference this time.

I hated fire.

"Look at those bubble blowers," Semias said. "Dancing around like fools, celebrating their new implants. It's not like they've never seen fire before." He turned away, disgust evident on his round, shadowed face. I'd caught him gulping down nutrition pills again today, probably stolen from some poor family in the Red District. I'd kick him off the team, but we were down a guy from last month's raid.

His name was Harell, Vance. Is that how you see it now—addition and subtraction instead of lives and people?

"Bubble blowers?" Daymond repeated. He absently fingered the scar on his cheek.

"You know. Kids. Whities. Newbies."

"They're only two years younger than you, Semias," Daymond replied.

"They probably *haven't* seen fire before," Ross said in a thoughtful tone, as if he'd missed the entire exchange. "Look at this security. I doubt NORA will let this tradition go on much longer."

I had to agree with him, but for different reasons. This was the wrong time of year to have a bonfire—the heat was already unbearable, and the fire made it a hundred times worse. No less than two-dozen monitors were stationed around the city square tonight, silver uniforms braided into the purple crowd, and the new graduates looked uncomfortable as they danced. They glanced often at the flames and the pile of blackening white uniforms, but stole glances at the monitors. If this uniform-burning ceremony was their graduation party, I actually felt sorry for them.

My team watched the crowd with envy and admiration. These guys had all grown up this way. The bonfire was a rite of passage for them, a point of no return. A last chance to be carefree and goof off, trying to impress the girls they knew they'd never see again.

A horde of blonde girls stood front and center, all wearing stiff, newly purchased purple uniforms and blazing green Ratings on their foreheads, chattering to each other like little birds.

Rating ceremonies were the worst. At least with criminals, I knew what they were thinking. It was the cold glares of green citizens I couldn't stand. Those who didn't look down their noses looked quickly away or pretended I wasn't there, which was just fine with me. Except today, a girl in the audience had stared me down in curiosity, even responding to my smile with one of her own. And, strangely, she'd later become a red. She was the talk of the entire city tonight.

"Poly's coming," Neb announced. "Looks like they caught the kid."

I straightened as Poly's team approached dragging a scrawny kid with messy black hair. He wore red girls' shoes that were too big and made him stumble. Those unfortunate shoes had cost him his freedom.

"I'm no smuggler, I swear," the boy said when they stopped.

"Sure, kid," I said. They always said that, but it didn't matter. Our job was to deliver him, not interrogate him. That made seven smugglers today. Hopefully that was enough to curb the Demander's appetite and let us leave this blasted city. The heavy rotten-lake smell was driving me insane. "We're going to test you now. If you pass, you can go home free."

He paused. "What kind of test?"

Poly retrieved his testing device from the transport and held it up to the flickering light. He'd helped invent it himself. It was simple, smaller than his hand—even though *everything* was smaller than Poly's hand—but he never let anyone else touch it. "Hold out your arm."

The boy's eyes went wide. "Wait. What does it test?"

"Food," I said. "If you haven't eaten real food recently, you have nothing to worry about."

"What is going on?" a woman shrieked, her voice bordering on hysteria as she pushed her way through the murmuring crowd. Apparently our presence had caught the attention of the graduates, and they watched us in fascination. The woman planted herself in front of me, hands on her hips, her long hair tucked over one shoulder. I stared at her in shock. It was Selia Dunstrep, wearing a yellow 629 Rating. She'd been in my clan—at least, when it had existed. Not only that, but she'd served in the Circle and worked with my father.

"Your mom?" I asked the boy. He trembled, his eyes shifting from the woman to me. Then he nodded.

Blasted woman, I thought. It would've been so much smoother if she hadn't come. Quicker than anyone could react, I leaped and yanked her arms behind her, locking her wrists together. She let out a surprised gasp and tried to jerk away, then gritted her teeth in pain. Her bonds were linked to her techband, so she'd feel that jolt every time she moved. I knew all too well how that felt.

"You are ordered to submit to a food test," I said.

"This is ridiculous! I just came to see—"

"Are you the boy's mother?"

"I—" Her mouth tightened in pain. "I will not submit to a test, and neither will he. We've done nothing wrong."

"The boy has already been tested." Poly watched his device, holding the boy's shoulder with his other hand. His deep voice rumbled over the growing noise of the crowd. "He's positive."

The boy stared at his mother in shock. Her mouth dropped a little. "It must be the device! He wasn't—you can't take … Please. I have other children at home."

Great. Our last smuggler had just become an entire family. I motioned for a couple of guys to assist. They hurried to obey. "We'll need to test all of you, then," I said.

Poly waved his device over the woman's skin, making her flinch. It took a couple of seconds for the result to appear. The light turned red. Positive.

"It's all my fault," she said. "Just let my children go. Please! They're innocent and still getting used to this place. Whatever the punishment is, I'll take it instead."

I forced my face to remain impassive, sending a quick techband message to the monitor station to request a search team for the woman's home. They'd be there within minutes. "Your family will meet you shortly," I told her. "Whatever happens, at least you'll be together."

"Don't you dare pretend to care about us." Her eyes flashed in the firelight, giving her a strangely demonic look. Her voice dripped with venom. "You're taller now, but I know who you are. You're Iron Belt Hawking's son."

"Daymond, put her in the transport."

"Yes, sir."

"Your father was a good man!" she snapped. Daymond grabbed her arm, but the woman twisted away. Her hair fell into her face as she spat the words. "He would be ashamed of you now, hunting down your own. Becoming one of them."

I refused to reply. It wasn't the first time a member of my clan had recognized me, and it wouldn't be the last.

"Sir?" the boy asked next to me.

I'd forgotten about him. "What?"

He winced at my tone but seemed to gather his courage. "Um, what will happen to us?"

I glanced at Poly, but he chose this moment to stand and walk away, flipping the screen up on his techband as if calling someone. With a heavy sigh, I leaned against the transport. Kids were the worst. I could handle hysterical mothers and angry, fist-throwing fathers—but when they dragged children into this stuff, nothing good came of it.

"Look, kid, I doubt we'll even catch the rest

of your family. Your clan members will probably hide them before we get there. That's what usually happens."

The boy shook his head. "No. We can't be separated. My mom said we have to stay together." He paused. "Was she right? Are you really a Hawking?"

I yanked the transport door open and motioned to the boy. He hesitated before stepping in and settling onto the oversanitized plastic seat. Parents didn't know everything. They meant well, but there was a lot they couldn't control. It was about time this kid learned that lesson. "I was, once," I said and slammed the door shut.

It wouldn't take him long to grow up. NORA would make sure of that.

5

My stepfather always complained that our unit was too small, even though it was bigger than most high-density blocks. But tonight I had to agree with him.

Konnor's voice wafted in through the vent, angry and loud. "I'm telling you, it's a mistake!"

"I thought so too," Lanah said. "But the official quashed that theory pretty decidedly. Poor Treena."

"Poor Treena? The timing of all this is just a little suspicious. Do you realize that Councilman Alden's medical report leaked today? Everyone knows about his heart problem now, and there's no way he'll retain his position. I'm next in line, Lanah. Me, a councilman! And then she goes and does *this* the day before Ratings!"

"We don't know why this happened, Konnor." Lanah's voice was soft.

"Yes. We do. Your daughter has managed to drag

our name through the mud and ruin my career, all in one day." He paused. "I suppose that's what I get for marrying a rejected woman with a baby."

Anger rose to the surface of my thoughts. Konnor was striking my mother where it hurt the most. He did that often when he was upset—sometimes with fists, other times with words. But as scary as his temper was, I knew the cold silence that followed was even worse. Those moments of cruel clarity were the true danger. Even Lanah knew better than to defend me now.

Indeed, there was no reply, and for a moment the only sound coming through the building's old ventilation system was the tapping of the air conditioning.

He would confront me soon. I could only guess what that confrontation would mean. For a second I had a flashback, a memory of hanging over a rail, looking down on the city streets below, feeling helpless as my sweaty five-year-old hand slipped farther and farther. *"Don't forget this feeling,"* Konnor had said. *"If you fail our family, I expect you to find your way back here. I expect you to make the noble choice."*

I sat in my room alone, fingering the tiny round mirror I'd borrowed from Lanah months before and never returned. Just fourteen hours ago I'd woken from a deep sleep, contemplating my future with Dresden. We were supposed to go to the academy together. He would study broadcasting, and I'd become a Rater.

We'd already bought a list of professors and their grading practices from a former student—it had cost Dresden over four hundred credits.

I felt sick. Education scores, volunteer hours, khel tournaments. It all seemed so silly now. What was the point? If it didn't matter, why had I dedicated my life to it all?

Why did it matter for everyone else but not for me?

I left the vent where I'd been listening and sat on my bed next to the pile of new purple uniforms, neatly pressed and folded. I hadn't changed into one yet. As a child I'd fingered my mom's dark uniforms, wondering how it would feel to be an adult, to wear a number that showed the world who I was. What was the protocol with reds in a green household? I'd never heard of it happening before. Reds didn't live in comfortable homes with families. They ended up in work camps and distant manufacturing plants. They didn't deserve the pills they took, the water they consumed. The physical space they occupied. Would they kidnap me in my sleep tonight and dump me in the Red District?

I picked up my mom's hand mirror. The reflection that stared back at me seemed completely foreign. Puffy circles under the eyes, redness around the pupils, a haunted expression. Most glaring, however, were the glowing numbers burned into the forehead: 440. Bright red—as if etched in blood.

The implantation process had been nearly painless. If I hadn't been undergoing the surgery myself, I would have been fascinated. The implant was simply a thin gray screen, so thin it was nearly transparent. It was placed under the first layer of skin. A tiny line in my skin was the only indication that any incision had been made. The line would disappear within days, they had said. If only the same could be said for the implant.

My hands itched to scratch it away, to tear at my skin until the numbers disappeared. Until I could see only myself again. But it wouldn't work. It was connected to the techband somehow. If I messed with it, it would trigger a painful electric punishment.

The tower came into my mind again, and I pushed it away.

The sudden rapping on my door made me jump. The mirror vanished into my pocket, and I sat down again. "Come in."

Lanah entered, her face drawn and her eyes swollen. She'd been crying too. The thought gave me a guilty bit of satisfaction. The bed sagged as she sat next to me and handed me a nutrition pill and some water. I tossed it down my throat and swallowed, ignoring the water.

"I have something for you," she began. "It's from your dad."

I leaned back against the wall, arms folded. "What, he's too good to come in and give it to me himself?"

She blinked. "No, I mean your biological dad. Jasper." Her hand fumbled in her pocket for a moment. "He wanted you to have this on your Rating day. I don't think even he anticipated how hard this day would be for you."

"My dad?" I repeated dumbly and sat up. "You've seen him recently?"

She put a finger to her lips and whispered, "No, no. He's in prison now. Before you were born, he showed it to me. It was a couple of weeks before … he left."

"He's in prison?"

"That's the rumor. I don't know for sure."

"But … why? What did he do?"

"Let's just say that Jasper was a traitor—to his family and his country."

I sat back, stunned. I was the daughter of a convict? "Why haven't you told me this before?"

"Konnor forbids it. He doesn't want any connection between us and Jasper. He'd go and burn my marriage record if he could. But I thought you should know. Maybe it will help you understand what's going on."

"So you don't think it's my fault."

"No. I don't." She took my hand and put something into my palm before I could pull it away. It was hard and cold. Did my con-man biological father think a gift would make up for a lifetime of pain?

I inspected it, tempted to throw it out the window. "A rock?" It was half the size of my palm, smooth and flat, the edges round.

"His favorite stone," she said. "Your father had a special interest in geology. He drilled a hole through it so you could wear it as a necklace if you wanted."

I gave a sarcastic chuckle. "Yeah, because I've always wanted a purple rock that belonged to the man who ruined my life."

She sighed. "I wanted you to know my theory, but we don't know anything for sure. Don't place all your problems on his shoulders quite yet."

I stared at her. After everything that had happened today, and after everything she'd been through, she was defending him? Before I could reply, her eyes grew misty, and she turned away.

It wasn't right. Lanah always blamed herself for other people's mistakes. She'd taken the heat for my stepdad—and *from* him—for as long as I could remember. But there was something stronger than guilt in her eyes this time. "You really did love Jasper."

She sighed, wiping her eyes. "I loved him, and I thought he loved me. Obviously I was wrong."

I couldn't imagine leaving Dresden for anything, especially if we were married. Well, that wasn't going to happen now. Jasper had taken Dresden from me, too.

"Ametrine—"

"Treena, Mom."

She paused. "Jasper gave you your name, you know."

"All the more reason to change it."

Lanah gave a wistful smile. "Treena, my mother always said I'd know whether a guy loved me by his willingness to sacrifice—that my well-being would come before his. The man you marry will give up what he wants most for you. That's how you'll know."

"Dresden is totally like that."

She bit her lip but nodded, her eyes flickering to the stone in my hand. She reached into her pocket and retrieved a thin piece of metallic string. She looped it easily through the stone, then latched it around my throat. We looked at each other for a long moment, then she pulled me in for a hug. I went rigid, and the embrace didn't last long. When she pulled away, her face was sad. "Jasper always said there was a time to run and a time to fight, and the trick was knowing the difference. I couldn't face it, Treena. I ran. But you've always been a fighter like your dad. Maybe that's the message you're supposed to take from this necklace. Just know that I support you, wherever you go from here."

She stood and kissed me on the forehead like I was five. I threw her an absent wave.

After she left, I stared at the rock in the dim lamplight. It was a deep purple, nearly the same shade as NORA's official color. Purple was really just half blue, half red, my teachers had said. Blue for the peace we now enjoyed, and red for the blood of those who had sacrificed their lives for our comfort. Was it a message from my dad that I should submit to

NORA's will? That I should wait for them to relocate me, slink into the shadows, and accept my fate?

The thought made my stomach churn. If that was what he wanted, I'd do the opposite.

I turned off the light but stayed awake in the darkness. A plan began to form in my mind, fuzzy at first, like the tendrils of fog that gathered in the early morning, and then firm and cold, like the strange purple rock my traitorous father had insisted that I receive. The rest of my life stretched before me in the thickness of night. I lay there, watching the hours click by on my techband, waiting for sleep to bestow the slightest bit of relief.

It never came.

6

The bonfire consumed my dreams, and the nightmare came again. It was hazy at first, like watching a projection through smoke, but then came into focus, burned into my mind as if with a branding iron.

I lay in bed on the verge of sleep, listening to my twin sisters' heavy breathing. I was just drowsy enough that I didn't hear the shouting at first. After a moment, there was a sharp crack as the door banged open.

"Vance, wake up!"

The panic in my mother's voice shocked me fully awake. "What?"

"They're setting the cabins on fire. Everyone's evacuating to the shelter. Go check on the other wing, then help your father!" She strode quickly to my sisters' beds.

Before I fully understood, I was running down the hall. My feet clapped all too loudly against the wood floor I'd helped lay one board at a time. Our entire settlement was wood. If there was really a fire ...

A faint smoke smell reached my senses, and horror forced my body into high speed. I reached the door and pounded on it. "Fire! Get to the shelter!" The voices on the other side told me that they were already awake. Two wings, all exiting safely.

I leaped forward again, headed for the lookout platform. The air grew thicker and heavier with every step.

All of our cabins were connected underground, but NORA didn't know that. My father was a brilliant leader. Our people would be gathering in the shelter now, where food and water storage could keep them alive for months. But we hadn't counted on fire. Cold and hunger, yes, but not fire. Such a stupid, naïve oversight.

When I reached the loft, I could barely breathe. The smoke was so thick that I wondered if my dad was even alive, but then his figure emerged. He was nearly unrecognizable, his face black as if painted, and he held a wet piece of cloth over his nose and mouth. He handed me something—a plastic canister with a band, obviously some kind of breathing device. I slipped it on, and suddenly the air was easier to breathe, though painfully hot and dry.

"Dad," I croaked. "We can't fight from here. We need to get to the shelter and make a stand!"

"The men are lining up now, ready to strike. Are

the women and children headed to the shelter?" His voice was crisp, hard. This wasn't a father talking to his son but a commander barking orders.

"Yes, sir."

"I sent Rutner to drench the northeast building in water, but that won't hold the fire long. We need to defeat the soldiers now, or evacuate and risk capture."

I glanced at the tree line, straining to see through the darkness and the heavy smoke. When my eyes adjusted to the black, I saw figures. Vehicles. They had us completely surrounded, and they stood around as if bored, like students with nothing to do after school. "Do they really think a fire will send us out with our hands up?"

Dad just let his shoulders slump as if I'd voiced his biggest concern. "Seems strange to me too."

NORA soldiers had attacked twice before, but they'd seemed reluctant to kill anyone. We'd taken out two dozen of their soldiers, and all they'd gotten for their trouble was a few stunned settlers. Why they needed people so badly in that swollen mess of a country, I had no idea, but at least we knew they wanted us alive.

"This seems like the perfect time for them to attack," Dad said as if talking to himself. "They've permeated our defenses, and now they're just standing there. What are they waiting for?"

I gripped his arm. "What was that?"

"I said—"

"No, no. Listen."

He started to protest, but a low rumble began to fill the air. It didn't come from the earth but from the sky. Dad went rigid. An expression of utter horror spread across his face, as if he'd just seen the reaper himself. His eyes fixed upon me, and for the first time in my life, I saw fear.

My father was afraid.

"What? Is it a bomber jet?" I glanced upward and caught a flash of light from above, then another. There were more than one, and they seemed to be circling us like ravens circling death.

Dad just stared at the sky. I wanted to shake him, to force him to snap out of it and tell me what to do. He opened his mouth to speak but coughed instead. I reached up to tear the mask off my face and hand it to him.

Dad just shook his head and swatted my hand away. "Bombers," he managed.

"But why would ..." The answer slammed into my mind like a fist. "They don't want to capture us anymore, do they?"

The wood groaned beneath our feet. The fire had reached the top of the platform now, climbing and snapping like a hungry dragon with ferocious claws. We only had a few minutes before the fire drove us out or the building collapsed under us. I hoped Rutner was protecting Mom and the twins. Was he ordering them to evacuate, or had they hunkered down, determined to die rather than give themselves up?

"The empress warned me this would happen" Dad said, his voice distant. "But I didn't listen."

"You've been communicating with their leader?"

"She tried to make a deal. I refused. I thought we were safe here, so far outside the borders. I thought if we defended ourselves, they'd see we weren't worth it."

"Why didn't you tell me this?"

He turned to me and gripped my shoulders, and suddenly the commander was back. "Get them out. Take them to the hunting shelter in the forest. You'll be attacked, but gather the men on the outside of the group. Hopefully a few of you can make it."

I stared at him, letting his words sink in. "What do you mean, you?"

He dropped his hands. "Maybe I can draw their fire, distract them for a bit, so you can break through their line." At the last word he broke into a fit of coughing and covered his mouth.

"It's too late for that!" My heat-singed voice sounded hoarse. "Dad, this building will burn down—if the air teams don't blow it up first."

He coughed into his wet cloth, and his face constricted. "Then you'd better hurry."

I tore the mask off, barely feeling the wall of heat slam into my face. "No, Dad. You're their leader. You're the first person who should be getting out of here!"

He shot me a stern look, an expression I knew well. "You have a lot to learn about leadership, son. It's not about privilege but about sacrifice. You're *their leader now. If I can buy you a little more time, I have to try. Now go!"*

He moved more quickly than I'd ever seen. One second he was standing there, and the next he grabbed the breathing mask and slammed it onto my face. I twisted away, but his strong arms shoved me off the highest level. It wasn't a hard fall, only about ten feet, but I landed on my back. I lay there, stunned.

I stared at the man who had raised me, the man who had taught me how to fight without weapons and to lead using only words, and an angry sob tore from my throat.

"Keep them safe, Vance," he shouted through the haze, and then my father turned back to his vigil on the platform. He pulled out his long-range rifle and glanced back at the darkened sky. Two more aircraft had joined the group, and they seemed to be gathering into some kind of formation.

With a growl, I bolted for the shelter. The only way to save Dad was to obey, quickly. Only when we broke through the enemy's lines would he follow. It would take every weapon we had, and we'd probably lose half the settlement—but if we attacked all at once, it was possible.

Together we'd have a fighting chance.

Keep them safe ...

7

The first rays of morning light shone through the window. The traffic was just beginning to flow on the street below; I heard talking and the shifting of gears as people rode past. It was Rating Day for regular citizens, but it was also Assignment Day for graduates. Today we found out what our Ratings truly meant.

Which was why my plan had to begin immediately.

I dressed in my new purple uniform, straightening the stiff shoulder seams in the mirror and trying not to look at the glowing red number on my forehead. If my plan worked, it would be fixed before my assignment came. Hopefully.

With a quick jog downstairs, I gulped down my pill and asked to borrow my mom's makeup. I only used it on special occasions. She stared at me, a strange look on her face. "Where are you going so early?"

"To meet Dresden," I lied. "He wants to talk. I won't be too long." If she knew the real reason, she'd never let me go. I swallowed hard. Dresden hadn't tried to contact me. A part of me was withering inside, the darkness of rejection spreading through my wounded heart. But there was still hope. If my plan worked, it could change everything. We still had a chance.

"All right." Doubt shone in her eyes. "Good luck. Call me if you need me."

"Sure, Mom."

The late-spring heat was already stifling when I swung onto my bike. It was a grim omen of the type of summer to come—more water restrictions and more greenery regulations. Lanah wasn't going to be happy. She loved her flower garden too much. She gave her allotted five plants some of her personal drinking water every day. I thought it was a little ridiculous, but she just said she missed the feel of real leaves. Whatever that meant.

It was fifteen minutes of hard riding before the Block came into view. It was a simple cube-shaped office building that housed most of the government officials in Olympus. My stepdad was summoned here on occasion for his job in Integration. I could only assume that the Rating Office was here as well.

After a few minutes I located a nearby bike rack and took a deep breath, smoothing my uniform. I wore no ornamentation, unlike the men and women who ascended the staircase and entered the building. They had bands of varying thicknesses and colors on their arms, and an older gentleman actually had multiple stars beneath his collar and a silver stripe across his chest. I squinted to see his face. The tribune himself, the empress's personal assistant, here in Olympus. I'd never seen him in person before.

I hesitated. What I was about to do was risky enough, but the tribune was here, of all people. It could just as easily go bad as good, and I couldn't afford to backslide any further. I watched the tribune disappear through the doors, surrounded by an entourage of guards and assistants. I could wait outside for a few hours, maybe, until he left.

No. I've spent my entire life doing what I've been told. It didn't work out. Now it's time to try the opposite.

The crowd was dissipating. I forced myself to take one step, then another. The doors loomed closer. At the last second I swooped my hair across my forehead, glad for the frizziness for the first time in my life, and strode inside.

No one noticed me at first. There were a dozen different hallways, but the entire crowd of people turned left when they reached the main hallway, all headed in the same direction like a school of identical fish. I felt odd stepping out of the crowd and into the massive center room.

This wasn't my first visit. I'd been here once

before as a child on a field trip. But the enormity and the grandeur of the room still took my breath away. A large dome in the center full of stained-glass pictures rose high overhead. The sun colored the glass so majestically that its rays shone down like pink spotlights. Glittery spots of dust made their way slowly down to the hard marble floor.

"Can I help you?" a voice asked.

I jumped. It was an older lady, silver roots peeking through her bleached blonde hair. She eyed my forehead with suspicion. I stood straighter, ready to plead my case.

The woman simply pointed overhead. "Visitors always stop and stare at the dome," she said. "Easy to tell who should be here and who shouldn't."

"I've come to see my Rater," I said quickly.

"Ah," she said knowingly. "Come to file a complaint?"

So this was a common occurrence. A surge of courage welled up inside me. "Yes."

"Do you know your Rater's name?"

The woman was small, but her voice was sharp. She had probably worked here for decades, asking the same questions of dozens of grumpy graduates like me. "I know his initials. RMR."

She raised an eyebrow. "Mr. Roulon. I should've guessed. I'll take you to his office, but I doubt he's there today. You can leave your complaint with his assistant." Her legs carried her quickly away, and I had to jog to catch up.

"What happens if I file a complaint?" I asked.

"He looks at your data again. If he thinks there's a discrepancy, he fixes it."

"But if not?"

The woman turned a sharp corner, and I nearly ran into a soldier in a gray uniform in my effort to follow. I mumbled an apology, but he just stalked away. My guide didn't look behind her as she spoke. "Then your Rating stands."

"That's it?"

She finally turned, her movement making me pull up hard. "NORA doesn't make mistakes. Get that through your head while you're young." With a quick yank, the woman opened a heavy metal door and held it for me. "Good luck."

To my surprise, the blond boy at the desk was only slightly older than me. Or maybe his freckles—a red mass of dots giving his face an orange hue—just made him look young. His eyebrows were reddish, which I guessed was his real hair color. The guy was bent over his work, arms moving frantically, knocking things over in his haste to tidy up.

A glass door behind him read "Rater Roulon." A framed photograph hung beneath the name, depicting a round-faced man with dimples. So this was the man who'd held my future in his hands, then tossed it into the wastebasket like a bag of old parts. I stood on the tips of my toes to see through the glass, but the room was empty. Mr. Roulon wasn't there.

The assistant finally looked up and rolled his eyes. "Of course. Today, of all days. Can you come back tomorrow?"

"No," I said, straightening. "I need to—"

"File a complaint, yeah. I'm sure you do. Hold on a minute."

With a final sweep of his arm, he wiped all the objects off his desk into a drawer. Then he punched something into the screen and grabbed my wrist, scanning the techband into the system. "Your name is … Ametrine Dowell."

"Treena," I corrected, feeling my determination drain away. This wasn't going to work. I needed someone above the Rater to look at my case. My Rating needed to be fixed before my assignment was issued, or I'd be shipped off without options. Why had the Rater chosen today to be gone?

"And your Rating score is—Oh." I pulled my hair aside to show him, and his eyes widened even more. Then I saw it—a small, nearly imperceptible downward turn of his mouth. Disgust.

"My scores are nearly perfect in every area," I said, forcing down a shiver. His reaction was understandable, but still. "My Rating is a mistake."

He turned to the screen again, his face suddenly closed and distant. "Even perfect scores wouldn't guarantee anything. They don't include the Rater's overall impression points or the interview score."

"Then *look* at my impression points and my interview score. I know you can't tell me what I got, but just peek at them really quick."

He sighed loudly, muttering something about a "high-profile job," and his fingers flew across the glass screen. Then he squinted, a puzzled expression on his face. "Your impression score is fine. Your interview score too, actually. One of the highest scores I've seen."

My heart skipped a beat. So there was a chance that this really was just a mistake, after all. He gave me a long look, and I simply shrugged.

He cleared his throat. "As a Rater's assistant, I can't change anything. The only thing I can do is make a note of your complaint. And, honestly," he said, leaning forward, "I've been here two years and seen hundreds of complaints. The Rater never overturns a Rating once he's signed it."

I shook my head. "I can't accept that."

The guy made some notes on the glass screen, then stood up. I wished the screen were visible from this angle. "Your best bet is to fulfill your new assignment in a way that exceeds their expectations. That may actually get you somewhere." He made sure the screen was powered off, then stepped around the desk. "Wish there was more I could do. Sorry."

With that, the assistant made his way to the door and opened it for me. I had no choice but to leave. To my surprise, the guy followed me out. The door's lock clicked behind us with chilling finality. He gave me a last look and headed down the hallway as if in a hurry to get somewhere. Sighing, I made sure my frizz securely covered my forehead once again.

Great. What now?

The assistant wasn't the only one rushing away. The hallway was a mass of purple uniforms. Excited conversation buzzed in the air. As before, they all headed in the same direction.

Curious, I poked my head around the corner. The crowd was entering a set of double doors at the end of the hallway. Two guards stood on either side of the doors, their eyes sharp and probing.

"Excuse me," I said, touching the elbow of a man passing near me. "What's going on?"

The man looked surprised. "The empress's visit, of course. Didn't you get the network message?"

I felt my eyes widen. "I must have missed it. Thanks." He was gone before I finished, pushing against the purple exodus that filled the hallway.

The empress? She was coming here? I'd never actually seen her in person, but every citizen knew what she looked like. I had studied her life story in history class, trying to figure out what she'd done to get the Rating that had propelled her to the throne at age eighteen.

A thrill of excitement surged through my veins as I forced an opening in the mass of people. A visit from the empress definitely explained the crowds and my Rater's absence. He would be here somewhere, headed for the auditorium. I tried to remember what his photo had looked like, tried to hold it front and center in my mind. I wasn't leaving this building without talking with him, empress or not.

"Ouch!" a woman cried. I had just stepped on her foot.

"Sorry," I mumbled, but the pushing of the crowd didn't allow me to do much else but follow. We inched our way closer, taking small steps and easing toward the double doors. The guards seemed alert, but they hadn't stopped anyone yet. Of course, everyone else around me was a green. I pulled my hair forward again, hoping the lights were bright enough that the red glow wouldn't shine though.

Right before stepping into the auditorium, one of the guards glanced at me. I looked away quickly, rubbing a fake headache, hoping he hadn't looked too closely. The seats were nearly full, all facing a polished wooden platform on the stage. A dozen more guards surrounded the platform. The redness of my new Rating would be extremely noticeable when the lights dimmed so I had to be careful. I passed under a blast of cold air conditioning and shivered.

Keeping my hand up, I caught a glimpse of the Rater's assistant slowly climbing the staircase to the left. Hoping the Rater would also be nearby, I followed, choosing a seat two rows behind him. It would only allow for a side view of the speaker, but it was the closest I could get to the front. A thrill of excitement shot through my body. I was about to see the empress in person.

Dresden will be so jealous, I thought with satisfaction.

I scanned the room for a few minutes, feeling my heart sink slowly to the floor. There were probably a thousand people in here, all greens, all blonde. It would be nearly impossible to find the Rater. A thousand people, I thought. It seemed strange. There couldn't have been more than a couple hundred who worked in the government building. Maybe the higher officials of the area were here too. That meant my father was probably in the crowd as well. Slouching in my seat and keeping a hand over my forehead, I glanced at the rows behind me. No one looked familiar.

The guard who had watched me enter began climbing the steps on the far side, searching faces. My breathing quickened. I forced myself to sit normally as he turned and headed my direction. Twenty meters. Ten.

But before he reached our section, the lights suddenly dimmed. The guard's outline froze and then retreated down the steps. I gave a sigh of relief.

The audience immediately quieted in anticipation. Within seconds the tribune rose to introduce the empress. When she appeared, we stood and put our fists over our hearts in respect. And then I gave a start. This woman, wearing a curvy, sequined uniform dress, looked different from the lady I'd seen in the transmissions. The face was the same, but the youthful intelligence she was famous for was replaced by irritation. She just looked … older. Her usual intricate braid was gone. Instead, her long blonde hair hung straight, with a few haphazard streaks of purple and silver. I knew that I was witnessing the birth of the latest appearance-points obsession.

Her hair wasn't what had surprised me, though. It was her unnatural, highly arched eyebrows. Too many face-lifts. I chuckled to myself. Tiny embedded jewels and intricate tattoos—and the highest Rating score in the entire nation, 974—framed her forehead. She had managed to keep her position for almost seventeen years. Her score had decreased, though. It had been 976 before today.

She nodded to us, a polite smile pasted onto her painted face, and then she tilted her head gracefully. "My dears, thank you for your greeting." The audience caught her meaning and sat down. "I have only a few minutes, so allow me to deliver my message. Then I will take a few intelligent questions."

She stood a little taller, as if gathering her thoughts. "You've likely heard the rumors about food smugglers, especially in this area, for several years now. It will not surprise you to hear that most of them are Integrants. These people attack our borders, steal precious resources, and smuggle food. In the past, we've allowed them a second chance through integration and the reform system. But that is not the worst of it." She paused dramatically. "Now they have repaid our kindness with an uprising within NORA's borders."

The shuffling sounds in the audience went silent.

"The smugglers don't see the danger they're perpetuating," she continued. "Since the beginning of time, food has been the common thread in every war. Battles rampant with death and horror have been waged over its acquisition, those with food always holding the power. Food used to be the root of illness, the source of poisons and toxins, and always fostered inequality. People had too much or too little and consumed the wrong kinds, which caused their bodies to become inefficient and their lives wasteful. I will not allow our nation to crumble under the problems we've worked so hard to eradicate. The nutrition pill is all we need. And I certainly will not allow these miscreants to hold power over our people or overthrow our peaceful government. It is time to act, to cleanse our streets of the black market forever." She paused for effect. "As of today, NORA is under martial law."

There were some audible gasps, but many covered their shock with polite applause. I sat back in my seat, stunned.

The empress waited for the clapping to stop before she went on. "In the past, citizens found to be in an unscheduled location during daily techband sweeps were simply docked Rating points. It's clear that a more effective form of remediation is necessary. Starting tomorrow, citizens caught anywhere they're not authorized to be will receive an electric punishment from their techband."

The crowd stirred, a low murmur sweeping the room like a shockwave. I remembered all too well pulling on my techband as a child, wondering if it would come off, and feeling a sudden electric jolt. That jolt, or punishment mode, happened anytime someone messed with their techband. As I got older, my professors had insisted that it was for our own protection. The techband held all our data—personal records, schedules, schoolwork, personal finances, and more. We scanned it to buy things and unlock doors. It was just part of life in NORA.

The empress was inflicting the tightest security measures NORA had ever seen. The consequence of disobedience wasn't simply a Rating reduction. It was pain. The woman who stood before us wasn't the humble, everyday hero I'd studied in history. A shiver spread through my body, and it wasn't from the cold.

A flicker of movement caught my eye. It was the suspicious guard. He stood against the wall now, arms folded, waiting. He looked ready to move as soon as the lights came on.

"Some will say this policy is too strict," the empress continued, turning toward our side of the room. Her high eyebrows made her look like a surprised deer.

"Know this. Where there is division, there is unrest. Our frequent wars with the outlands are devastating enough. We cannot afford to battle amongst ourselves any longer. It is time that our children felt safe in their own streets. Once that is accomplished, we may reconsider."

The audience was silent, everyone turning the idea over in their minds. A woman near the front stood and bowed. "Excuse me, Your Majesty. If I may … When will the new policy be announced to the public?"

The empress frowned. "This evening, at 1700 hours."

Several other people stood and bowed, and the empress sighed. "Very well, you may ask a couple of quick questions."

The standing figures started to talk over each other, but a man from the back shouted, "Does this apply to everyone? Government workers? Children?"

The empress pushed back from the platform a little, her lips pursed. "Yes. Those in the military and administrative positions will have an adapted version of the punishment, for obvious reasons."

As the man sat, a dazed look on his face, a woman jumped up. "Your Majesty, may I ask a question?"

"Speak," the empress ordered impatiently.

The lady looked around the room for a second, as if unsure about her question. Finally she blurted, "Is this policy in reaction to what happened to your Rating today?"

The audience froze as every eye turned to our leader. Her expression darkened as she raised an eyebrow—if that was even possible—and stared at her questioner as if considering how to squash an insect. The questioner shifted her weight nervously, then looked away.

The tribune stepped forward on the platform. "We are out of time," he began, but the empress waved him away. She gripped both sides of the podium tightly and leaned forward. "As stated under law, I will remain your leader as long as I'm the most highly Rated individual. That does not appear to be changing anytime soon. I am most insulted by your insinuation."

The woman jerked back as if she had been slapped. Then she slowly sat, sinking low into her chair. I knew her Rating would be affected by her outburst, even though she'd only voiced the question most of us wanted answered.

The empress stalked off the stage. We stood and saluted again, but she didn't give us a second look. The commander cleared his throat. "The empress has been very generous to deliver this message in person. She relies on you, her most trusted and most highly Rated citizens, to ensure that her message is well received. You are dismissed." He glared at the humiliated woman in the audience before following the empress out.

I tried to imagine the impact this announcement

would have on NORA. Since Olympus shared a wall with the integration camp, it would affect us the most. An alliance between the food smugglers and the Integrants must have been threatening, indeed, to prompt such stern retaliation.

The audience began to disperse, the noise level rising as the crowd filed out the doors. I watched the crowd, looking for a round-faced man with dimples, but he was nowhere to be seen. The guard who'd been watching me stood in the middle of the doorway, a steady rock in the midst of a flowing river of people. He wasn't about to let me get by again.

Pushing down a rising sense of panic, I turned my head and looked for another exit, but there was nothing. I started making my way down the stairs, holding my forehead again, but that must have been what the guard was looking for. Out of the corner of my eye, I watched him push his way forward. I was in big trouble now. If I was arrested for sneaking in, there would be no Rating reconsideration.

With a quick glance at the platform, I noted that the empress and all her guards were long gone. That meant there was a back door somewhere. I reached the bottom of the platform and leaped up onto it. The guard picked up the pace behind me. Leaping again, I threw myself behind the curtain the empress had disappeared behind. The guard shouted something, but I couldn't understand his muffled words.

Ahead was a dark hallway. At the end of it, light

shone around the outline of a doorway. I sprinted down the hall, nearly tripping over my feet. *Please be unlocked.* With a mighty heave, I threw all my weight against the door. It opened more easily than expected, sending my feet stumbling forward.

Suddenly I found myself in a heap on the floor in front of a pair of silver-sequined high heels.

"Sorry," I muttered, looking up. Several guards stood immediately in front of me, stunners aimed at my head, protecting the woman at whose feet I lay. Her two arched eyebrows stared down at me, framing eyes that registered irritation and confusion. Then her painted lips curved downward like a disapproving parent.

It was the empress.

8

My jaw dropped as I stared, horrified. Her sternness melted away as she realized my mistake, and an amused light reached her mascara-plastered eyes.

"Don't move," a stocky officer said, his stun gun still trained on my head.

"She's little more than a child," the empress said, studying me. Her manicured fingers reached out to brush my hair away from my Rating, and then I heard a sharp intake of breath. Every stun gun in the vicinity was immediately aimed at me—the center of a semicircle of unwanted attention. The empress made a *tsk-tsk* sound.

I heard the door open behind me, and the suspicious guard nearly bowled me over. When he saw the empress, his face went a sickly white, and he stood uncertainly, as if unsure whether to grab me or stand at attention. He chose the latter.

I felt nauseated as I raised my hands in surrender, still sitting on the ground. "I'm so sorry. I didn't know—"

"Don't talk in Her Majesty's presence, red," the tribune snapped.

"I haven't seen a Rating that low since that serial killer from Alta," the empress mused, still studying me. "And such a pretty face—proportional and intelligent. What a waste."

"Please—" I began, and the tribune stepped forward with his arm raised to strike, but the empress put a hand up.

"Let her speak," she commanded. "Stand up, red."

I stood. "I didn't mean to follow you, Your Majesty. I just came looking for my Rater, to ask for a reconsideration." My voice wavered. It was too late to be shy now; if she had me arrested, it was over. "But now that you're here …"

She gave a soft chuckle. "My dear, I don't oversee Ratings. I'm no councilwoman."

"I know," I said quickly. This was my last chance. "But my Rater won't change it, and there's been a big mistake."

"NORA doesn't make mistakes, child," she said, folding her arms. "You must have done something to deserve it."

I thought again of my biological father and gulped. It was probably the last thing I wanted this woman to know. "My scores are nearly perfect," I said, knowing as the words left my mouth that I'd lost the battle. The guard behind me grabbed my arms and locked them behind my back. It was over.

"Wait," the empress said suddenly. Her eyes narrowed, and she circled me like a vulture examining its prey, her pointy shoes tapping sharply on the hard concrete. "What is your name, child?"

"Ametrine Dowell."

A flash of recognition appeared in her eyes—or was it my imagination? Her face darkened. My wrists felt clasped together in some sort of device, which sent a painful current of electricity shooting up my arms when I moved too quickly—probably connected to my techband somehow.

"Ametrine, hmm? An unusual name."

"My father named me."

A strange look came over her face, but she hid it quickly. "Well, Ametrine, I see a certain stubbornness in you. Perhaps that alone is the cause for your Rating. You should accept your fate with grace. It will make your life a lot easier."

Her words should have made me more docile, but they made me angry. It couldn't end like this. I hadn't done anything wrong, and they were determined to make me into something I wasn't. I looked up at the empress. My eyes met hers, steady and undefeated. I was ready. "This is wrong, and I won't accept it."

She looked down her nose at me for a moment, eyes flickering to the red numbers on my head. "I can see that." We were inches away now. The tattoos on her forehead were laced with golden thread and tiny precious jewels. I didn't know where to focus. "Well, you did get past my guards. How you did that," she said, shooting a glare in the sheepish guard's direction, "I can't imagine."

"We'll take care of her immediately, Your Majesty," the tribune said in a terse manner.

"No. She's coming with me." She waved her delicate hand. "This one is interesting to me. I'm sure we'll find something to talk about."

Before I knew what was happening, two guards shoved me toward the largest transport I had ever seen, its reflective, reinforced steel designed to deflect bullets and stunners alike. Despite its size, it smoothly hovered above the ground as they forced me inside, whacking my head against the doorframe before I fell onto the seat. I rebalanced myself and looked out the window. The guards stood at attention. As the empress set a dainty foot inside, I caught the last part of her whispered conversation with the tribune.

" … absolutely unacceptable. If I'm not safe here, then where?"

"He'll be stripped of rank immediately."

"No. I want him executed."

I gave a little gasp, which resulted in a painful jolt from my bonds.

"Yes, Your Majesty," the tribune replied sharply, his voice tight. She climbed in with a sweet smile and watched the two armed soldiers sit on either side of her. The guard who'd chased me stood stiffly as the transport eased away, but his face had turned yet another shade of pale. Maybe he'd heard their conversation as well. He knew what was about to happen. And it was all because of me and my stupid, selfish stubbornness.

"Please—" I began, about to plead for his life, but she cut me off immediately.

"So, Ametrine," she said in a bored tone. "Let's have a little chat."

It was my first ride in a transport. Most citizens rode their bikes to their assignments, but the privileged few got driven around. My stepfather was one of those. I'd asked him once to take me for a ride, but the request had only made him angry. "Work hard and get your own someday," he'd said. Somehow I'd never imagined my first ride would go quite like this. I took a deep breath and tried to ignore my racing heart.

The interior was of soft leather, white and almost silky to the touch. It smelled of disinfectant and lipstick. There were only two small windows on either side made of reinforced, double-paned glass. The realization gave me little comfort.

The city sped past quickly. We were headed west, toward Brighton, surrounded by several armored transports on either side, in front, and behind. I was still confused as to why she'd insisted on my presence here. I could tell that the guards on either side of her didn't understand it either. I was the one who deserved to be executed. And yet, I was sitting here, relaxing in the empress's transport. Not in comfort, exactly—but still alive, at least.

Why had I sneaked into that meeting?

"You want a higher Rating," the empress said. "Why do you think you deserve it?"

My mouth was dry, but I couldn't help but blurt out, "Please, Your Majesty—the guard *tried* to do his job. He nearly caught me before—"

"*Nearly* doesn't cut it here," she snapped. "And neither does *try*. He had his chance. If I can't count on my personal guard to protect me, who can I count on?"

The guards stiffened, but they continued to look ahead. Their faces were chiseled and tanned like models. It seemed the empress liked to surround herself with visual perfection, even when it came to her guards.

"Well?" she asked. "Answer me or you'll share his fate. Why do you want a higher Rating?"

Could she really do that? Execute an innocent citizen just because they failed at something? I nearly snapped at her again, but I knew it wouldn't help. Why did I deserve a higher Rating? I thought about my accomplishments. Something told me she didn't care about all that. "So I can be with someone."

"Ah. A boy worth risking everything for, right?"

I blinked, wondering if her words were an act, a ploy to get me on her side. But it was true. Dresden was worth it. "Yes."

"What is his Rating score?"

I paused. "942."

She whistled. "That is a problem, isn't it?"

She's toying with me. I kept my mouth shut.

"The way I see it, you only have two choices." She turned to look absently out the window. "You fulfill your assignment well and work your way back up." There was a hint of a smile on her pouty red lips. "Or you can accept a special assignment—one that will be very worth your while. If you fulfill it, of course."

Trying to hide my sudden interest, I slouched against the seat. The movement, slight as it was, sent an electric jolt up my arm. I swallowed. "What assignment?"

"It's dangerous," she cooed. "Risky, foolhardy, and downright painful. But I have a feeling you're up to the challenge. And," she leaned forward to whisper, "if you can manage it, I'll personally order a Rating reconsideration for you."

I took a deep breath, taking a moment to consider her words, my mind whirling. A second chance, from the empress herself. Was this really happening?

She sat back, watching my face. "I have a personal law-enforcement team stationed in the capital city, Aiguille. They take care of things for me, things the monitor force doesn't have the competence for." One of her guards swallowed hard, glancing at her out of the corner of his eye, but she went on. "We've recently discovered that a member of the team has been leaking information to the Integrants. Unfortunately, I don't know who it is. The team is far too well-trained and valuable a resource to disband." She gave a wry smile. "They call themselves EPIC—Empress's Personal Intelligence Contingent."

"You want me to join them? To catch a spy?"

"Exactly."

I thought back to the Rating Ceremony. "Are they the ones in black?"

"Yes. You've seen them, I assume?"

"Just one." I hadn't understood how a red could serve in the military. Now I understood. Had the guy from the ceremony been handpicked by the empress too? "So I travel around like they do and catch criminals."

The empress looked bored. "Smugglers, mostly."

"How much time do I have?" I asked.

"Two weeks."

"That's not very long."

She sat back, crossing one leg over the other. "My dear, I could stop this transport and have you dumped out the window right now. Or, if I were in a bad mood, I'd simply order you to fulfill this assignment. But being the benevolent creature that I am, I've given you a choice. And, to be honest"—she examined her manicured fingernails—"it doesn't seem like the choice should be all that difficult."

My mind spun, trying to take it all in. A dangerous assignment, a secret ploy to uncover a government spy. I'd barely had the guts to visit my Rater this morning. Not only was the empress's offer the quickest option, but it was the only *real* option. Whatever assignment came my way would be in the dregs of society, probably working in manufacturing or refuse. It was extremely hard to work your way out of that. It would be years—a decade, perhaps— before I became a yellow.

And then there was Dresden. His face flashed into my mind—his laughing blue eyes, the hint of curl in the light hair above his collar, his strong cheekbones. The feel of his arms around me. I couldn't imagine a life without Dresden.

The empress's painted lips curved into a smile as she watched my face, as if knowing she had convinced me. And as much as I hated to admit it, I knew it too. I felt a little dizzy. Dresden and Tali would be getting their assignments today, which meant they'd probably be gone within days.

"Can I tell my family good-bye?"

Her hands clasped into fists, but her voice was controlled. "Of course not. Your family will be notified. You'll only be gone two weeks, after all. Assuming you survive."

I gripped the seat with my thighs to steady myself. "Survive?"

"Of course. I told you it was dangerous. We've lost several soldiers in the last couple of years. Smugglers can hide weapons as well as food, you know. And then there's the danger of the traitor discovering your mission and taking you out. So, yes, *if* you survive."

My stomach twisted. All I'd wanted this morning was a second chance. Well, this was it. This was *my* assignment, my one and only opportunity to change the future. I'd worked too hard to have it all taken away from me. A surge of determination grew inside me, and I lifted my chin. "I'll do it."

"Excellent." She flipped open her techband. "Ruben, take us to the train station."

PART TWO

9

My legs moved to a rhythm, predictable and steady, and I barely noticed the citizens and vehicles around me. Running was a huge relief after a difficult mission and cramped transport ride. I required my team to run with me every week for conditioning, but that was only a small part of it. For one precious hour, I could leave the past behind.

Someone behind me sucked in a ragged breath and then coughed. I smiled. Tormenting Semias, who had to stop every few minutes to catch his wind, was yet another perk.

We were three miles from the bunker—I refused to think in kilometers—when my techband suddenly vibrated. Murphy was back with the newest recruit, no doubt.

I slowed to a walk and accepted the call, wondering what the latest unskilled and sorry trainee would be like. "Vance here."

"I thought we talked about the running thing," Murphy said, using his most authoritative voice. "You scare the citizens. I probably have a dozen formal complaints on my desk already. "

"What's wrong with scattering the stuffy businessmen on their way home? They could use a little more exercise anyway."

He muttered something under his breath. "Get out of the bike lanes and onto the sidewalk. Meet me at the furniture store in five minutes." The screen went blank.

I forced back the irritation. We'd passed that a mile back, and since he could track us, he probably knew it.

"Time to sprint, boys," I shouted, smiling at the groans that followed.

When we got there, Murphy leaned casually against his transport. Casual for him, anyway. He probably stood at attention in his sleep. The guys, still heaving from their run, crowded the transport for a look at our newest recruit. I pushed my way through and froze as Murphy opened the car door. The passenger stepped out and stood, blinking in the bright sunlight.

A girl.

The other guys quieted, and someone cleared his throat. The girl was of a slight build, with searching dark brown eyes. Her hair was pulled back into a tight ponytail, although the front part was swept over her forehead and pinned into place. I saw the soft red glow of the numbers underneath. She shifted her weight from side to side as if wishing she could run away or climb back into the vehicle. She looked at me, and I stiffened. The girl from the Rating Ceremony.

Daymond cleared his throat. "You're the new recruit, then?"

The girl nodded, her eyes still glued on me. It was hard to tell she was the same person I'd seen in Olympus. Her shoulders slumped a little, and her haunted eyes darted around like a cornered raccoon; her new purple uniform hung poorly on her petite frame.

The Demander had gone too far this time. If he thought sending a girl would hold us back, he was dead wrong.

"This is Ametrine Dowell," Murphy announced. His voice held a hint of amusement at our reaction. "Treat her well, boys. And good luck to you, Ametrine." He strode around to the driver's side and climbed in. The transport pulled away and disappeared into traffic. She stared after it, looking a little lost.

"A girl," Daymond said. "What the fates were they thinking?"

"She's pregnant," Semias said, staring at her. "That's the only explanation."

Ametrine gasped and whirled to face him.

"Don't be stupid, Semias," Ross said with on his I-know-everything air. "They send pregnant girls straight to the medics, then to the work camps."

"How do you know? Experience?" Daymond

asked. Ross opened his mouth, but Daymond talked over him. "Well, what are we supposed to do with a girl?"

"I get her first," Semias said. His eyes slid slowly down her body.

The guys instantly went still. The girl froze. Before I even realized what I was doing, I had slammed Semias against the store wall. His expression was stunned, then turned murderous. He was several inches taller and thicker through the shoulders, but my hand tightening on his esophagus effectively encouraged him to be still. "One more comment like that," I spat, "and it'll be your last."

He swatted at my hand and gave me a death glare.

Daymond jumped forward and extended his hand to Ametrine. "I'm Daymond. You've already met Vance, leader of Team Two. I guess you're one of us now. You'll meet Team One back at the bunker."

I pulled away from Semias, who was peeling himself off the wall, and nodded. Handshakes were a NORA thing. "Don't mind Semias. He's all mouth, especially when it comes to stuffing himself."

Semias swore under his breath.

"You'll be with me until you're trained, Ametrine," I told her.

"Call me Treena."

Neb pulled on my sleeve like an eager toddler. I tried to ignore him, but the tugging became more insistent. I shot him a glare.

There was an unnatural hint of color in his cheeks. "I just thought of something."

"What?"

"Um, where's she gonna sleep?"

Someone coughed, and I felt anger rise up inside me again. What was the commander thinking, sending a girl? This really complicated things. "We'll put her in the bathroom—I mean, washroom."

"Excuse me?" Treena said.

It was suddenly very quiet. "But," Neb continued, "what if we have to—you know—"

"I'm sure she'll share."

"Hold on," Treena said. "There's no way I'm sleeping in a washroom."

"Three-quarters pace, men," I ordered. "See you at the bunker."

The guys looked grumpy, but they got the hint and took off at a jog. Semias lumbered along after them at a walk. If only I could get Poly to take Semias. He wasn't ready to advance yet, but ... a girl? This was going to be tough.

I motioned for her to walk with me, but she shook her head. "No. Let's run. Why are you treating me like a porcelain doll?"

With a shrug, I started to jog. Her legs were shorter, but she kept pace pretty well. "The bathroom offers a lock and privacy. I don't trust these guys, and neither should you."

She looked at me out of the corner of her eye, and I

knew exactly what she was thinking. If she couldn't trust yellows, could she really trust a red? For a while there was only the sound of traffic and the steady rhythm of our breathing. After about a mile, she was still keeping up. At least they'd sent me a girl who could run.

"Fine," she said after several minutes. "I'll sleep in the washroom until they're used to me. But only if it's clean."

I gave her a sideways look. She'd just joined the most dangerous military unit in the nation, and she was worried about sanitation. "We do our own cleaning, so I can't promise anything. But it could be worse. You could be sleeping in the stairwell."

She shot me a glare. Treena looked like any other NORA girl, but I sensed an intense anger under the surface. She was obviously not happy to be here. What could she possibly have done to warrant 440? And why had they sent her here, of all places?

There was only one way to find out.

I clicked my techband screen up and called Daymond. His face came into view, bouncing with his strides. "Yep."

"Change of plans," I said. "Let's stop at the Red District. I think it's a good time to get Treena's initiation out of the way."

"Yes, sir," Daymond said with a grin.

It gave me great satisfaction to see Treena swallow hard.

10

I'd been here before.

At least that's what it felt like. The Red District in Aiguille was similar to the one in Olympus: very few bikes and hordes of people shuffling around, their eyes darting sharply, missing nothing. Dozens of children dodged through the crowds, laughing and playing, their uniforms dirty and unfitted. I wrinkled my nose. The roads were black with filth, the buildings shorter and dusted with various shades of grime. The street cleaners obviously didn't come here either.

The citizens' faces showed a practiced boredom, but they clung to their kids with the ferocity of a mother bear. The EPIC team lined up on the curb, still sweaty and panting from their run, and suddenly there was a stillness to the crowded square, as if we'd dampened the sound. Nearly all motion stopped. A few people actually turned around and headed quickly in the opposite direction.

"If you were trying to sneak in," I said, "you failed miserably."

Vance glanced meaningfully at his guys. Two of them broke off and trotted after the people who had left. Then he turned to me. "You ready, Treena?"

I nodded, even though I wasn't. Without a thought, I patted the hair covering my Rating.

"Today you're a beggar," Vance said with a chuckle, and he smoothed my hair out of my face. His fingers were calloused but gentle, and it sent a tingle down my spine. "If there was ever a time to show your Rating off, it's now."

"No one will believe she's a beggar," Semias said with a frown. "She looks too clean. Her uniform looks fresh out of the package."

Vance opened his mouth to argue, but Daymond— the one with the scar—spoke up. "I actually agree with Semias this time. She doesn't look desperate enough."

"I'm happy to dirty her up a little," Semias said, still staring at me. "We want her to look authentic, after all."

I glared back. "Do. Not. Touch me."

"Semias," Vance said quietly. "You and Day sweep the north alley. I'll contact you when you're needed."

"Yes, sir." Daymond shot me an apologetic look before striding away. Semias just smirked and shuffled after him.

I let out an exasperated breath. "You don't need to

protect me."

Vance ignored my comment and reached into his pocket, pulling out a set of tiny black devices, then fastened one to his ear. It looked like an earring. "Put this on so we can communicate. I'm staying out of the way, but I'll be there in seconds if it sounds like you need help. Any questions?"

A million, actually, but few he could answer. I knelt and rubbed my hand in the dirt, then brushed it onto my uniform. "So, I'm supposed to catch a smuggler? Is that all?"

"You can catch more than one," he said with a slight smile, "if you'd like. Semias arrested three at his orientation."

That wasn't exactly what I'd meant, but it seemed simple enough. "Do I get a weapon or anything?"

"No. You haven't been trained to use one, and it would be too conspicuous. That's why I'm listening in. You'll be fine, though. They won't hurt you."

No weapon, no help. My mission was to identify the traitor, and I couldn't do that unless the guys trusted me, which meant passing this test. If Semias could do it, I could. I hesitated, then stepped up against a shop corner and leaned against the building. Sure enough, a layer of dirt attached itself to my uniform. I rubbed against the wall on all sides like an itchy cat, then nodded in satisfaction. "All right, I'm ready."

"Good luck."

It wasn't long before I stood on the first floor

of a high-occupancy apartment building, trying to decide where to start. I chose a random door—plastic, covered in dark fingerprints, and much too thin to provide its owners any sense of security. Everything was the same gray color. I felt an overwhelming urge to find a rag and start scrubbing like a crazy person.

Instead, I tapped on the door, trying to look hunched over and miserable. There was no answer. A mixture of disappointment and relief flooded through my body as I moved on to the next door. No answer. If nobody opened up for me, would I fail the initiation? Or would I just have to do this again another day?

At the sixth door, an eye almost completely covered with mousy gray hair appeared at waist level. "What?" a tiny voice whispered. A child.

"Uh, I—just wanted to know if you have any extra nutrition pills? I'm really hungry."

The door opened a little wider, and I could see two eyes now. "You talk funny. Like the soldiers." She—I assumed it was a girl—glanced at my forehead. "'Cept soldiers don't have the red numbers. Just the green ones. Lemme ask my papa."

The sharp crack of the door slamming made me jump.

"Treena," Vance's voice said over the feed. "You in?"

"Not yet," I whispered. "Give me a minute."

"Let me know the second you get inside."

"I will, I will."

"Lady," the kid said through the door. She messed with the knob, and the door swung wide open. The girl couldn't be more than six years old. "My papa still gots the sickness, you know? But he says you can have one of his pills. They taste gross anyway." She held the tiny gray pill up for me to see. The material inside was coarse and cheaply made, like the ones Tali used.

Part of me wanted to take it and run away. If this kid was a smuggler, I didn't want to know. I accepted it, rolling it over in my palm. The outside was a little slimy from her hand, but she beamed up at me with a brilliant smile.

"Thanks, cutie." I forced a smile and started to turn away.

"Wait," she said. She leaned forward and whispered, "I have a potato. It smells bad, and it has the white pokey things, but you can have it. I'll go get it for you."

The word *no* got caught in my throat as she dashed off again. A potato. We'd done a unit on illegal substances in school, and I knew it was some kind of root-based food. Smugglers grew a lot of them because they were easier to hide from scouting planes.

Food. This girl and her father were smugglers. Or customers, at least. A sick feeling anchored me to the spot, and I felt numb. Could I destroy a family? Could I achieve my goal at the expense of a six-year-old kid? Did I have it in me to send an innocent child to the work camps so I could have my Rating changed? Was it right to take my happiness from someone else?

I suddenly felt nauseated, and I swallowed hard. Of course it was right. I hadn't written the law—I was just enforcing it. It wasn't like she'd be harmed, exactly. Just sent elsewhere. Surely the work camps weren't much worse than living in the Red District.

The girl returned, hands cupped around something small and brown. Her face radiated excitement. "I like it because the white pokeys look sharp, but they're not. See? It doesn't even hurt."

"You can't give this to me."

"Yes, I can. Papa said I could use it how I wanted, so you can have it." She thrust it into my hand and pulled away.

Smugglers were supposed to be evil-looking Integrants, violent and greedy men with scars and tattoos. Not little girls. I slipped the potato into my pocket. "Thank you. You'd better get back to your dad now."

Footsteps echoed up the stairs behind me, and I turned in surprise. Neb, Ross, Daymond, and Semias appeared out of the dim light and headed toward us. My heart sank into my toes.

"Vance said you needed backup," Daymond said.

"Your first door, huh?" Neb said. "Not bad."

Before I could speak, they leaped past me and through the doorway.

"Look out! There's a—"

It was too late. The shock on the girl's face turned into horror as the guys nearly ran her over. She hit the wall and fell to the ground. The EPIC guys just stomped past her, weapons up and ready.

"Are you okay?" I reached out to help her, but she stiffened and slapped my hand away. "Don't touch me. You're a soldier!"

"I'm so sorry," I mumbled.

Shouts from deeper inside the apartment told me her father had been discovered. Within seconds, a pale-faced, skinny-figured man was shoved into the hallway, his arms already fastened behind him. He wore a wrinkled, worn uniform that desperately needed washing. "We haven't done anything wrong," he insisted, his voice weak. "I have no food here."

"Daddy," the girl exclaimed. "I gave her the potato. I didn't know!"

He glanced at me, and his face went dark.

Suddenly there was a shrill cry from a back room, and then another nearly identical cry. The father groaned. As Neb went in to investigate, the little girl ran to her dad and wrapped herself tightly around his leg. "Daddy, why did they tie your arms again? Daddy, hold me."

"Twins!" Neb exclaimed, and came out holding two screaming babies wrapped in tattered blankets. One was flailing, and he struggled not to drop it. I started forward to help him.

89

Semias, who held the father's elbow, shoved the little girl aside, and she stumbled to the floor. "Someone tie this kid up, will you?"

"Leave my daughters alone," the father snapped. "They're innocent. They can stay with a neighbor while I'm gone."

"You aren't coming back," Semias said. "Possession of an illegal substance is punishable with a one-way trip to the work camps. Your kids will be fostered out."

The father growled and lunged for Semias.

Semias was ready. He stepped aside and shoved the man sideways, slamming him roughly into the wall. With a grunt, the man fell to one knee and struggled to right himself. Before he could blink, Semias had his stunner pointed it at the man's face. The sickly man breathed hard as the two stared each other down. Their Ratings were only twenty points apart, I noticed.

"Welcome to NORA," Semias whispered and pulled the trigger. I gasped. The little girl screamed as her father crumpled to the floor. The twins' wailing rivaled hers in volume and intensity.

Daymond groaned. "Was that necessary, Semias? Now we have to carry the guy."

I gaped at them in disbelief. I'd never seen someone get stunned before. Semias knelt down and grabbed the girl's shoulders, wrestling her arms together to bind them. Her sobs had turned into hysterical shrieking.

"Nice try," Daymond said. "You're taking the old man. You shoot 'em, you carry 'em. I'll take the girl."

Semias grumbled, but he backed away.

"Treena, come get a baby," Neb said.

I shuddered, stepping over the unconscious man, and took the more upset of the two babies. Her cheeks were wet with tears as she gasped for breath between screams. Pure terror reflected in her dark eyes. I pulled the hole-filled blanket up to cover her again.

"Four at once," Ross said. "You hold the record now, Treena. Not bad for your first time."

"Shh," I told the baby and pulled her close, bouncing to give her some measure of comfort, to stop the crying. "It'll be okay."

But the truth was, for this family, things would never be okay again.

"You sent them in, didn't you?"

Vance didn't respond. We watched as the captured family's transport disappeared into the late-afternoon traffic. The father had been deemed dangerous, which required two monitors to escort them as well as the driver. I was relieved that someone else was taking them to their fate; but I'd almost rather have chosen that above walking home next to Vance.

Something very close to rage surged through my veins. "It wasn't necessary. I had it all under control."

He met my gaze. "Under control. That's what you call it?"

"How do you know I wasn't playing along? Maybe I was just biding my time."

"But you weren't."

"You don't know that."

"It's not what you expected, is it? You thought you'd be catching the bad guys, when really, you *are* the bad guy. And you couldn't handle that realization."

My mouth dropped open a little. "Well, technically we're enforcing the law. That doesn't make us bad."

"Technically. But you're missing the point. There's one rule in EPIC, Treena, above all else. Until you believe it, you won't survive here. The law comes before the people—before Integrants, before smugglers, and even before EPIC. We fulfill the job no matter what. That's the lesson you're supposed to learn here."

My anger surged, then exploded. "Don't you dare lecture me about following the rules. I've obeyed every stupid law that's ever been written. I spent my entire life following orders and pleasing people, believing that if I did my life would be perfect. Look where that got me!"

He gave me a long look. "Whatever happened in your past, this is the time to be very careful. You think you're safer here, unwatched? You really think the empress would allow a bunch of reds and yellows to roam the country without very close supervision?"

"Just two reds."

He let out a frustrated breath. "Some of my guys have died, Treena. This life is dangerous. We had to send you in unarmed for initiation, but I'll issue you a weapon as soon as you're trained. Smugglers won't hesitate to kill you if it means their freedom. Add that to the fact that most of the nation hates us, and you'll see why it's so important to follow orders exactly." He started to turn, then paused. "Oh, and by the way, you'll want to dispose of that potato before we get back."

"She was just a little girl," I whispered. "I couldn't trade her happiness for mine."

Vance's expression hardened. "You'll get over that soon enough. Time to head for the bunker. Try to keep up."

With that, he turned and jogged away.

○━●○━●○━●○━●○

Major Murphy, the stern-faced man who had met me at the train station, had told me about the bunker. But I hadn't expected it to be an actual bomb shelter far beneath the Council Building. Had the guys chosen this place, or was it all NORA could offer them? Was it intended to protect EPIC from the world, or was it the other way around?

We must have descended a dozen staircases before we reached the bottom. My ears felt fuzzy as the stairwell grew darker and the air became heavy and cool. It was hard to believe that we were only a few kilometers away from the empress's palace and the famous square where Peak had first delivered the Standards. This felt like an entirely different world. At the very bottom was a dirty concrete wall and a single door. With a shove, Vance flung the door open and held it for me.

The front room wasn't what I had expected. There was no furniture at all, and workout equipment lined the walls. A thick, rectangular training pad sat in the middle of the floor. The stale air smelled like sweat and urine.

On the wall closest to the door was a shelf full of stunners. Helmets and gear had been shoved haphazardly into the bins below, and a combat boot lay on its side on the floor.

"The bedroom is down the hall, and the washroom is to the left." Vance still held the door for me, and I realized that I was standing there like an idiot.

"Lovely," I muttered and stepped inside. "Home sweet home."

"You'll get used to it." He closed the door, pushed on it, and slid some kind of metal device closed. It snapped with a click.

"What's that?" I asked.

"A dead bolt," he said. "It's not exactly NORA approved."

"A lock? But why?"

"I don't trust NORA's locking system."

There was a slight hesitation in his words, which made me realize that it wasn't the locking system he didn't trust. What kind of guy led a group of misfits, arrested children in the name of the law, and locked himself underground? A part of me—a very small part—was intrigued. There was distant laughter from the other room, and I remembered that there was a whole other team I had yet to meet. More stares and more doubts.

"Wait," I said before he could walk away. "Do you think I can do this?"

Vance hesitated. That was all I needed to know. So much for a good first day in EPIC.

"Training starts tomorrow," he said. "You'd better get some rest."

11

I slammed the screen closed in frustration. My techband's error message displayed no matter who I tried to call. Either we were too far underground to receive a network signal or I wasn't allowed to contact anyone. Something told me it was the latter.

The guys were still using the washroom. I sat on the dirty floor in the hallway next to the bedroom door, my knees propped up casually. After initiation, what was one more dirt stain? Besides, soon I'd receive a black uniform instead. As far as the guys knew, I'd passed with flying colors. Vance hadn't told a single person about my failure, which both relieved and bothered me. If he thought I owed him anything, he was flat-out wrong.

I sighed and clicked the screen open again. While on the train, I'd gotten one last note from my mother. It was a text message, not a real recording, but better than nothing. I scanned the list and found it again.

As you asked, I told your friends you got a second chance. They're excited for you. Dresden is going to the academy, Broadcast Division. He says to tell you good luck and he hopes to see you there soon. Taliyah's assignment is laundry for the military. She leaves tomorrow and says to keep fighting for what you want. Your father and I wish you the best. Mom.

P.S. I sure hope you're doing this for yourself and not for Dresden.

Dresden's assignment wasn't a surprise. He was probably packing right now, getting ready to board the morning train. At least we'd be in the same city, even if I couldn't contact him. There was a heavy ache in my chest. He was moving on without me. And I was sleeping in a washroom, arresting children and searching for a spy.

And then there was Tali. Laundry wasn't the most glamorous of jobs, but she'd always wanted to get out of Olympus. It was a change of scenery, at the very least. If only I could have said good-bye.

Laughter floated down the hallway from the bedroom. I got on hands and knees and snuck a peek—if they weren't dressed by now, it wasn't my fault—just in time to see Ross stepping out of the washroom with a towel around his waist. I pulled back, my cheeks burning.

Team One had been nice enough during introductions, but now the guys basically pretended I wasn't there. I didn't complain about that. In a way, I imagined myself being pretty comfortable here. At least everyone seemed to see each other at the same level despite the hundreds of points that varied between them. It was almost like Ratings didn't even matter.

Minutes later, Vance peeked his head around the corner and nodded. His dark hair was combed neatly back, and he wore a gray T-shirt. The old-fashioned soap smell that always followed him was stronger now.

"It's all yours." He handed me a folded black uniform. "Hope you find it clean enough to suit you."

I shot him a look and stood, trying not to notice how his T-shirt accented his rock-hard chest. A few steps through a noisy room full of laughing, half-dressed men, and I entered my new "bedroom." The mirrors were still misted with steam. A blanket and pillow—both off-white, and both well used—sat by the door. That was the extent of my bedding for the next two weeks.

"Lovely," I muttered and went back out to the bedroom. I swiped the pillows off the two nearest beds and strode back into the washroom. If I had to sleep in here, at least I'd be relatively comfortable.

I decided to camp out under the sanitation sinks

jutting out from the wall. It had a clear view of the door, and the floor wasn't wet there. I slid the door closed and shoved the lock into place before settling down on the hard tile.

Now, if only I could do something about the smell. Stuffing the pillows under my body and the clean one under my head, I pulled the blanket over my shoulders. The blanket smelled. Didn't they sanitize their fabrics down here?

Night had fallen long ago, but the guys didn't quiet down a bit. They were discussing the day's events, and occasionally the sound of arguing floated through the door. I strained to hear and caught a word here and there: Mission. Frenzy. Rating Day. Council.

The word *council* made me think of Konnor. His plan to unseat the current councilor of integration made me uneasy. If by some miracle he did get the position in the next few days, my parents would have to move here. He'd be working in the very building above us. I wasn't sure how I felt about that. It would be nice to see my mom again—I didn't like leaving on such uncertain terms—but it was nice to be out of the house, even if it was … this.

I hope you're doing it for yourself and not for Dresden, Lanah had said. Was she really more worried about my motives than my safety? Wouldn't most mothers have said, "Be careful," or "I love you" at that point, and not lectured about a boyfriend?

And why not do it for him? I'd had a huge crush

on him for years. I'd tutored him into the top ten for academic scores, and he'd trained me to become a pretty decent khel player before we finally hooked up. Together we made up a perfect person.

My fingers found their way up to my forehead again, and I jerked them away. *Who are you kidding? Dresden is a perfect person without you.*

My thoughts soon grew fuzzy, and a warm sense of comfort spread throughout my tired body. My last thought was *One day down, thirteen to go.*

o—●o—●o—●o—●o—●o

A harsh banging shattered my dreams, and I sat up too quickly, completely disoriented. My head whacked something hard with a painful thump.

Groaning, I held my head in my hands so it wouldn't explode. Where was I? It was so dark I couldn't tell if I was dreaming or awake. My head throbbed as it all came back. The washroom. EPIC. The mission. But what was that pounding noise?

I stood slowly and made my way to where the door should have been, feeling along the wall with one hand and holding my sore head with the other. It took a few seconds of fumbling to find the lock, and then I opened it a crack. "Hello?"

"Time to train," a gruff voice whispered, and a hand yanked me through the door.

"What? Let go of me!"

The hand dropped. "Let your eyes adjust for a

second," my captor whispered. "You're about to run into a wall. Here, follow me."

"Vance?"

His hand reached for mine, more softly this time, and pulled me through the darkness.

It really was Vance. "But where are we going?"

"Training," he said as if it were the most natural thing in the world.

Neb was waiting for us in the training room, bleary-eyed and shirtless. Other than the three of us, the room was empty. The lights that had seemed sufficiently bright yesterday were barely adequate now, and shadows haunted the corners of the training arena. Now that my heart had slowed a bit, my mind was finally working right.

"You really are serious?"

"Our team has missions day and night. The sooner you get used to it, the better. Besides, the training room is all ours."

"If I accidentally murder someone tomorrow out of exhaustion, I'll blame you," I muttered.

Neb barked a laugh, then clamped his mouth shut when Vance shot him a look.

"Why is Neb here?" I asked.

Vance paused. "Observation."

I opened my mouth to reply, but suddenly understood the real reason. Vance was, in a small way, being a gentleman by refusing to be alone with me.

"I still don't know why you're really here," Vance

said, walking to the far corner. "But I'm going to find out right now. Let's see what you can do." He tilted a padded black cylinder and rolled it toward us. I eyed it with confusion. "This is a training stand," he said. "I want you to pretend it's a person. Punch it, kick it, whatever."

I raised an eyebrow. This was training? Beating up a black piece of padded foam? This would be interesting. With a mighty heave, I threw my fists at it. I nearly fell over as the stand twisted under my weight. With a flush of embarrassment, I set myself again and kicked at it, almost missing altogether. Then I tried to use my shoulder to shove it aside. It didn't budge. The thing must have weighed as much as a transport.

Neb was trying so hard not to laugh that his face was bright red. Even Vance had a smile tickling the corners of his mouth. I felt utterly and thoroughly humiliated. Putting my hands into fists, I faced them. "What?"

"Well, that answers *that* question," Vance said, and Neb finally exploded with laughter. His snorts were so ridiculous that I glared at him, rubbing my sore shoulder.

"So why did they send you, then?" Vance muttered. "If you're inexperienced, there could really only be one reason."

"What's that?" Neb asked, leaning calmly against the wall.

"A tool," Vance said. "They want us to use her as a decoy or something. The Demander and the empress must not be satisfied with our performance."

You could say that. I kept my face impassive.

"If that's the case," Vance said slowly, "it's even more important that you learn to defend yourself, Treena. Neb, come here."

Neb jumped to attention like a lapdog. I almost expected his tongue to start flapping. "Yes?"

"Teach her the basics. Just punches and kicks for today. Tell me when she's got it." He didn't wait for an answer but retreated to the corner of the room where he'd gotten the stand. Then he sat on the floor, back to us, rigid and straight. I watched him in confusion.

"What good are kicks and punches when someone points a stunner at you?" I muttered. "I thought we'd be doing shooting practice or something."

"They didn't give me a stunner until I'd been here a month," Neb said. "Gotta prove yourself first. Now I'll show you how to punch. Make a fist and bend your thumb around the front."

It was hard to pay attention to Neb's droning when Vance was training across the room. He had spent the first ten minutes sitting still, completely ignoring us. I watched him out of the corner of my eye while he stretched. Neb was making me punch the black stand—the bag, as he called it—and soon I could make it buck backward a little. It was a small feat, but it was progress. Then we moved on to kicks. It was about then that Vance started fighting the air.

It was the strangest, most intoxicating thing I'd ever seen. His breathing deepened and came out in short bursts as his arms and legs whipped through the air—faster and faster. Soon his entire body was a black, dancing blur. Even Neb had stopped talking and stared in awe.

Vance dropped to the ground and spun as if kicking the feet out from under an invisible opponent and then leaped forward with a yell. Then there was a series of bullet-quick punches just before he leaped again, avoiding an unseen attack. His arm whipped out behind him as if he were holding off another man to his right, and his leg swept out again as he turned. Three quick kicks, each in a different direction, and another yell. I hardly dared blink.

I'd watched Dresden get sweaty playing khel hundreds of times, and his tall, lean body was carefully toned. But there was something raw about Vance, something wild and powerful. His build was shorter and wider than Dresden's, yet somehow he seemed much quicker. And there was something unsettling about his eyes.

Suddenly those eyes were on me, and I realized I was staring. With a quick clearing of my throat, I turned back to the bag. Vance straightened and wiped his forehead. His shirt, wet with perspiration, clung tightly to his hardened frame. "Let's see what you've learned."

"You just want a break," I said and swallowed hard. Vance had taken off his sweaty shirt. I tore my eyes away and locked my gaze onto the bag. My cheeks were hot as I kicked it again with a grunt. After Vance's performance, he probably thought I was the weakest, silliest girl he'd ever met.

He didn't smile. "Show me a punch."

I hit the bag as hard as I could. It didn't budge.

Vance shook his head. "No, I mean punch me." He put a gentle hand on my shoulder and eased me toward him.

I shrugged. "Fine." With a heave, I threw my fist toward his chiseled stomach still glistening with sweat. He grabbed my fist before it connected. "Not there. If I were trying to attack you, that wouldn't even slow me down. Aim here." He pointed to his solar plexus, where his rib cage met in the center.

"All right," I said slowly and struck again. This time I nearly touched his skin before he swiped my fist away. I hadn't even seen his hand move.

"Better. Your aim is actually pretty decent. You're putting your whole body into it, but you still don't have much power."

I blinked. "Um, I'm not a huge person. What else am I supposed to do?"

It was a sarcastic comment, but he stood straighter, his expression thoughtful. A flash of movement in the corner caught my eye. It was Neb, trying to imitate Vance. He kicked and punched the air, but his movements looked awkward and disconnected. There was nothing of the smooth and flowing dancelike movements Vance had just demonstrated.

"What was that?" I asked. "I mean, what you just did."

My question pulled him out of his thoughts. "Oh, just something my father taught me. Martial arts. It's a kind of combat."

"Will you teach me?"

A flicker of surprise flashed across his face, but he covered it quickly. "I've never taught anyone before."

"Really? But you're the trainer."

"I show everyone the basics, but these guys prefer boxing. They think all you need is a hard-enough punch to the face and your opponent is out for the count."

"Isn't he?"

Vance gave a sideways smile, really looking at me for the first time. "Sometimes."

I pulled my arm up for a stretch, feeling my muscles stiffening already. I'd be very sore tomorrow. Or, rather—looking at my techband—later today. We'd burned an hour already. The other guys would be up soon. Somehow the realization made me want to enjoy these quiet moments while they lasted. I felt Vance's eyes on me as I settled myself in front of the bag again, pulling my arms behind me for a series of punches. After a couple of minutes, I felt my body warming up comfortably, my breathing becoming quicker and more rhythmic. I had almost forgotten about Vance when he spoke.

"Yes."

"Hmm?"

"Yes, I'll teach you." He grabbed the bag and leaned it onto its side, spinning it effortlessly out of the way. "But I want you to practice on a real person from now on."

I hid a smile. "Fair enough."

"And," he continued, "you need to throw away everything you have been up to this point."

"Excuse me?"

"Watch," he said. I barely saw his arm move and realized he was throwing a punch. My body instinctively leaped backward. Vance's fist stopped just short of where I had stood. "See that?"

Adrenaline coursed through my veins as I gaped at him. "What was that? You showing off now?"

"You retreated."

"What else should I do, get hit?"

"That's just it. You've been taught by NORA to be docile and obedient, to run away from conflict. Conquer that reflex. Smugglers will only attack if they think they can beat you. Fight back, and suddenly you're not worth the effort."

What did he mean, *you've* been taught? The guy had obviously been in this dungeon too long. And

I was anything but docile. "Fine, then teach me to defend myself. But I'm not sitting around until I get attacked, Vance. I want to get in the first strike."

His expression was thoughtful as he nodded. "Deal."

We practiced for another hour before I couldn't take any more. My body was stiff and sore from what felt like an actual beating by the time the first guy awoke. My "room" was quickly occupied by a group of sleepy, dirty, sour-breathed men who just kicked my pillow aside. There would be no nap this morning.

Day two had begun.

o—●o—●o—●o—●o—●o—●o—●o

While the men did their business, I ran through my stretches, sitting on the mat in the training room. "Two weeks," I muttered. It felt like forever. There were twelve guys, six on each team, which meant I'd have to rule out one guy per day. I sighed. It didn't make sense to hide in here, pretending like I wasn't a part of the group. It was time to start asking questions and getting to know the team. I forced my aching legs to stand and started for the bedrooms.

The sound of muffled voices, low and deep, stopped me. It came from the stairwell. I moved to the door, straining to hear. The voice was unfamiliar.

Curious, I put my ear right up against the heavy door, but it didn't seem to help. I sat against the wall and grabbed my feet into a leg stretch just in case someone walked in. I could only pick out a word here and there. *Promise. Tomorrow. Resistance.*

I perked up, straining to hear over the sounds of the guys getting ready in the other room. What conversation was so secret that a guy had to sneak into the stairwell?

He must have finished his call, because the talking stopped and I heard the snap of a techband screen closing. I leaped back and grabbed a weight, pretending to have been lifting for a while, although I didn't have to pretend the shakiness. A bulky man from Team One entered and nudged the door shut. I couldn't remember his name. He glanced at me, murmured a hello, then disappeared into the bedroom.

Neb peeked in from where the large man had just gone. "The guys are done. You can have the washroom back now."

"Who was that again?" I asked.

Neb looked down the hallway, then shot me a strange look. "That's Poly. He's the official leader of EPIC, although he's given Team Two over to Vance. Why?"

"Nothing. Just hadn't met him yet, is all."

Neb nodded and turned back. I followed slowly, reviewing the bits of conversation I'd overheard and committing them to memory.

Poly, the Team One EPIC leader, was my first real lead.

12

At least the girl could take a fast shower. I'd walked in ten minutes after she had, and she was already in the bedroom, all dressed.

She glanced up at me and froze. Her uniform hung crooked on her slender neck, nearly exposing a bare shoulder. Her wet hair fell down her back, messy and wild. Her hand was extended over Daymond's bed, and various personal items were spread across the blanket.

The horror in her expression made me raise an eyebrow. "Looking for something?"

She jerked her hand back and shoved it into her uniform pocket. "I—uh—just needed … I was looking for a comb."

My mouth twitched. "A comb."

"I left mine." Straightening her back, she stared at me.

She hadn't brought anything with her, which seemed weird for a girl. Even the guys had a few belongings from home. It was yet another puzzle piece in the mystery of her past.

"You can use mine." I retrieved a black, fine-toothed comb from a bag under my bunk. She held back when I approached, as if unsure she should accept, but I gave what I hoped was a friendly smile and handed her the comb.

"Thanks," she muttered and inspected it before working it through the tangles on her head.

I sat on my bed and watched. Her hair seemed darker wet, more of a light brown color than the standard fake blonde.

That thought disgusted me. Treena was no different than every other NORA girl. I was fascinated because of her Rating, but that was it. Besides, there was an important matter that needed discussion. I took a deep breath and plunged in. "Why were you spying on Poly?"

She stopped, the comb frozen midswipe. "What?"

"Trying to get the mission details in advance?"

"No. Of course not."

"It's probably weird for you being the only girl, but the same rules apply to you as the rest of us. When Poly receives orders, he'll share them with us when he's ready."

She sighed as if angry at herself. "I don't really care what our orders are. I'm stuck here, like it or not." She bent over and began swiping at her hair with my comb again.

An uncomfortable silence filled the air as I processed her words. Most new trainees were excited to be here, but Treena obviously wasn't. She'd also failed her initiation, although I had passed her anyway. The other EPIC guys hadn't hesitated at all on their first mission. They'd been totally fine—even eager—to arrest anyone who broke the law.

She whipped her hair back and straightened, and for the first time I noticed her necklace. It was a delicate silver strand that disappeared inside her uniform, held there as if by something heavy. When she saw me looking, she tucked it out of sight again. A gift, maybe?

A realization hit. "You have a boyfriend. That's why you're here."

"What?"

"Let me guess," I said, my voice flat. "Blond, just like every other pill gulper in NORA. Really smart. High Rating, of course."

"That's none of your business."

Yes. Definitely a boyfriend. "You just joined my team. You're spying on our leader and poking through our things. I'd say it's definitely my business."

If she'd been pale before, now she went bright red. The rush of color to her cheeks only confirmed that something was up. I was definitely going to find out why she was here. I'd protect her, but I wouldn't trust her.

If only she wasn't so blasted nice to look at.

I stood and walked out, calling over my shoulder, "Keep the comb."

13

waited exactly two minutes after Vance left before entering the training room. So much for being clever. Even if I could find the spy, how could I go to the empress without proof? If Vance already suspected me, my time alone would be limited from now on. I had to be more careful.

As I walked in, Poly tossed me something. I caught it in one hand and examined it. A nutrition pill, but twice the size of my regular ones. I wiped it clean as discreetly as I could, then popped it into my mouth. Seconds later, a fullness filled my stomach, but there was also something else. A sudden burning sensation.

"What the fates is in that pill?" I asked.

"Caffeine," Neb said. "The capsule gives you constant energy for about four hours. We only get these ones right before a mission."

"We have a mission? Like, this morning?"

He opened his mouth to answer, but suddenly our

techbands vibrated as one. I flipped my screen.

EPIC Team: Report to
chopper pad immediately.

Chopper pad. That could only mean one thing—air travel. I swallowed, trying to keep my breathing under control.

I should've gotten more details from the empress before I agreed to this.

"Like, right now," Neb replied with a wink. "Let's go have some fun."

o–●o–●o–●o–●o–●●–o

The helicopter pad at the top of the Council Building was already buzzing with activity. Two shiny helicopters with four rotors on top of each caught the sun, their reflective armor so bright I had to shield my eyes. Obviously this mission wasn't going for stealth.

A dozen tan-clad workers trotted around, loading them with equipment. The other EPIC members stood aside, already dripping with sweat. Was it hotter today, or was I already getting used to the cool underground bunker?

Probably the million stairs we had to climb to get up here, I realized. Thank the fates for my khel training, or I'd have given up by floor fifteen. I focused on my breathing and ignored the shiny death traps they called choppers.

Vance and Poly stood next to the pile of supplies, speaking with Major Murphy. The stoic man who'd brought me here seemed unusually animated about something, flailing his arms wildly as he talked. Occasionally Poly would ask a question. I wished I could overhear the conversation, but Vance had made his opinion on eavesdropping quite clear.

"Where's Poly from?" I asked Neb, who had followed me to the rail.

"He doesn't talk about it, but he's a medic. At least he was. There's a rumor that he couldn't save a famous green's baby, and they sent him here to punish him." He grinned. "Just don't ask him about his name."

"Why?"

"He hates it. His real name is Palani, but Poly just stuck. At first he kept telling us that Poly means something in his father's language, but he wouldn't say what." He turned and motioned toward the city. "Amazing, isn't it?"

The view was incredible, I had to admit, despite my determination to stay far away from the edge. One tower poked out from the rest of the modern part of the city like a shiny, pointed finger. Lesser buildings clustered around it, although they were probably still hundreds of stories high, then flattened out like an outside circle, ending at the older district where we stood. It was beautiful. Which one was Dresden in right now?

"Let's go," Vance shouted. Poly was already climbing into the first chopper, and Vance gestured for his team to enter the second. I let my feet follow them and tried to think of something else, anything else. The floor of the aircraft just looked so … thin.

I was the last one. I glanced longingly at the doorway that led back downstairs. My mission was to catch a spy, not pretend like I belonged here. Maybe I could fake sick. My body was certainly shaking enough to make it believable.

"Does the princess need help getting in?" Vance asked.

I shot him a glare as I jumped inside. He grinned.

We weren't even seated yet when the door closed and the noise started. A loud pulsing began from the chopper, and then the world became a whirlwind of sound. I held my breath, resisting the urge to scream and cover my ears, feeling a surge of adrenaline. My body seemed to feel the sound deep down inside, and the vibration spread through me like electricity, accentuating my wildly beating heart.

The rest of the team fastened themselves into their seats like they'd done this a million times. After fastening mine, I forced my hands down and gripped the seat front as if the thin floor would fall away at any moment. Neb watched me curiously from across the aisle. I just turned away and focused on a metal screw in the floor.

Daymond, seated to my right, handed me a

headset. I nodded gratefully, although it was too wide and barely stayed on my ears. It muffled the sound a bit, but I also realized that it made communication possible over the noise.

"So, where we going this time?" Semias asked with a bored air. "Mopping up another botched military mission?"

"Get over yourself," Daymond muttered, then he caught my eye and shook his head like an ever-patient parent. I tried to smile, but it probably looked more like a grimace.

Vance finished checking the gear fastened to one wall and plopped down into the last empty seat. "It's another smuggling operation. Large group this time, so we'll have to be alert." His eyes flicked to me. "They found a smuggling hub in a Meridian warehouse. An informant says there'll be a drop in a couple of hours."

Everyone else nodded, and I sat up. *Meridian.* The closest military base to the border. It was famous for its skirmishes with outlanders. Konnor had gone there before, but with no less than three bodyguards. My fingers tingled from lack of circulation, so I unclasped them from the seat and tried to relax.

"A large group," Ross mumbled, his voice so low I could barely hear it.

"Won't be any different than catching three or four," Vance said. "Formation is the same as always, but Treena goes with me. Semias and Day, stay together this time. That was a blasted close call last week."

"Wasn't my fault," Semias grumbled. The safety belt puckered the fat under his uniform, making him look like an infant in an ill-fitting child seat.

"You wandered off to steal something and left my back exposed," Daymond said. "The guy missed me by centimeters. How is that not your fault?"

"We'll position—" Vance began, but just then the helicopter lurched, the noise rising in pitch. The windows on the right side filled with a view of the city. It was all so *small*—the streets, the bicyclists, everything. I tried not to imagine the door sliding open and sucking us out, the helpless feeling of falling, the horror of wind flying past.

I forced my breath out slowly and tried to focus on anything but the windows.

"Anyway," he continued when the chopper steadied out, "we'll position ourselves at the transport station and catch them in the act. Shouldn't be too hard."

"Why haven't the monitors done it, then?" Ross muttered, voicing my own thoughts.

"They've tried," Vance said. "Apparently the infiltration goes pretty deep. Either they're rewiring cameras and scrambling communications or the smuggler network has spies embedded deep in Meridian's security."

"What about the empress's new techband

regulation?" I asked. "Why don't they just zap those who aren't where they're supposed to be?"

Vance's mouth twitched. "Zap?"

"Punishment mode. Whatever."

He suddenly looked serious, a deep irritation crossing his features. "I don't think *zap* is the best choice of words, Treena. The empress is essentially electrocuting her citizens. You probably don't even know what getting zapped feels like."

"Of course not. Why, do you?"

Daymond belted a laugh. "You know what? I like her."

"What about us?" I asked, eager to change the subject. "Can we get za—I mean, trigger punishment mode? By being in the wrong place, I mean."

"We're exempt," Neb said with a satisfied smile.

Vance sat back, a disturbed look on his face, but he didn't say anything more.

14

The base was huge, and my relief at landing was overshadowed by the fact that I was surrounded by people who fought and killed for a living. We had been given silver uniforms to blend in. The guys had changed into theirs on the chopper, but I had hopped out and slipped mine over my new black uniform. I wasn't about to strip in front of five guys, team members or not.

Several buildings laid out in a giant triangle, all identical, surrounded us. The guys were well trained. Vance gave them their locations, and they disappeared into the crowd of silver uniforms crisscrossing the sidewalks. Poly's team had disappeared minutes before. Vance nodded to me and began striding away. I followed.

We approached what looked like a series of linked warehouses. Huge docking doors, all closed, lined the north side. When we entered, I blinked to adjust to the sudden darkness. It was narrow and packed full of storage on either side, with metal shelving and neatly catalogued signs. The roof was glass, but it rose up sharply in the center to allow a tall platform to stand majestically within view of the entire series of buildings. A lone figure stood over the rail. A supervisor, probably.

"Very little traffic here, and low visibility," Vance muttered. "Perfect for a drop."

The center platform wasn't just a supervisor station but also a crane of some kind. There was a heavy metal arm attached, although it rested silently against the back side. The supervisor leaned over the railing of the center platform and exchanged words with a worker below.

A buzzer sounded, and the supervisor began the climb down from the tower. Break time. He stalked toward the door, ignoring the workers who stood back to let him pass and ignoring us as if we weren't even there.

Vance mumbled, "North corner, two-yard—meter, whatever—square box with a gray blanket over it. Hide there until I come."

"Oh no," I said firmly. "You are not handling this alone. I'm your partner."

"Exactly. I'll position myself across the way. Just tell me on the feed if you see something." He kept walking nonchalantly, as if he were merely a worker on his way to the locker room.

I let out a frustrated breath. I didn't have much training, but it didn't mean I was useless. The fear I'd harbored earlier festered into irritation as I found the plastic container he'd described and settled myself behind it. Flanked by the corner, I would be out of sight even to the supervisor on the platform, but I could still see everything. Vance had chosen this hiding spot well.

Four minutes later, the giant crane gave a metallic groan, swung its arm around, and reached for a crate full of barrels. I perked up. The supervisor had already left, and there didn't seem to be anyone up there. Was it programmed to work during break time, or was this connected to the drop?

The crate must have been heavy, because the electric engine groaned under its weight. After making a pile of several similar crates near the closed docking door, the machine creaked to a stop. There was a sudden silence, followed by a strange clanging sound. Curious, I leaned away from the box to get a better look.

Someone was climbing down the platform pole, his hands and feet a blur. He disappeared behind a stack of crates before I could get a good look at his face. Seconds later the heavy loading door began to open.

I waited, expecting Vance to leap into action, but no one came. "Vance," I whispered into the feed. "Someone's here." There was no reply. I glanced around the room, wondering where he had hidden himself. Was this the drop, or had he rushed to the aid of his guys the next building over? Why hadn't he told me exactly what to look for?

A scraping sound from across the room jerked my attention forward. Carrying a cloth bag, the figure climbed over some boxes. He struggled to hold the bag, then swung it over his shoulder so he could jump to the floor. He wore the same gray military uniform we did, only it hung loose, and his face was blackened with dirt. A yellow, although I couldn't make out the numbers.

Suddenly an arm covered my mouth and yanked me backward. I squirmed and tried to elbow my attacker, but he stepped easily out of the way and put me in a chokehold. His grip tightened, and my vision began to spin. A twinge of panic flew through my mind. *Need ... air ...*

I wanted to scream, but I couldn't get anything out. My throat was in a vise—being squeezed, closed off. My body lurched as black spots appeared in my vision. I threw my head backward. It didn't free me, but it allowed me to turn enough to see part of the man's face. I forced my eyes to focus. A stubble-lined chin. Heavy black eyebrows framing muddy-green eyes. The hint of a hungry smile.

My thoughts had almost completely slipped into darkness when a dark figure leaped over the crates. The movement jerked my attacker's attention away, and the slightest bit of air slid into my aching lungs. It was the boy, the dirty one with the bag. He swung it over the crates with difficulty but stood up straight and dropped it on the floor. "Stop!" he hissed.

My captor dumped me to the side. I gulped in huge breaths, forcing my throat to reopen, trying to focus. *In. Out. In. Out.*

"What's wrong with you?" a gruff voice whispered behind me. He pointed to the strange red and green balls that now cluttered the dirty floor. "You don't just drop an entire bag of apples. Bruised apples cut our profits in half!"

Smugglers. And I was powerless to breathe, much less report it.

The boy shook his head in response and removed his hat. "They'd eat year-old moldy bread at this point. Bruised apples won't matter." Choppy, dark hair. Something about the figure was strangely familiar. The face was dirty, so it was hard to tell, but that voice …

"Tali?" I squeaked.

"Hi, Treen." She stepped softly over the scattered balls on the floor and pulled me into a crushing embrace. The gruff man moved to gather the food back into the bag, eyeing us with disdain, but Tali ignored him. "I thought I'd never see you again."

"You're—you're a smuggler?" My thoughts were still foggy, but I stared at the food on the ground. It seemed unlike any other illegal substance I'd learned about in school.

She laughed, the sound musical and happy. "I've wanted to tell you so many times. Wait—this is your special assignment? You joined EPIC?" She shook her head. "Fates! A bunch of soldiers, all to yourself! Why didn't I think of that?"

I glanced around, but Vance was nowhere to be seen. "Tali, you have to get out of here. When my team finds you, you'll be—"

"What, given a low Rating? Sentenced to laundry transportation?" She shook her head, bitterness evident in her eyes. "There's nothing more they can do to me, Treena. In fact, they gave me the perfect cover. I get to travel all over and make deliveries."

My jaw dropped. I didn't know what to say. Then it hit me. Her late-night shifts at the dock moving merchandise. Her anger at the system.

I was a lousy best friend. Perhaps the fates had brought us together so I could make Tali see reason. "Do you know what the punishment is for smuggling?"

"Oh, Treena," she said, and I almost expected her to make a *tsk-tsk* sound. "Work camps don't scare me, even the worst ones. I'm making a difference here, you know? Haven't you ever been part of something bigger than yourself? Something you believed in so strongly you'd give your life for it?"

"I … uh …"

When I failed to answer, she gave me a long look. "Oh, come on. It shouldn't be that hard. Listen, if you let me 'capture' you, maybe I can talk them into letting you join us."

I stared at her, stunned. "What?"

"I know you want Dresden, but, Treen, they'll never let you be with him now—even if by some miracle he still wants you. Please believe me. There's something coming, something big. And we can be part of it together."

My stomach sank. Not only did she refuse to leave this group, she was trying to recruit me. Even worse, a part of me wanted to go with her. But that would shut the door on my dreams forever, and I couldn't do that. I couldn't choose Tali over Dresden. She shouldn't force me to make that choice. I glanced at the yellow Rating on her head before I realized what I was doing.

Tali watched me, and irritation passed through her expression. "You've changed, you know. The Treena I grew up with was fun and carefree. Then you went all point-crazy. Do you even see people anymore, Treena?" She leaned forward and spoke more softly. "Or do you just see their numbers?"

I recoiled like I'd been slapped, and a searing heat spread throughout my chest. Tali had always been my best friend, the one person I could confide in. If anyone had changed, it was her. How could I trust her now, after years of lies? What kind of friend pretended to be one person at school, then turned on her own country?

The attacker stepped up beside me and waved his hand dismissively. "Time's up. The other EPIC team's evaded our trap. They're on their way here."

"Don't worry," Tali whispered. "We haven't killed anyone. They're just knocked out."

The man grabbed my wrist, twisting it painfully, and I cried out. He wrapped something rough around my hands, fastening them tightly behind my back. He reached to put something in my mouth.

"Wait, Ben. I'll give it to her," Tali said.

"Right. I'm not an idiot."

"Give it over. You can't go shoving girls around like that. All you have to do is say please." He glared as she swiped something out of his hand and showed it to me. "It's just a knockout pill, Treen. You'll wake up in a few hours. Open wide."

I stared at her. She gave me a pointed look, the kind that said I was being stupid. Could I trust Tali? The man watched me carefully, and I knew there wasn't time to think. I opened my mouth a crack. She pretended to stick the pill into my mouth, but palmed it instead. I pretended to swallow, then swayed and fell onto my side.

"See?" Tali said. "Manners. You go ahead. I'll pick up the apples and catch up."

Our act must have fooled Ben because he walked away muttering something about girls under his breath. Tali gathered the apples back into her bag before rushing to my side. "Surprised he bought it.

You've never been a good actress."

I sat up. "You're making a huge mistake, Tali. EPIC will catch you sooner or later."

"Maybe, maybe not. But at least I'll go down fighting. See you, Treen. I hope you figure out what you want." She turned and sprinted away.

o—●o—●o—●o—●o—●o

After Tali left, I heard voices across the warehouse. I let the facts run through my mind. Tali was alive, and she had just helped me. Tali was a smuggler, and I was supposed to catch smugglers. My team was gone. My wrists were tied. Was I supposed to wait for Team Two to come, or did I dare risk capture again by running to looking for them?

"Treena," a deep voice on the feed said, so suddenly that I jumped. "Do you copy?"

"Yes!" I exclaimed. "Yes, I'm here, Poly. Where are you guys?"

"Thank the fates," he said. "I think they've taken out the rest of Team Two, but we're closing in. Just hang on."

"I am."

"What was that?" a male voice asked from the loading dock.

"I heard it too. From over there, I think."

Fates. I lifted myself higher on my knees, just in time to lock eyes with two men. I jumped up and sprinted toward the exit, back the way we'd come.

"Don't let her escape!" a voice echoed behind me. I put on a new burst of speed and sprinted with every ounce of energy I had left. My raspy breathing grew heavier and more desperate as the doorway grew closer. My boot caught on something and I stumbled.

It was just the break they needed. A hand clasped my shoulder, and I shook it free only to have my arm grabbed. I fought, but it was too late. Three men had me secured in seconds. A tall yellow with lean features stood between me and freedom, his techband screen still up as if I'd interrupted a conversation. He glanced back at the screen. "Wish you could see this, Mills. It's a girl EPIC soldier. And a red, no less." He leaned over me, and I felt his hot breath on my cheek. "What'd you do, pretty little lady? Must've been pretty bad to be pegged as a red so young."

I struck. It took one kick, more a desperate toss of my leg than a true strike. It wasn't powerful, but it landed true. The techband screen nearly tore right off. Its owner gasped in shock and grabbed his hand in horror, his mouth working soundlessly. In slow motion, he sank to the floor. I hadn't shattered the screen, but the impact had been enough to trigger punishment mode. The hands gripping my arms suddenly loosened.

I was up and running before his companions knew what had happened, stumbling for the exit. Poly and his team *had* to be in position by now. I was out of time.

Incoherent shouting followed, and the wild footsteps behind me moved faster this time, taking advantage of my awkward strides. *Why did Tali let them tie my hands?* I summoned every ounce of speed I could, leaping toward the door with a yell, but it wasn't fast enough. A hand whipped out and hooked around my waist, yanking me to a near stop. I turned and swung my elbows upward, hoping to make contact with the man's face, but he was ready. He grabbed my shoulders and shoved me roughly to the ground. I landed with my nose in the dirt.

"Stupid girl," he said, then grabbed a handful of my hair and pulled, lifting me painfully to my feet. I yelped, but he didn't let go.

A skinny man sneered right in my face. "We're out of knockout pills, but no biggie. Let's find out if reds bleed like the rest of 'em."

He straightened. I realized what he was about to do, but my shaking, oxygen-deprived body was frozen in place. Just as his fist cocked, a figure jumped out from behind a crate.

"No!"

I felt the impact. Then everything went black.

15

After leaving Treena hidden, I did a quick perimeter check. Very few workers lingered here—they mostly trotted past without even glancing at me. I wasn't sure what to make of that. Either I was well disguised, or they knew exactly who I was and pretended not to see. In either case, nothing seemed out of the ordinary.

I found a corner stacked with dusty crates and crouched down, intending to get a location check on my guys. But just before flipping open the techband, I caught sight of something etched on a metal box in front of me. I squinted at it, then froze. Two curvy lines with a square in the middle. An iron belt. The sign of my clan.

I rocked back on my heels and brushed my hand over the uneven surface. Someone had used a laser to mark the box, and by the absence of dirt and rust, it had been done recently. That could only mean one thing.

I leaped up, searching wildly for the men I knew would be here. This end of the room was completely empty of workers now. A perfect time for a drop, although I knew now that wasn't their true intention.

If my clan wanted to talk to me badly enough to set all this up, it meant they were ready for us. It meant my men were in danger.

Your men are armed, I reminded myself. *It's the girl who isn't. And you just left her alone.*

With a curse, I sprinted back toward Treena's hiding place.

They were already there. Ten of them surrounded Treena, who lay on the ground.

A thick guy yanked her up by the hair. She glared at her captor with determination, breathing hard. Marshall, my clan's metalworker, said something—I couldn't hear what, from my position—and then cocked a fist.

I jumped up. "No!"

His fist made contact, and Treena crumpled to the ground. I swore and leaped forward, shoving Marshall against a stack of crates. I nearly landed a punch to his already bloodied nose before he had sense enough to block me. He spun out of my grasp and swung a fist toward my head. I redirected his punch toward the ground, stepped in, and kicked him hard in the groin. He collapsed with a moan.

"Punching a teenage girl in the face, Marshall," I muttered. "Are you really that insecure?"

"Vance," Anton, my former best friend, said. "Wondered when you'd show up." He stepped forward as if to pat my shoulder, but one look at my face made him pull his hand back.

"Nice of you all to gather in one place," I told him. "It'll make my job much easier." My gaze flickered to Treena, her unconscious body twisted on the ground, her face turned toward me. She looked peaceful, her dark eyelashes even more apparent against her smooth skin. A nasty red mark marred one cheek.

"Oh, you won't arrest us," Anton said. "We have a message for you from the clan." His voice was smooth, confident. He barely looked like himself. His hair was too short, his teenage tufts of beard had been shaven away, and a bright yellow 611 glowed on his forehead. Strangely, his wrist was bare. No techband.

"Our clan doesn't exist anymore," I said.

"Just because they scattered us doesn't mean we don't exist. We're gathering again, and our freedom will come very soon. You're lucky we're even telling you of our plans. Most of them didn't want Vance the Lapdog included at all."

"I'm no lapdog."

"Not a well-trained one, I'll admit," he said, grinning at the others, "but a lapdog in every sense of the word. Don't you want to hear the message?"

That stopped me. I glanced around the group.

Half of them had familiar faces; they were men who had families and vocations. Men who had followed my father with loyalty. Now they watched me with hatred and disgust. They couldn't blame NORA for their fate. It was too big, too far above them. But they could blame me, a seeming traitor who had defected to the other side. I was just one person, and I was right here.

"No, I don't," I said.

"Amnesty. They'll allow you back if you leave now. Undefect yourself, Vance. Come help us overthrow that stupid empress and her clones. If you tell us everything you know, we can succeed and be home within the month."

"Home." I nearly spat the word. "There is no home. Remember, Anton? It's just a pile of charred rubble now. Besides, you'll lose. The empress—"

"Implemented her new law too late," Graydon interrupted. His slender form made him appear taller than he was. "We've ditched the techbands, Vance. The military workers have to keep theirs to get us in, like this unfortunate fellow." He nodded toward a body on the ground. "But the rest of us are free. She can't punish us now unless she catches us."

"And she won't," Anton said. "Not this time. Join us."

I glanced back at Anton, who watched me carefully. Maybe too carefully. He'd never been a good liar. He stood a little too straight now, his face shiny with sweat, his manner nervous. It was interesting that they had chosen my best friend as their representative. If they thought that would get into my head, they were dead wrong. Unfortunately, Anton had brought nine men with him, men who now encircled me like they would a prisoner.

It wasn't much of a choice at all. If I left, the Demander would kill my family. They were no safer now than that awful day two years ago. Besides, I'd spent every day since then being manipulated and used. I would not switch from one master to another.

"No," I said.

Anton's mouth actually dropped. "No?"

"No. And I suggest you get moving. Team One should be here in …" I glanced at my techband, "hmm … about twenty seconds."

"I'm getting sick of this traitor's mouth," Darrell said with a growl. He pushed himself off the floor and lunged in my direction. I stepped aside and let him stumble past, then twisted his arm into a wristlock. In seconds his arms were fastened behind his back. The cuffs weren't as effective without the techband connection, but he wouldn't get far. *One down.*

"You chose the wrong side, man," Anton said. "They'll never let you go, and you know it. Join us and we can take her down together. Besides, something's coming. You don't want to be here when it does."

"I'm on nobody's side, Anton, yours or theirs. It's just me."

"Let's go, Anton," a smaller man said. "If he really does have backup—"

"Nah, he's bluffing. We took out his team, remember? You'll regret turning us down, Hawking." Anton motioned to two of his men, who started to approach. That was Anton—he never did his own fighting. I let my anger flow freely, feeling the surge of fire in my veins. As soon as they attacked, I struck—a kick, an elbow to the temple, a blur of motion. I took a punch to the nose and returned the favor with a shot to the ribs. Within seconds both men were moaning on the floor, wrists bound. *Two and three.*

"Oh, come on, Anton," a smaller man said, backing away. "We'll put out a call for the people to take care of him. He won't last a week."

"Yeah," another guy, Gregor, muttered. "Just tell Mills that Vance has turned on us. Again."

Anton glared, and his hand itched toward where he'd once kept his pistol. He didn't have one now, of course. Pistols would give them away in a second, not to mention how a gunshot echoed for kilometers.

Kilometers. Now I was even thinking like NORA. That was unacceptable.

"Don't move." I snatched up my weapon, aiming it at Anton in one swift motion. The color drained from his face. The other guys spun and began to run. I kept my weapon trained on his chest.

The footsteps faded into the distance as Anton's guys found their way outside. The sound of distant yelling broke the silence. Poly's team was closing in. The settlers had taken out five of us, but it looked like we'd get all ten of them, in addition to whomever Poly had found. The cold satisfaction that accompanied my thoughts shocked me out of my anger, and I lowered my weapon.

Anton dropped his hands and cocked his head to listen, his expression hardening. "You have your revenge," he nearly spat. "I should have known you'd betray us again. That's just who you are. But if you want me, you'll have to shoot."

I wanted to. Man, I wanted to shoot him, if only to make myself feel better. But the adrenaline surge was wearing off now. I tried to imagine him a foot shorter, his hair long over his ears, his face freckled and tan. Anton had once been the best trapper in the settlement, and I'd gone with him to catch rabbits and squirrels before we were technically old enough to be alone in the forest. We'd almost trapped a bear once.

He stared at me accusingly now, as if I'd been the one to set fire to the settlement and destroy his way of life. The innocent Anton was gone forever. I could tell he was thinking the same thing about me.

"Climb the platform pole," I said. "I'll tell them I checked it myself. But try to trick me again, and you won't even make it to the safety of prison." Without waiting for an answer, I strode past him and made my way to Treena's still form. Anton scrambled away.

I turned her onto her back as gently as I could. Her

chest rose and fell in a steady rhythm, and she looked fine except for the deep purple bruise. What kind of leader left his most inexperienced soldier alone to go meet with the enemy? Treena had even followed my orders despite her objections, and she'd paid the price for my idiocy. She'd trusted me to protect her.

That was her biggest mistake.

16

S he's waking up," Poly said.

With a moan, I tried to force my eyes open, then slammed them shut again when the headache hit. I was lying on a hard floor—the washroom? One eye allowed a sliver of light in, just enough to see faces above me.

"Welcome back," Vance said softly.

"What happened?" I tried to ask, but it came out as a groan. My jaw wouldn't work right. The pain was terrible—a throbbing in my cheek, my head, and even my teeth.

"Triggering punishment mode on his own techband," Neb muttered. "That was brilliant, Treena. I wonder if it works the same way if you mess with someone's implant?"

His words disintegrated in my foggy thoughts. What was he talking about? I tried to sit up, and Vance reached out to steady me with a gentle hand, but I shrugged him away. "Where are we?"

"We're still at Meridian. Take it easy," Poly said. "You may have a concussion. Fates, what I wouldn't give to have my pharmacy rights back—a pronopolyne pill would have you up in no time. At the very least, you'll have a bruise for a few days."

"Bruise?" Daymond mumbled. "If that's just a bruise, I'm emperor of NORA. She's lucky he didn't cave her face in."

"I think I can stand." I pushed myself up. The ground swayed for a second, and I closed my eyes against the light. "Where is everyone?"

"Escorting our smuggler friends to town," Vance said.

Neb broke in. "Vance kept them distracted until Poly could get there. He got three of them by himself."

Poly turned to me. "We think one of them got away, Treena. Do you remember how many there were?"

I glanced at Vance. He was staring at the ground. "Ten?" I guessed.

"All males?" Poly prodded.

I hesitated, then nodded, instantly regretting it when the pain slammed into my head again. "Yeah. Why do you ask? Did you catch any women?"

"Nah," Poly said. "Just making sure we got 'em all."

I let my breath out slowly. Tali had escaped. I hoped she knew what she was doing.

"There are no available choppers," Poly began, "so we're taking transports back. I'll escort Treena—"

"No." Vance interrupted. "I'll take her. Can she walk?"

"I don't see why not," Poly replied. "She probably has a huge headache, though. She may need someone to steady her."

"How about you stop talking about me like I'm not here? I can walk fine," I said.

"Come on," Vance said, avoiding my eyes. "It's parked out front. This way."

To my dismay, Vance insisted on riding back with me. I wanted to tell him he was the last person I wanted to ride with, but he hopped in and slammed the door before I could protest. We watched the military base disappear into the distance.

It was several minutes before I broke the heavy silence. "Where did you go?"

"Perimeter check. And you didn't obey orders."

"Excuse me?"

"I told you to stay down and notify me if you saw something."

"I did say something. You never answered. Besides, they jumped me from behind. What was all that 'stay together' junk, anyway, if you were planning on ditching me?"

He stiffened. "I thought you'd be safe there. I wasn't gone ten minutes."

"Good, then you caught the big finale. You know,

the part when I was running for my life and you sat behind a crate and watched? I hope it was a good show."

He turned to look at my face, his brown eyes flashing. "They paid for it. Besides, they wouldn't have hurt you. Just knocked you out with their pills, just like the others."

I snorted and pointed to the swollen mass of my cheek. "Wouldn't hurt me! You don't think this hurts?"

"If you hadn't fought, he wouldn't have assaulted you."

"Didn't you train me so I could defend myself?" I yelled. "Didn't you, just this morning, tell me to attack rather than run? What the fates is the matter with you?"

"You were completely surrounded and unarmed. The smart thing would've been to surrender and wait for backup."

"You *were* my backup. For all I knew, everyone else was dead."

"I can't protect you!" he thundered. The poor driver jumped, then eyed us in the rearview mirror. Vance sighed and lowered his voice. "I mean—I won't always be around, Treena." He ran his fingers through his hair in frustration. "Just forget it."

The anger drained away. "I never asked for your protection."

"Yeah, well, I never asked them to send a helpless,

untrained girl that I'd have to protect."

"I am not helpless."

"I saw the whole thing, Treena. You have courage, but your skills aren't there yet. Until they are, it's my job as your trainer to keep you safe. Those smugglers weren't the murdering kind. They were just proving a point."

I stared at him in disbelief. "If I didn't know better, I'd think you were on their side."

His jaw tightened as he turned away.

We ignored each other for the rest of the trip.

17

So, what now?" I asked Neb when we walked into the training room. My argument with Vance had only compounded my headache, which was now affecting my vision. Vance had stormed off into the bedroom, so I decided to wait awhile before going to bed. Or, rather, to my pile of pillows.

He shrugged. "Downtime. I'll probably go work out."

Ross chuckled as he walked past. "You? Since when?"

Neb glared at him, and I hid a smile. "Practically every day," he shot back. "I can lift my own body weight. I can probably lift you, Treena."

"I'll take your word on that," I said.

Ross, still wearing a grin, opened a closet near the door. There were several chunks of black metal resting on the shelves within. He typed something into a keypad, and one of the masses morphed into a set of weights. He grabbed them and headed for a bench in the corner, and Neb stepped in to take his turn.

There was no way I was working out. The dull ache in my head made me feel grumpy, and the confidence I'd felt this morning had drained completely away, taking with it some of my resolve. Tali was—had always been—a smuggler. How had I not known? What other secrets had my best friend hidden from me? She'd been a little distant since I'd started dating Dresden. Had my absence driven her to a life of crime?

And the bigger question: What could I do about it? If Tali wouldn't listen to reason and leave her group, at least I could keep her secret. The empress would never know. My friend had nothing to do with the EPIC traitor. I hoped.

The traitor. With all the craziness, I had nearly forgotten about my mission.

There were four guys out here now, all positioning themselves on benches or chairs for a solid weight-lifting session. They seemed so relaxed. I decided to take a risk. "I've been wondering something."

"What's that?" Ross said with a smirk. "She does talk. I was beginning to wonder."

I ignored him. "Why are you guys here? You all seem fairly normal. Or are you even allowed to talk about your past?"

The room quieted, and they suddenly seemed

intensely focused on their exercises. Daymond, who was on all fours doing push-ups, rocked back and gave me a long look. "Of course we're allowed to talk about it. It's just that most of us aren't here because we're particularly noble. We just saw an opportunity and took it."

"How do you know?" Ross asked, settling in for some bicep curls. "I'm very noble."

Daymond snickered. "Everyone has their quirks. The problem is that ours aren't exactly NORA approved. You already know about Semias's pill addiction."

"Shut it, Day," Semias snapped.

"Ross constantly pretends to be someone he's *not*," Daymond continued pointedly.

"Not true," Ross said without pausing.

"And Neb is here to work on his confidence."

Neb, who had been stretching, froze. His head snapped up. "I can't believe you just said that."

"That's pretty much my story too," I said quickly, hoping they wouldn't pry. "But everyone has issues, and that doesn't explain why you're here. You seem like decent guys."

"Except for Semias," Ross said.

"Day was a chopper pilot," Neb broke in. "Caused an accident or something, and that's where he got his scar."

Daymond's face darkened. "You know nothing about it, Neb. I didn't cause anything."

"What? She deserves to know the truth. She's one of us now."

Was I? Today I'd done nothing but hinder my team. Tonight I'd sleep in the washroom, and tomorrow I'd probably stumble my way through training yet again. I didn't belong here, and they knew it.

I quickly changed the subject. "I know this sounds weird, but do any of you feel sorry for the smugglers?"

Someone snickered, and Neb smirked as if I'd said something funny. It was Daymond who spoke up. "They're criminals. That would be like asking a cat if he feels sorry for mice."

I switched tactics. "Yeah, but have you ever thought that maybe you and the mice were on the same team?"

They looked at each other, perplexed. Neb cleared his throat. "What's your point, Treena?"

"Just curious, I guess. Never mind."

The guys started talking amongst themselves, and I sensed that my interrogating was over. It hadn't gone as well as I'd hoped. If I wanted information, I'd have to be much more subtle—without sneaking around, spying, or asking direct questions, apparently.

I reached my corner and sighed. Two days down, and what seemed like a lifetime left to go.

18

I'd known Treena would cause an uproar, but this went way beyond my expectations.

I lay in bed, too angry to sleep, listening to the heavy breathing of an exhausted team. I checked my techband. Four a.m. My two years were up today, and the Demander would be expecting my answer. The problem was, I had no idea what that was myself.

When he'd offered me the deal, I'd planned to escape by now. There hadn't been a doubt in my mind that I could. I hadn't taken into account that even if I did, my clan would never allow me back after the things I'd done to my own people. Some choices were final. Working for NORA had eroded my future just as surely as it had destroyed my past.

Poly had taken me in without question, even after being told who I was. The last two years hadn't been all bad. But it wasn't possible to continue as we were, not with my clan pursuing me as they had today.

Sooner or later I'd have to choose a side.

I'd grown up watching my father guide his people, make sacrifices for them. They loved him, and he'd ultimately given his life for them. He was the type of man I'd always wanted to become. Tonight, I felt further away than ever.

Anger simmered in my chest. I hadn't asked to be an EPIC leader. I hadn't asked to be here at all. I was sick of people toying with me, dangling my mother and sisters in front of me like a prize.

Suddenly I knew what I had to do. I dressed quickly and silently. It would be light soon, and the commander would be in his office. He didn't think anyone knew how early he went to work, but I knew. I made it my business to know.

Just before I reached the hall, the bathroom door creaked open. I froze. It was quiet for almost a whole minute. Finally, I headed for the training room. Seconds later there was a light footstep in the hallway. "Don't you ever sleep?" Treena asked.

I groaned inwardly. "Not when I can help it. Do you sneak up on people often?"

"I got pretty good at stealing in khel, since I was too short to score much. You know, since I'm so innocent and helpless and all that."

I caught the coldness in her tone. It was well deserved. "Fair enough."

"Going for a walk?"

"Running an errand. How's the bruise?"

"I'll live."

"We'll have to skip training today."

"Where are we going?"

I gave a frustrated sigh. "*We* are not going anywhere."

"I'm coming with you."

"You don't know where I'm going."

"I don't really care. I've got to get off that hard floor for a while—it's killing my back. If that means coming with you, so be it." She took a step forward. "Besides, the exercise would be nice."

I thought about our mission yesterday and how Treena had nearly outrun men twice her size. She most certainly did not need the exercise. "Don't suppose you'd follow an order to stay here."

"Nope."

"You're the most exasperating girl I've ever met."

"Thanks." I could hear the smile in her voice.

For a minute I considered ditching her, but I knew she'd just follow and get me in trouble. "You coming like that?"

She looked down as if realizing she was still in her nightclothes. I couldn't see the blush, but I knew it was there. "Give me two minutes."

She dressed surprisingly fast and started toward the door with a single glance in my direction. I shook my head and headed for the corner of the weapon wall. She followed. I ran my fingers along the drywall, relying on touch to find the vent. A wire poked out slightly around the frame. A slight pull and the entire section of drywall came out easily. It was just large enough for a person to crawl through.

"A secret passage?"

"Not as interesting as you imagine. It only goes about twenty feet back and then meets up with the ventilation shaft. It goes up at an angle, and there are grips here and there, but it'll still be hard. You sure you're up for this?"

"Why can't we just walk out the door?"

"They monitor it." I watched her, wondering if she would lecture me on the greatness of NORA or turn and run to tell Poly I was sneaking out. She met my gaze, steady and determined. There were questions in her eyes, possibly the same questions that I had for her, but she didn't ask them.

She exhaled slowly. "Okay. Lead the way."

Twenty minutes later we emerged and climbed into the warm night air. The moonlight was incredibly bright, almost blue in hue compared to the blackness of the compound. I doubted Treena had ever been out this early in the morning before. She couldn't tear her eyes away from the sky.

We turned right and headed downtown. Treena stared upward so often that, at one point, she tripped over an uneven piece of sidewalk. I grabbed her elbow to steady her. "Thanks," she said, looking at my hand. She swung her elbow up and away to break contact.

"You look like you've never seen stars before."

"I haven't." She gestured at the sky. "Not like this. We could see a few in Olympus during the winter when it got dark early, but curfew kept us indoors at night. This is amazing."

"One of the perks of EPIC, I guess. We get to see more than most people."

We traveled for several blocks before she spoke again. "This is a long walk, isn't it? Why don't you ride bikes? Or call a transport?"

"Bikes are too restrictive, and reds can't call transports."

"But I came in one."

"Because it was ordered by a green. We use them for missions all the time, but Poly or Major Murphy have to call it in. Reds live very differently from everyone else, even in EPIC. You'll get used to it."

That seemed to bother her, and she fell silent. We walked for half an hour before reaching the modern part of the city. The stores got taller as the electric signs became brighter and more insistent. Everywhere we looked, there were ads for useless Rating-raising products and procedures. I refused to read them. This was Treena's world, not mine. She watched the signs with childlike fascination.

Suddenly she stopped short, gaping at something overhead. I followed her gaze to an ad board above a bike shop, a picture of a young green. His teeth were unnaturally white, his Rating bright against the drab gray background. He smiled as he spoke the words that appeared on the screen: *Kolor Bikes—Because Impressions Matter.* The figure smiled, then winked, and the sequence began again.

Treena gasped.

"What's wrong?" I asked.

"Do you know who that is?"

"Everyone knows who that is," I said dryly. "Dresden Wynn, record-breaking graduate. I think he's more popular than the empress right now. You all right?"

"Yeah," Treena said. "Just need a minute."

She didn't explain, and I didn't make her. She stared at the sign for a long time, a funny look on her face, breathing hard. Girls. I'd never understand them.

Finally she nodded and we continued, neither of us in the mood to talk. Traffic was thickening already, bicyclists with their purple-clad riders, and transports with their important passengers. We reached the most crowded part of the city where the brilliant skyscrapers towered high into the sky. The solid steel academy building, with its sharply cut corners, rose high above the rest, absorbing the pinks and oranges of the rising sun. Even I had to admit it was a stunning sight. A sign, high and bright with the NORA symbol above it, flashed overhead:

NORA ACADEMY OF LEADERSHIP
TAKING EXCELLENCE TO A NEW LEVEL SINCE 2065

Treena gave a little gasp, nearly bouncing in her excitement. If she thought this was a sightseeing trip, she was dead wrong. Maybe I shouldn't have brought her along after all. I shoved the front doors open, pursing my lips, wondering how to get her to stay in the lobby. But she returned my gaze, her eyes hard and determined.

I pushed down the irritation and held the door open for her. A slight smile graced her lips as she sauntered past me and through the heavy golden doors. "Opening the door for a girl, huh? What is this, the 1900s?"

I grunted.

Despite the early hour, the building was already bustling with activity. I'd been here twice before, but the inside—with its shiny metal walls and gold-trimmed ceilings—was still as captivating as the outside. Some said it was real, but I knew it wasn't. It was too clean, too uniform in color. Treena walked in awe alongside me, eyeing the overpolished floor as we approached the security desk. The young guard sat, alert, her eyes sweeping everyone who passed through. When she saw our Ratings, her eyes widened. I swiped my techband and nodded to her. The security gate swung open. With a shrug, the woman waved us past.

We passed the main lifts and headed down a separate wing of the building. The sign above the hallway entrance read, *Leadership Academy: Military Division.* We made our way to a smaller lift and rose to level 89. But the doors didn't open immediately. "Authorization," an automated voice demanded.

"Vance Hawking, for Councilman Denoux," I replied.

"Unidentified companion detected," the voice said. "Identify."

"Ametrine Dowell," she said. "His … assistant."

There was no sound for a minute or so, and I wondered about Treena's presence here. Maybe it would have been better if she'd stayed in the lobby. But then the digital voice replied, "Entrance authorized." The doors opened.

Flanked by two soldiers, a short, red-faced man with a wide build greeted us, his lips pulled downward into a frown. "You have nerve, kid, coming here. Your privileges are for emergencies and summons only."

Treena stood there, dumbfounded, staring at the Demander himself. I knew what she was thinking. It was the same reaction I'd had upon meeting the man two years ago. The man who commanded NORA's military forces should be strong and tall, not short, balding, and whiny. He was probably a relative of the empress or something.

"Did you miss me, Denoux?" I asked. "It's been two years since our deal. I've come to announce my decision."

"Deal?" He huffed a little. "You make my orders sound like some kind of bargain, Hawking, and I don't make deals with Integrants."

Rebecca Rode

I realized my body was in a defensive stance and forced myself to relax. "Except me, apparently. I've kept my end for two years, and I'm done. You will send me to join my family in the work camps immediately."

Treena's head whipped around, her expression guarded.

"You are a soldier!" Denoux snapped. "Soldiers are discharged when there is no use for them anymore. And frankly, you haven't finished your assignment. I recruited you to capture smugglers, to finally end the food trade once and for all."

"To end the … You want me to catch every single smuggler singlehandedly?"

"Of course not. That's why we assembled a team to help you out. Poly is the official leader, of course, but everyone knows you're the experienced one. Not that there isn't room for improvement." His expression turned smug. "We all heard about your failed mission yesterday. They captured your entire team, as I recall. And yet somehow you're fine."

"They knew we were coming."

He leaned forward. "Interesting, isn't it?"

I took a step forward. "They knew, and still our group of thirteen arrested twenty-one documented smugglers with no military backup. I'd say we fulfilled our mission."

"Twenty-one smugglers out of hundreds left out there. You're barely worth your weight in nutrition pills, boy." He stabbed my chest with a pointed finger. "You're getting better, but you have a long way to go yet."

"Since I joined, we've caught four hundred and eleven," I said, forcing myself to speak evenly, "not including the ones we arrested yesterday. I'm not here to argue. I won't wait around another year or even another week."

Denoux snorted, spraying moisture several feet. Treena wiped her cheek. "Let me explain something. Ignore the fact that you're an Integrant. You're a red, and reds don't bargain. They obey. They snivel and cower and respect their superiors because they have no other choice. You're lucky we spared your life at all."

"I never asked you to."

He paused, giving a dramatic sigh like a parent enduring a difficult child. "You forget that I was there, boy. I still remember that night—the stillness of the trees, the heavy smoke. The screaming prisoners. And young Hawking, fighting for his life. Scared. Oh yes, you were terrified. You saw death looming over your head, and it frightened you to the point of madness. As much as you'd like to think of yourself as a hero, or even a victim, I know better. You took the easy way out." He stood taller and whispered, "You're no different than the rest of us."

My fists clenched so tightly they shook. My instincts screamed to take over, to leap onto Denoux and pummel him. With a flick of the wrist and a word, this man toppled civilizations and destroyed lives. There was nothing—*nothing*—I wanted more than to take his life, as he'd taken my father's. The guards on either side of him raised their stunners. One clicked his into fatal mode.

"Vance," Treena said softly.

I let out a slow breath, fighting for control. This was not the time. "They'll do fine without me."

A satisfied smile crossed his face. "I must decline, young Hawking. Your day of freedom is not today. The dynamics of our military are changing, and apparently your sad little band is an integral part of the empress's latest plan."

"Sir," a full-figured woman said, coming up behind him. "The empress has given preliminary orders for the next mission. She demands an immediate response."

Treena began pulling me toward the lift.

"You'll obey orders, Hawking," Denoux said as the doors opened. "Or I'll take you out, empress or not." Then, more quietly, "Revoke his security privileges immediately."

I stepped inside. The doors clanged shut.

Silence.

"I can't believe you talked to him that way," Treena finally said, her voice shaking, "and got away with it."

I leaned my head back against the wall and drew in a long, slow breath. She was right. That conversation hadn't gone as expected, but at least I'd escaped without arrest. I was still free to figure out a new solution. I would have to find my mother and sisters on my own. Once I found them, we would bust out of NORA forever.

When we stepped out, the main floor was packed with students headed for their classes. I started to push forward, but with a shake of her head, Treena eased me gently against the hallway wall. We stepped back to wait.

"So you're an Integrant," she said with a nonchalant air.

Before I could reply, an unfamiliar voice spoke up. "Treena?"

"Dresden!" she gasped.

A guy walked toward us, moving with the typical overconfidence of an academy student. A silver pin was clipped to his shoulder above a double-striped arm rank. His Rating actually was that high.

Bike Boy.

"It is you!" Dresden said, his voice registering disbelief. "What are you doing here?" A group of students, probably his friends, pulled up behind him. They stared at Treena's forehead.

Treena wrapped her arms around his waist. The guy made Treena look even smaller. "It's good to see you, Dres," she said.

"How are you? And what happened to your face?" Dresden looked at me as if unsure what he was allowed to say. "Is it—you know, the assignment?"

Treena dodged the question and nodded toward me. "This is Vance, my trainer."

Dresden gave my Rating a long look. "Interesting."

"Congrats on the ad board, Wynn," I said. "Although I think you need to lay off the tooth polish. Those shiners were two shades short of psychedelic."

"Speaking of which," Treena said, glaring at me, "you're a celebrity now, huh?"

He grinned. "I have four sponsors. One of them is for a khel supply store, even. Not exactly what I pictured for my future, but I'll take it."

"I'm so glad you're happy."

The friends behind him started to whisper to each other, eyeing my Rating, and then Treena's. They turned away in disgust. A crowd was starting to gather. I knew from experience that this wouldn't end well. "We should get going, Treena."

"You'd better keep her safe," Wynn said in a deeper voice.

"She's safe with me," I said.

"Oh, and Treena," he said, grabbing her elbow. He lowered his voice to a whisper, but I could hear every word. "Be careful. You don't want to ruin your face for good, in case you get reconsidered. Appearance points count for a lot, you know?"

She had a funny look on her face when he pulled away. "Thanks. See you soon."

19

When we stepped outside, the heat slammed into my face. I adjusted my too-big uniform again, wishing it was any color but black. Luckily the buildings created long shadows in the streets, which meant a little shade on our walk home.

Home? I shook my head. That dungeon where I slept was not home.

"So," Vance began as we walked. "That was the boyfriend. Bike Boy, love of your life."

"I told you before. It's none of your business."

"You have secrets."

"You have more, apparently."

We passed a stout little man unlocking his shop. His gaze latched onto us as we approached, and I noticed a Greens Only sign in the window. His eyes narrowed when he saw our numbers. If Vance noticed, he didn't react. How did he live like this—spending day and night protecting people who treated him this way? Not a citizen, not a soldier, but an outsider.

I fell into step beside him. "Do you often subject yourself to humiliation in front of your female trainees?"

Vance gave me a sideways look. "Only the prettiest ones."

I felt the heat rush to my cheeks. "Not the most effective way to get a girl, you know."

"Yeah," he said. "Especially when they're already taken." I opened my mouth to reply, but he was grinning. His smile turned mischievous. "Bike Boy seems very … athletic."

"He is. His team won the central khel championship the last three years. He taught me how to play better, and I tutored him in math and science. We evened each other out, you know? I thought our scores would be—I, uh, thought things would be different."

He looked up at the sky. "You owe me an apology, then."

"What?"

"I was right about him. Perfect grades, perfect attendance, perfect volunteer hours—"

"He's more than that," I said quickly.

"Blonde hair, blue eyes, blinding white teeth—"

"You never mentioned the teeth, so I owe you nothing. Besides, you saw him for, what, a minute? Other than appearance, you don't know him at all."

"Don't need to. One of you is pretty much the same as the next."

I stopped and glared at him. "Okay, you'd better explain yourself now, because I'm sick of taking the brunt of your problems. I wasn't there *that night*, and neither was Dresden, or any other citizen you glare at on the street. Yet you act like we had something to do with it, whatever *it* was."

"Don't worry about it, Treena. Just live your life." He started walking again. "Enjoy your little rainbow world full of happy people and order and numbers and forget about those of us who see it for what it really is."

With a growl of frustration, I trotted after him. "What do you think it is? Because in case you haven't noticed, we're both reds. I have just as much right to complain as you."

He barked a bitter laugh. "Oh? So NORA killed your father, burned down your home, and forced you into slavery too? Then I apologize."

I froze. I thought about what the commander had said, and then it all started to come together. I caught up just as he turned a corner and startled a pair of high-heeled ladies as they tapped their way to work. They gaped at his Rating, then hurried past.

"I want to hear the story," I said.

"No. You don't."

A monitor patrol car went slowly by in the vehicle lane. A sour-faced monitor, a woman, caught a glimpse of our Ratings and glared at us through the glass. The vehicle slowed nearly to a stop, and I could almost see her brain straining for a reason to stop us. Which group had higher jurisdiction, EPIC or law enforcement? They served the city, but we served the empress. Our two goals didn't necessarily conflict with each other, but the anger in her expression proved that our two groups didn't mesh well. After a moment, the vehicle finally sped up and disappeared into the growing mass of bicyclists.

A week ago, he would've been right about me not wanting to know. I'd walked through Konnor's integration camp several times without being curious about the people I passed. They were outsiders who had escaped the dismal outside world and come to NORA for a better life. Weren't they?

"You said NORA attacked you and made you a slave?" I asked.

"Seriously, Treena. Don't pretend like you care."

"Fine, then, don't tell me everything. Just tell me about your dad."

His gaze grew distant, and it was nearly a block before he spoke. "He was clan leader over almost a thousand people. The Hawking clan was the largest and most powerful in the outlands."

"Impressive. Where did they come from?"

"We accepted anyone who wanted protection. Our fortress was supposed to be impenetrable, and people traveled for weeks to join us."

"But it wasn't."

"It was—for the first two NORA attacks. But the

third time we were taken completely by surprise. They destroyed our surveillance cameras and killed the guards, so nobody knew they were there until they'd lit the fires. My dad stayed behind to hold them off and ordered me to organize our people for an escape."

His eyes met mine, and the depth of emotion they held made me instantly guilty for having brought it up. "He didn't make it, then?"

"No."

"And you didn't escape, obviously."

He didn't answer, but it was enough of a reply.

"And you didn't cooperate, which would explain the Rating." I couldn't believe it. NORA attacked settlements? "I thought Integrants came on their own, to escape the violence of the outlands."

"Some do, but most of us are prisoners. We're not allowed to talk about our past. It's part of the integration process—pretend you're happy to be here, and you get out of the compound faster. Only I skipped the integration part."

"How's that?"

He snorted in disgust. "There I was, fighting desperately for my life and trying to help my people escape, and the Demander thought, 'Hmm. There's one who can fight. I should add him to my collection.' He brought me in, held a knife to my mother's throat, and threatened to kill my family, one by one, if I didn't cooperate."

A knife? Those were illegal in NORA. Knives

were tools of the Old America, tools of the violent and uncivilized societies of the past. But then, threatening peoples' lives was illegal too. The commander was the councilman over our entire nation's military, and he was breaking our own laws.

"I refused, but he insisted it would only be for two years." He chuckled bitterly. "What kind of idiot would believe that?"

"I didn't know your family's lives depended on your job here. I bet they see you as a hero."

He shrugged. "I promised my dad to keep my family safe. I'll do anything to fulfill that, even if it means playing their stupid numbers game."

"Game. That's a good way to put it." I paused for a pedestrian to shuffle by. "What did you think about the Rating system when you came here?"

"When I was dragged here, more like. I didn't get it, and I still don't. I mean, why do you let yourselves be controlled by some stranger's opinion of what you're worth? Why can't everyone be valuable for who they are and not just how well they conform to some random ideal?"

My face burned. "I don't know."

He sighed. "Sorry, but you asked."

I had, and I deserved every word. Even stranger, I agreed with him. It sounded ridiculous when he put it that way. "What are you going to do now?"

"No idea. Just don't tell anyone. Poly's the only one who knows about all this, and I'll tell him we failed to reach an agreement."

"Sure." I pushed a wayward hair behind my ear—
I'd left it down today, and it hung past my shoulders—
and smoothed it down, staring at the ground. "Keep
my secrets, and I'll keep yours."

"You've got a deal."

20

When we got back, the guys were awake and using the washroom. I curled up in the training room and closed my eyes, which were suddenly heavy from lack of sleep. As uncomfortable as I was, it didn't take long for my mind to drift into slumber.

The end-of-summer air was growing cooler. I was five years old, just weeks away from Level Two school, and I had just told Konnor about my first failed exam. I'd only missed six questions, I reasoned, but he wore a thunderous expression. I winced, ready for the blow I knew would come, but he simply grabbed my wrist and yanked me out the door.

Minutes later, his neck glistened with sweat as he pulled me toward the tower's front doors. He held my hand tightly, roughly. I asked why we were here. He mumbled something about showing me the view.

It was early evening, the building empty, the

hard floors and blank walls echoing the sound of our footsteps. We entered the lift, and Konnor pushed the highest button. Number 82.

My stomach felt tingly for a while, and then the doors slid open, exposing us to a hot, heavy wind. The roof. He pulled me immediately toward the rail.

"Look down," he said. I shook my head. He yanked on my wrist, but I clung to his leg with my other arm. He reached down and grabbed my jaw, forcing me to look down over the city. "Eighty-two floors up. You won't learn physics for another three years, so I'll translate: that's about six seconds of air time before you hit."

I didn't understand, but I hugged his leg with renewed strength. He peeled me off with a grunt and lifted me off my feet. Whimpering, I reached for him, but he lifted me slowly over the rail. I stood right on the ledge now, held up only by his arms. My whimpering turned into sobbing.

"As a kid, I always wanted to fly." His voice was soft, distant. "I hoped to be a pilot. I even volunteered at the plant where they assemble military choppers. I'm not complaining. My current assignment has much more stature. But my position is precarious, Ametrine. My position is as precarious as yours is right now."

I shook so badly that I thought he might drop me on accident. I felt the hard ledge under my feet, firm, but Konnor still had full control of my fate. With a *flick of his wrist, I would fall. My eyes dropped to the ground, which seemed a hundred kilometers away. The bicyclists on the street below looked like tiny moving toys.*

"P-p-please," I said. "I'll never fail again! I'll get perfect scores, and I'll be your good girl."

"My good girl?" His voice hardened. "You were never mine. You're another man's child, and yet I support you and pay the consequences of your failures. Ametrine, your actions affect your entire family. Six missed questions seem small now, but failing a class—or even one test—can mean an entire Rating point. Understand?" He let my right hand slip a little and I gasped in horror, squirming to grab the rail with my free hand.

"Yes, sir!"

"I'm not convinced. Show me that every time you think about falling short, or letting up, or giving up, you'll picture this scene right now. Look down, child, and memorize it. Let me help you get a better view." I let out a wail as he lifted my feet over the ledge. He lowered me then, feet dangling, alive only by his grip on my arms. My body shook violently, and my cheeks were wet with tears. I looked down once more, wishing that someone would look up and see us. Wishing they would help me, that they'd lift me into their arms and take me far away.

"Whether I like it or not, you are a Dowell," he said. "Dowells do not fail. If such a thing were to

happen, I expect you to make the right choice." He *nodded toward the ground. "We all make sacrifices for those we love, and sometimes this, right here, is the noblest choice a person can make."*

He began to lift me toward safety, but his grip loosened and slid toward my sweaty hands. So slippery. Just before my feet made it over the rail, my tiny fingers slid out of his grip.

I woke up gasping. It was the same nightmare I'd had for years, and I always woke up right before hitting the ground. The training room was still empty. I was alone. My lungs sucked in air, and I forced myself to focus on breathing. In. Out. *You didn't fall.* In. Out. *That was a long time ago.*

After a moment, I stood and made my way down the hall. It was strangely quiet. The bedroom was empty as well. Where had they gone? I flicked open my techband and noticed that I had a text message. It was from Vance. Apparently we were allowed to communicate with each other, at least.

```
Went for a run. You were
sleeping so soundly. I
didn't want to wake you.
Train on your own, and
we'll see you in an hour.
Sorry to lock you in.
Orders.
```

I gave a frustrated sigh. The guys had watched me sleep and then excluded me. No, not all of them. Vance had used the word "I." He had decided to protect me, to set me apart from them once again. Noble but irritating. The guy could've just woken me up.

I read the message again, stopping on the reference to the locked door. Just to test it, I stood and yanked on it. It was locked tight. Who had ordered me locked in? Didn't the empress trust me to fulfill her mission? My head throbbed with the beginnings of another headache. I decided to take advantage of my solitude by taking a shower.

I'd barely had time to strip down and climb into the shower when my techband started vibrating.

EPIC TEAM: TO CHOPPER PAD IMMEDIATELY.

"So much for that," I muttered and turned off the water. I toweled off quickly and slipped into a clean uniform.

A banging sound on the door made me jump. "I know. I'm coming."

"Treena, let me in," Vance's voice said in an urgent tone. "I need to talk to you."

The second I unlocked the door, he pushed it open and strode inside, locking it firmly behind him. It was so unexpected that I stared at him. "What?"

"I just read the details of the mission."

"What's wrong?"

He looked at me, searching my face. I felt a warm blush creep across my cheeks. "Our next mission isn't chasing smugglers," he said. "Tonight, for the first time, we're heading up an integration mission."

"What does that mean?"

"We're capturing an entire settlement."

I had to force myself to breathe normally. He nodded at my reaction and leaned his shoulder against the shiny tile wall.

I thought about the girl with the potato, and my heart sped up. "But I thought yours was the largest settlement. You mean there are others still out there?"

He let out a heavy breath. "After they took my clan out, the smaller groups got scared and started to combine into one big settlement for protection. It was a good idea, and they would've been pretty safe, except for one thing—their location, high in the Himmel Mountains. They planted themselves right next to the Peak River."

The Peak River was the main artery of Aiguille's water supply. I nodded. No wonder the commander was concerned. "I know it'll be hard for you and probably bring back some horrible memories, but in some ways it may not be so bad, right? If we're heading up the mission—"

"It means that we're on the front lines, doing all the work. Taking the losses."

I rocked back, stunned.

"There's something else. The orders mentioned you specifically."

"Me?" A sick feeling swelled inside me.

Vance turned to face me head-on. "You know all about me, but I know nothing about you. What did you do?" He looked angry now. "Why is your Rating so low? I'm sure you know more than you're telling."

"I didn't do anything," I said, my mind whirling at the sudden change of subject.

"Right. A girl like you, with a boyfriend like Bike Boy, doesn't just become a red. Start talking."

"I really don't know! It must be my biological father. He's in prison."

He considered that. "No. Your score might take a little hit because of him, but nothing like this, and you know it."

"I'm not lying." Vance was acting so strange— almost obsessive. I tried to change the subject. "What did the orders say?"

"There are only two reasons they'd send you here," he grumbled, almost to himself. "One, there's something about you that our team needs. Since you have no combat training or military experience, I have to assume it's because you're a girl. But that doesn't explain the Rating. Second, whatever you did to earn a 440 was so bad they're throwing you intentionally into harm's way. There's something I'm not seeing here."

"Vance."

"What?"

"What exactly is my part in the settlement mission?"

He looked at me, his face drawn in resignation. "They want you to be the bait."

o—●—o—●—o—●—o—●—o—●—o

The flying part was getting easier at least. Or maybe I was just too distracted by the impending doom to worry about falling out of the sky. As terrifying as a crash would be, at least there was a tiny chance of survival. But me, alone, at the hands of an entire outlander settlement? It was suicide.

We flew east toward the mountains, far outside NORA's borders. Below us somewhere were the ruined cities of what had once been the United States before the two government parties had declared war and nearly killed each other off. Supposedly my grandparents' generation had salvaged what they could and left the rest to waste away.

The vibration of the metal beneath my feet was a little more familiar this time but I still wished it wasn't so dark. In other circumstances, I'd be thrilled to finally see what a real forest looked like.

I glanced down at my clothing. This time we wore horrid brown coats and combat boots. Mine were way too big. It seemed that destiny wanted me to drown in men's clothing for the remainder of my two weeks in EPIC. Assuming I survived that long.

When the chopper landed, we filed out quietly. The cold wind literally took my breath away, whipping my hair into my face and stinging my eyes. The coat did little to keep out the cold. Poly's chopper landed in the next clearing over, then both the machines rose together. They'd deposited us on the opposite side of the mountain from our destination to avoid detection, which meant we got to hike for several hours before arriving. That was fine with me. If we had to navigate the entire continent before arriving, I'd be perfectly content.

"Don't forget what I told you," Vance whispered as we started after our guide. I'd clung to every word of his instruction on the way here, knowing it was my lifeline. "Any questions?"

"What if they don't buy it?"

"I'll be right behind you, hidden in the trees."

I shot him a look, and he shook his head. "I'll cover you this time, I swear."

Another gust of wind pulled a sharp smell into my senses. I leaned forward and took in a deep breath. It was the trees. Even in the darkness I could see their branches outstretched like fingers guarding the frozen earth. NORA trees stood straight and tall, each with the same number of carefully spaced branches, but the twisted trunks out here were raw and beautifully asymmetrical.

The ground wasn't flat like at home either. It was uneven and covered in debris, sometimes turning sharply upward and other times rocky, sloped, and slippery. I focused intently on the ground so I didn't fall. We had hand lights, but they barely lit up two meters at a time.

"Step onto your heel first," Vance said, "and rock toward your toe. It'll help you step quieter."

I glanced at him, but he was already looking away. Looking up, actually. A peaceful calm had settled over his features. He looked almost reverent.

"This isn't exactly the way I imagined it," I said. "It's so cold. Why isn't there any snow?"

He shook his head. "We only get snow on the peaks. And even then it's only for a month or two in the winter."

"Oh. Well, have you ever seen it? I mean, what does it feel like?"

He scanned the forest, stepping confidently as he considered my question. "Only twice, on hunting expeditions, and I've only seen it fall out of the sky once. It was …" He gave a sideways smile. "Cold."

I rolled my eyes. "Thanks for that."

"Anytime."

We'd hoped the exercise would warm us, but I was numb by the time we reached the clearing. I checked my techband for the time before remembering that it didn't work out here. According to Poly, punishment mode could still be activated if the techband was tampered with, but it had no network signal. It felt strange to be off the radar.

The soft white glow of a handful of lanterns greeted us. The lights were concealed deep within the branches of the trees, so they didn't do much more than guide us to the dark outline of the waiting group of soldiers. From what Vance had said, these three hundred were only a third of our troops on the mountain. Apparently NORA wasn't taking any chances this time.

Poly motioned for us to stay here as he and Vance pushed their way through the ranks. Major Murphy waited stiffly in front of a makeshift shelter in the center, arms folded, wearing the typical armored military uniform. A shorter figure came out of the shelter and stopped next to him. I squinted, trying to see better in the low light, wondering why the man seemed familiar. I leaned toward Neb. "Is that who I think it is?"

"Commander Denoux himself," he said in wonder. "I can't believe it. He's overseeing this mission? This must be really important. "

A sick feeling crept through my stomach, but there was nothing I could do now. I'd already agreed to this. Well, I'd been ordered to do it, and that was the same thing. Nine hundred soldiers waited to be led by the commander and the EPIC team. Was this the commander's way of punishing us for Vance's earlier outburst? But if that was the case, what was my part in all this?

If the empress really needed me to catch a traitor,

why march me in front of an armed settlement?

After a few minutes, Poly and Vance approached with somber faces. Everyone was alert, stretching sore legs and arms and checking their weapons.

"Why is the commander here?" Neb asked when the EPIC leaders reached us.

Poly glanced away. "This is the first time we've combined forces with the military. He wants it to go smoothly."

"He doesn't trust us," Daymond said.

"So what are the orders?" Semias grumbled.

Poly glared at him but continued. "The settlers are getting smarter. They won't be taken easily. The perimeter wall is made of NeoSteel, electrified and too smooth to climb. We can't go in with an aerial attack or we'll destroy too many targets. So a decoy is our only choice. Treena, you will pose as a beggar, approach their front gate, and convince them to let you in. Once you're inside, get this device as close to the center of the camp as you can." He handed me a small metal rectangle and pointed to a switch on the side. It gave off a warm vibration even through my gloves. I stuck it in my pocket, feeling another wave of nervousness as Poly continued. "It should disable every electronic lock within a two-hundred-meter radius of the center point, allowing us to surround and penetrate the camp. EPIC will be the front line. These soldiers aren't familiar with settlers at all, so they've been ordered to follow our lead. Oh, and, men, set your guns to stun. Under no circumstance will you shoot to kill."

"I don't like this," Vance muttered.

"Just obey orders this time, Vance," Poly growled. "Time to get your personal feelings out of the way."

"How many people in the settlement?" I asked.

"Preliminary estimates are a thousand," Poly said.

"A thousand!" Neb exclaimed, his voice cracking.

"Poly," Vance said. "I can't lead a unit of NORA soldiers. You know how they see me."

"You can, and you will," Poly said, his voice low and hard. "I understand your feelings, but if you care about these people, you'll stun as many of them as possible. It's the ones who fight back that will get hurt."

"But the soldiers—"

Poly whirled to face him. "You *are* a soldier. Act like it, or I'll turn you over to the commander."

Vance recoiled, his face hard. Our group was silent for a moment, everyone suddenly very interested in the ground.

"Yes, sir," Vance said.

The order came to move out. The hike to the structure was slow. There was no clear-cut trail, and at times we had to climb over sharp rocks and leap across streams—all in the darkness of night. I had a dozen cuts and bruises under my uniform, but I didn't dare stop for fear I'd end up at the bottom of a ravine. I caught Vance's gaze once, but he turned away in frustration, his body stiff as he looked into the night. No doubt this was bringing back awful memories for him. Except that he was the attacker this time.

After a couple of agonizing hours, the scouts detected four watchers up in the trees, two men and two women. I didn't know what was happening until the scouts retrieved the bodies from the ground, their movements coldly efficient. I felt sick. The lookouts were probably parents, moms and dads trying to protect their children from danger.

Before the wall was even visible, the order came to halt and take cover. Poly scattered the EPIC team to various checkpoints, then spoke to someone in sharp whispers on his feed. My heart thudded so painfully I could barely hear anything else.

Finally Poly nodded to me.

I took a deep, ragged breath, and Neb and Ross whispered their encouragement as I walked slowly past. Vance clenched his fists and watched me go.

My body shivered violently as I forced one foot in front of the other, feeling hundreds of eyes on my back. The walk to the gate felt like several kilometers, but it probably only took a few minutes. It was the longest walk of my life. The giant steel wall was just in front of me now. A reinforced metal gate at least six meters tall lay silently in the distance between two trees. A faint electric buzz sounded from somewhere. These people were serious about their security.

There was no sound behind the wall. Maybe the

settlement really didn't know we were here. I didn't dare touch the wall, let alone knock. It was too dark to see anything, so I just stood there and called in a shaky voice, "Hello?"

No answer, but I heard shuffling. Finally a head popped up over the wall. It was a boy, maybe thirteen or fourteen. "Stay where you are and put your hands up."

I complied. At least he hadn't shot me on the spot.

"Bert," the boy whispered, and I saw a small radio in his hand. It looked old and clunky. "There's a girl here. She has red numbers on her head. Want me to shoot her?"

"Please," I said, trying to hide my sudden horror. "I'm so cold. Do you have an extra blanket? That's all I ask."

"Shut up, girl," the boy said. "Don't move. I never miss." He tapped a long wooden stick—a rifle, probably—and halfheartedly aimed it at me.

"If you won't give me a blanket, can I at least go through your garbage?" The word *garbage* seemed strange on my tongue, but Vance had insisted. If I said *refuse*, they'd get suspicious. "I haven't eaten anything in days."

The boy hesitated. "You're from NORA. How'd you get out?"

"They destroyed my settlement a couple of years ago—burned it down, integrated us. I worked with the smugglers for a while, but we got attacked in

Meridian. I was lucky to get out in a transport full of apples."

The boy stared at me, bug-eyed, his gun still trained on my head. "The Meridian hub was attacked?" The gun lowered a bit. "Hang on a sec." There was a one-sided whispered conversation again, low enough that I couldn't hear anything this time.

My legs shook so badly I worried they'd give way. After walking for hours, standing still was utter agony. The device in my pocket seemed to burn a hole through the thin layer under my coat, despite the rest of me being past feeling. *Just get inside, Treena. Deploy the device and get out—that's all they want.*

"My backup is on the way, but first I'm supposed to ask you a question," the boy said. "If you're really an Integrant, what was your clan leader's nickname?"

Oh no. My stomach sank. Vance's last name was Hawking, I remembered. But surely that wasn't what the settlers wanted. I wore an earpiece—the earring kind again, so I knew Vance was listening. But revealing this code word meant betraying his people in a very big way. All he had to do was stay silent, and I'd be arrested. Or shot. Our entire operation would be buried before it even began. There was no sound in my earpiece except the muttering of soldiers in the background.

Please, Vance.

"Well, girl?" the boy said. He clicked something on his weapon and closed one eye as if to aim.

Please.

"His name was Sebastian Hawking," Vance whispered, his voice hoarse. "His nickname was Iron Belt."

Hiding my relief, I repeated the words. The boy looked surprised, but he lowered his gun and raised his radio to his lips. "She passed, Bert. Another one of Old Man Iron's clan."

The gate didn't open immediately. I shivered for several minutes while he conferred with two men who had joined him. The three figures kept turning toward me, then talking some more.

I was about to speak when a section of the wall opened. It swung inward into blackness, revealing an opening just large enough for a person to slip through. The large gate had been a decoy.

I allowed myself a tiny shred of hope. If they were going to shoot me, at least it wouldn't be here.

Several heartbeats later I made my way to the wall and stepped inside. It wasn't three people who greeted me there but eight, all armed and suspiciously staring me down.

A woman stepped forward. "Hold your arms out. I'm checking you for weapons."

"Sure," I said and obeyed. She ran a detector across my arms and down to my feet. I held my breath, but it didn't make a sound when it ran over the unlocking device in my pocket. Luckily Poly had insisted I come unarmed.

"Nothing registered," she said.

"See? Told you she'd pass," the boy said. "Can I take her in?"

The woman hesitated. "Valor, go with them. Keep your weapon trained on her, just in case. I'll meet you inside."

A balding man nodded and stepped forward. The boy barely seemed to notice and motioned for me to follow him. "I'm Lowry. My Uncle Drumlin's the clan leader. Least, he was, before we combined. I guess our clan doesn't really exist anymore."

"This is huge," I said with genuine awe at the settlement that opened up in front of me. Even in the darkness, I could see hundreds of dark structures. Cabins. They surrounded a huge building in the center. I'd never seen so many wooden buildings in my life. We used concrete and steel in NORA. I'd heard that some cities to the east had real trees, but I'd never seen them. Here, there was hardly anything in sight that *wasn't* made of trees, a stark contrast to the modern wall that enclosed the place. The low rumbling of a generator grew louder with each step. The ground was packed hard from foot traffic, so it was much easier to walk here than in the forest.

"Four times larger than yours was," the boy replied with a proud tone. "I'm supposed to take you to that center building. That's the kitchen. Bet you're excited to have real food after so long, right?"

"Absolutely," I said, feeling the nervousness flare

up again. *Uh-oh.*

"I hoped they'd let you in right off. Red numbers are fine. It's the ones with green numbers you have to watch out for, you know?"

"How long have you been here?" I asked, eager to change the subject.

"Almost a year," he replied proudly. "Built two of these cabins with my dad. NORA doesn't know it, but our buildings are lined with metal stolen from their own military base. We have fire extinguishers in each building, and every person has an air mask in case they try to use knockout gas. It's crazy high-tech. This is the safest place for you, trust me."

"Impressive. You really think NORA would attack you here?"

"My uncle thinks so, but I doubt it. They wouldn't dare."

"Lowry," the older man, Valor, said from behind us. I had forgotten he was there. "Quit running that mouth of yours. She hasn't been cleared yet, you know."

"Sorry." The boy shot me an apologetic look, then leaned closer and pointed to my forehead. "Does that thing hurt?"

I touched my Rating with one gloved finger. I didn't even notice it anymore. "No." *Yes. Every day, but not in the way you think.*

"Weird. Well, they'll probably take it out tomorrow, regardless. Here we are." He headed for a steel door in the north-facing wall of the largest building. Four short knocks and the door opened with a moan. A figure stood in the darkness of the opening.

"This is her," Lowry said.

"Let's get started," a deep feminine voice said from the doorway, and she stepped aside, holding the door open for me. Her smile was forced, her eyes strained and tired. They'd probably woken her up for me.

"Doing what?" I asked.

"Why, your dinner. It should all come back to you pretty quickly. Assuming you are who you say you are."

I forced my shoulders to relax. "That sounds great."

The door slammed shut behind me.

21

W hat's taking her so long?" someone grumbled. "She must be close enough by now."

"They're making her eat something," I said, only half listening. I mentally kicked myself for not preparing her better. Of course they'd offer food. It was the best way to test a former settler. Treena wasn't handling it well—she was choking like a goat trying to swallow an entire transport at once. "Chew carefully for twenty seconds, then swallow it just like a pill. Wash it down with water if you need to."

The men in my charge stood there, shifting their weight from one leg to the other, muttering quietly to themselves. One of them shot me an icy glare. I stood a little straighter, meeting his expression. I was the youngest guy in the group, an Integrant, and a red—yet they were supposed to obey me. Blasted commander.

"Whoa there, honey," the woman's voice said

over the feed. "Take smaller bites."

"I'm sorry," Treena responded, her mouth still full. "It's just that it's been so long—my jaw must've—ugh—forgotten how to chew."

"Interesting." The woman wasn't fooled, and it was obvious in her voice. "I'll take you to your room, then."

"Thank you. It's been a really long time since I've eaten." Treena's voice sounded a little off. "But my stomach hurts a little. Do you mind if I walk it off?"

"In that case, it's straight to your quarters for you. There will be plenty of time to explore in the morning after you've rested. And after you've been cleared, of course."

"What exactly does that mean?"

"Your former clan will have to identify you."

There was a pause. "That will be nice. Um, can I use your washroom really quick?"

"Our what?"

I cursed, straining to hear better.

"Uh, bathroom," Treena said quickly. "Sorry, they had me trained pretty well."

The woman's voice hardened. "Just up these stairs."

There was nothing on the feed for a while, then Treena thanked the woman. A door opened and closed. There was the sound of heavy breathing, then a big thud. Silence.

"Treena," I whispered. "Are you all right?"

Another moment of quiet, and then the sound of heaving. Ah. So she hadn't been faking her stomach sickness after all.

"What's going on?" someone asked—a captain, by the bands of rank on his arm.

"She just needs a minute," I said.

The captain grumbled something, but he sat back again to wait.

Soon a shaky voice came back on. "Sorry, Vance. Don't know what came over me, but I'm ready now."

"Are you sure? You can always—"

"Yeah, I can do this." She coughed. "Here goes. Three. Two."

"All units, ready," I said, and the command was repeated down the ranks.

"One." It was almost a whisper.

A buzzer sounded somewhere, and Murphy's voice yelled over the feed, "Attack!" Suddenly the ground thundered with the sound of hundreds of heavy feet running through the darkness, all headed for the wall. Then the shouting began.

I looked longingly at the dark and welcoming forest. It would be so easy to slip away and hide. But if I did, my family would be executed. I was as much a prisoner here as I was within NORA's borders.

The soldiers assigned to me watched me with dark expressions. They seemed to know what I was considering. Had the commander assigned them to me, or me to them?

It didn't matter right now. I'd promised Treena protection this time. Our superiors had insisted that Treena enter unarmed, as there was no way a real refugee could have obtained a weapon. They obviously weren't concerned about what would happen to her once her betrayal was discovered.

"On our way, Treena," I said into the feed. "Just hold on."

When we arrived, the wall was much higher than I'd imagined. The gate was still closed, and it buzzed loudly with electricity, causing the soldiers to slow down in confusion. A section of the wall stood open, just large enough to allow one person through at a time. I groaned. This would take forever.

A familiar click sounded above my head, and I froze. A dozen rifle barrels sat atop the wall, and one was aimed right at me.

I barely had time to spring out of the way before the shooting started. The thunder of bullets and screams of dying men echoed sharply across the sleeping forest. So much for the element of surprise. Amid the chaos of rifles and stunners exchanging fire, I saw that the thin doorway was closing now, shoved by men from the other side who had finally realized that the locking mechanism was disabled.

We didn't have time for this.

I leaped over and shoved my way through just as it slammed shut. Surprised grunts were replaced with cries of pain as I let myself loose—a sweep to the leg, an elbow to the face, the crunching sound of breaking bone. A thud as someone fell, then another. And another. There were only two men holding desperately to the door now, both watching me wide-eyed, knowing they were next. One of them looked upward and shouted for help from their armed comrades.

I twisted around them, reaching instead for the solid metal lever above the shorter one's head. It was similar to the one on NORA's border wall, almost like they'd stolen the technology. I plunged it downward. The wall emitted a deep moan, and the buzzing of electricity sputtered and died. The two men stared at the lever, then at each other, and took off running and shouting just as the door burst open.

"The wall is clear," I shouted. Only one of the gunners at the top of the wall remained, and he was facing the other direction. I took off at a sprint.

An alarm started to wail somewhere. If the gunshots hadn't already awakened the sleeping settlers, the alarm would.

"Open this door, now!" the woman screamed through Treena's feed.

"It won't lock," Treena said into the feed, her voice strained. "Must be the device jamming it like all the other locks. She's going to kill me, Vance. Fates! I can't hold this much longer!"

"Is there a window?" I asked, lengthening my stride.

"Well, yeah."

"Prop something against the door," I said, panting, "and then climb out the window. See if you can find handholds along the exterior of the building. I'll be there in half a minute."

"But Vance, I can't—I'm not good at heights."

"Do it now!" By the banging sounds on the feed, the woman was seconds away from pushing through. I checked behind me, surprised to see that my troops had gotten past the wall and followed. "Head for the center structure!"

"Okay," she said in a tiny voice. She sounded sick again.

Around us, soldiers banged on smaller cabin doors. These people were well trained, though, and many answered with a rifle shot through a window. The few who did come out, bleary-eyed and confused, were stunned unconscious and now lay in a heap.

A figure jumped out from behind a building, fired a shot that struck one of my soldiers, and ducked out of sight again. A surge of pride filled my body before I remembered that resisting would only be more dangerous for them. It would be too easy for a soldier to "accidentally" slip the stunner into fatal mode and return fire. Even now I could see the crazed, murderous look in some of their eyes. I shouted, "Five men per cabin, but drag the stunned settlers to safety until the fighting stops. Remember that the cabins are probably connected underground. The rest of you, follow me!"

My orders were repeated through the ranks, and a few actually broke off and obeyed. I saw Treena immediately. She clung to the window frame, struggling to place a foot in the mortar between the logs but slipping with each attempt. A woman yelled out the window, fist shaking, and then she reached down as if to peel Treena's fingers off her perch. I took aim and fired—one shot, and the woman spun backward and disappeared. Treena whirled around to see, nearly throwing her off the four-story building completely.

"Someone help her!" I yelled, frantically searching our equipment for another ladder—a wooden one, or a long object—but nothing was long enough. "We need some kind of net!"

Instead of obeying, a line of soldiers surrounded me on either side, gazing upward at the flailing girl, and one of them slowly raised his weapon. My eyes went to the window, but there was no one else there.

He took aim—right at Treena.

"Wait! Don't shoot!"

He fired, but I swept his leg just in time, throwing him off balance. He landed flat on his back with a grunt. "What's wrong with you?" I snapped. "She's on my team!"

"Fates, just following orders!" the man gasped.

"I never told you to shoot her!"

The blast from the stun gun must have hit close because Treena lost hold of the windowsill with one hand. She swung precariously from the other hand before regaining her hold. Daymond finally jumped into action, twisting two rope ladders together to form a makeshift net, and tossed it to Ross. They stretched it taut below Treena's desperate form.

I didn't have time to watch, though. The fallen NORA soldier was getting up, and the others had noticed the scuffle. They circled me like carnivores before their prey.

"You're not talking about my orders," I said. "You're getting them from someone else."

"What kind of fool would follow a red?" a fat-nosed soldier asked, grinning down at me like a boy at mealtime. "At least you're smart enough to understand that much." He raised a fist, but my instincts took over. When he stepped forward for the punch, I gave him a swift kick to the knee, dropping him just before the guy behind me attacked. Out of the corner of my eye, I saw Treena let go.

"No!" I shouted, but Daymond and Ross were ready. They stretched the rope ladder as taut as it would go, and Treena fell perfectly into it, back first, spreading her weight out like a winged bat. She hit the ground, but the net seemed to have broken her fall just enough. She sat up right away, looking dazed but unhurt.

It distracted me just long enough for a couple of soldiers to grab my arms. I tried to whip around, but a third soldier wrapped his arm around my throat and put me in a headlock. I kicked backward to break away, but the arm tightened around my throat. My vision blurred, and I mentally kicked myself. Any idiot knew not to get distracted. These men weren't sloppy smugglers but trained soldiers, hardened from decades of careful training.

The captain who'd pretended to relay my orders approached. "Stupid red. I hoped you'd give me a reason to do this." With a smile that looked more like a grimace, he raised his gun and aimed it at my head.

"Stop!" Treena shrieked as she struggled to untwist herself from the net, but it was too late. The impact exploded into my brain like a transport train.

22

I woke up in the commander's tent, my wrists fastened to the side of the bed. My guys—well, and Treena—huddled near the opening, dirty, tired, and looking grim. I did a quick mental count and relaxed. Everyone from my team was there. They were so engrossed in conversation that no one noticed I was awake.

"Anything can happen in a battle," Semias was saying. "He probably disobeyed an order. They would've had to shoot him."

"No," Treena said quickly. "I was watching. I felt the rush of air from a stunner, then Vance started yelling at them, and the soldiers turned on him right as I fell. If you guys hadn't made that net when you did …"

"Bet it was supposed to look like an accident," Daymond said. "That's why the soldier tried to shoot you while you were still hanging."

197

Semias groaned. "Fates! This is ridiculous. Listen to yourselves. How do you know the guy wasn't aiming at someone behind you, Treena? Maybe someone was in the window, ready to attack, and the soldier was trying to save you."

"Then Vance would have helped instead of attacking the soldier," Daymond replied. "Face it, Semias. The soldiers were jealous of EPIC, so they tried to take us out when no one was looking."

"Not *us*," Ross said. "Just Treena and Vance."

"Who'd be jealous of two reds?" Semias muttered. "You're all insane." He stalked out without a second look.

"Good morning, sunshine," Daymond said, finally noticing me. Treena's eyes lit up, and she headed to my side. She lifted a hand as if to grab mine, then pulled it back at the last second, looking flustered.

"Did we win?" I croaked.

"No EPIC losses, but sixty military casualties," Daymond said. "About two hundred settler deaths, mostly suicides. The rest are unconscious and headed for NORA already."

Two hundred. It was far worse than I'd expected. I tried to sit, but something pulled at my wrist. "Why am I tethered to the bed?"

"They said you attacked your own soldiers," Daymond said. "The commander was furious. The entire unit was backing it up, so it's their word against ours. Luckily, Poly smooth-talked him into waiting for you to wake up and tell your side of the story."

I forced myself up into a sitting position. A fresh stab of pain in my side made me wince.

"Poly also said it wasn't safe to move you yet," Treena said, "since you were hit in the head. He feels really bad, Vance. Says he should have listened when you tried to withdraw as a unit leader."

"Yeah, well, I'm glad he realizes that." I swung my legs around and pulled on my bonds, but they were tight.

"I'll go tell Poly you're awake," Daymond said, motioning for the others to leave as well. Treena moved to follow.

"Wait," I told her. "Are you all right?"

She looked at the floor. "Compared to you, yeah. My stomach still hurts a little."

"Ah." Every Integrant knew the pain of hunger, the hollow sickness nutrition pills caused at first. For a stomach accustomed to real food, the pill wasn't enough. It had taken me a year to get used to it. But I hadn't thought about the reverse situation. Treena could very well be the only person to experience food after only ever living on pills. "Your stomach may take a while to recover. You've just changed the delicate chemistry of your digestive system."

"Don't worry, I'm fine. Better off than some." She took a deep breath, probably remembering those she had just betrayed. I knew the feeling. "Thanks for the rescue. I'm sorry you got hurt because of me."

"Not hurt. Just zapped," I said with a forced grin. "It's not the first time."

"I figured." She returned the smile, but it disappeared quickly. "When I saw them aim at you, and you still watching me, making sure I was safe—" Her face crumpled. "I don't know. It was like something in me snapped. When you fell, one of them kicked you. I stole Daymond's stunner and charged at the guy like a crazy person." She chuckled bitterly. "If it weren't for Daymond pulling me back, they'd probably have shot me, too."

That explained the pain in my side. "Guess you're one of the team now."

"Am I?" Her voice was distant. She reached up and grasped her necklace, something I'd noticed she did often.

"What's that jewelry?" I asked. "A gift from Bike Boy?"

She shook her head. "My dad."

I allowed myself a twinge of satisfaction. "You must miss him."

Her voice grew hard. "I never knew him. He left before I was born, but he told my mom to give this to me on my Rating day. Some father, huh?" She removed the necklace and placed it into my hand, the delicate strand hanging down between my fingers. The stone was still warm from the heat of her body.

"But you wear it every day. Why?"

Her eyes finally met mine, level and determined.

"The purple reminds me of NORA. I think he was trying to tell me that I should trust the system."

"And look where that got you. I see why you don't like it." I stared at the stone for a moment, then held it up to the light. "What about the gold, then?"

She brought her head closer, staring at the stone in surprise, and I caught a whiff of pine needles. "What in the fates? I can't believe I've never noticed that before. Must be the mountain light or something."

I lifted it over her head with my free hand, and she guided it into place with a grateful smile. My wrist brushed against her soft cheek, and she leaned in just a little. I cleared my throat and pulled my hand away. "If I were a father about to leave my family, I don't know that a rock would be my first choice for a gift. But then again, at least he left you something."

"What was your dad like?"

"Honestly? Stern and overprotective." She laughed gently, and I continued. "But a great man. My entire clan adored him. They'd do anything for him, and he felt the same about his people."

We fell silent, and I sensed the unease in her demeanor. Her eyes flicked toward the door. Before she could leave, I blurted out the first thing that came to mind. "I was wrong about you."

"What?"

"After we ran into Bike Boy, I accused you of being just like every other shallow girl in NORA. But I've never met a girl who would march into a settlement, unarmed and alone."

"That makes me either incredibly brave or incredibly stupid." She shrugged. "I was wrong about you too. I've always thought that outlanders were cruel and violent. You wouldn't believe some of the stories I grew up with."

"I haven't eaten a baby in years," I said. "Well, unless you count that one last week." She groaned at the joke, and I sobered. "We're not cruel, necessarily. But violent when we have to be. While we're on the subject, I've always thought citizens like you were stuck-up, selfish robots with numbers on their heads."

"You weren't far off."

"We were both wrong," I said softly. "And right."

Our eyes met, and her lips softened into a shy smile. A wayward lock of hair hung over her face, and I had a sudden strange urge to gently brush it back into place.

"Vance?" a voice called from the doorway. I whirled to find Neb standing there, a strange look on his face. He glanced at Treena, then back at me. "Um, Poly's on his way, and the commander isn't far behind."

"Thanks."

A furious blush stained Treena's cheeks, and she moved quickly toward the door.

"Treena," I called after her. "You realize what happened today, right?"

She stopped. "What do you mean?"

"Someone tried to kill you."

She stared at the floor. "We don't know that for sure."

"Yes, we do. And I will find out who it was and why. They will not succeed. Not as long as I'm around. Understood?"

Treena didn't return my gaze. "Yes, sir."

23

I felt sick.

It could have been anything, really—the jostling, deafening chopper I sat inside, or Vance's injuries, or even the real food. But when I thought of what we had just done, my stomach twisted. Two hundred innocent people had lost their lives tonight, and the survivors were prisoners. Dozens of children were probably waking up right now, scared, torn from the only homes they'd ever known, all facing a future of poverty and competition.

All because I was willing to do anything to raise my Rating. NORA had used me, and I'd been completely willing to be used.

I gripped my seat, shivering despite the coat I wore. Team Two sat slumped in their seats, fully asleep, their belts the only reason they weren't sprawled out on the floor in heavy slumber. Semias's head had fallen completely forward, a long string of drool swaying with the movement of the chopper.

Vance wasn't with us. He was probably still being interrogated. Two days ago I wouldn't have worried for him. But now I knew how precarious his situation was. If he was found guilty, would they execute him? Or would they punish his family instead?

Poly sat rigidly next to me, his dark eyes staring at nothing. As the official leader of EPIC and the person who had appointed Vance, Poly was partially accountable for Vance's actions. I thought back to the conversation I'd overheard on my first full day. I hadn't done anything to investigate the EPIC leader. Somehow, after today my Rating reconsideration felt further away than ever.

"What will happen to Vance?" I asked Poly.

For a moment I didn't know if he was ignoring me or if he simply hadn't heard my question. I opened my mouth to ask again, but his eyes finally focused on me. "I don't know."

"He was only protecting me. They'll give him another chance, right?"

He leaned forward so quickly that I recoiled. "Did a soldier really point a gun at you?"

"I didn't see it, exactly," I admitted. "But I felt the blast go past me. What I don't understand is why the soldiers attacked him afterward."

He shook his head and sat back wearily. "They were just looking for an excuse. I was a fool. It wasn't the first time he's been attacked, although usually it's his own people who try it."

"His clan members have fought him?"

Poly gave me a long look. "Don't worry, he can take care of himself. Well, except for this last time. Must've been too many of them."

Or he was distracted. I remembered how he'd refused to tear his eyes away from me, making sure I was all right. "Why did you choose Vance as your first?"

"You sure have a lot of questions about Vance," Daymond said from across the way. He lay crooked in his seat with one eye open. I'd forgotten that everyone could hear our conversation through the feed. "All these guys and you like the Integrant. Girls are strange creatures."

"I just wondered about his loyalty," I snapped. "How do you guys know he won't turn on you and save his friends?"

"Vance has captured four times more smugglers than anyone else," Daymond said. "And most of them were Integrants. If he's a double agent, he's not doing a very good job."

We fell into silence again as the chopper hit a bit of turbulence. I gripped my seat tightly and took a deep, slow breath, trying to keep my mind on our conversation.

Poly had resumed his glassy-eyed stare, so I tilted my head back and tried to clear my thoughts. Finally, sleep came, but with it came dreams of a guy—not the one I'd come to win but the one who had just sacrificed himself to save me.

The one guy in NORA I should never, ever want.

24

It was dark by the time I got back, and both teams were asleep. My body moved sluggishly, and I knew I wouldn't last long without a little sleep myself, but my thoughts were still sharp. When I walked into the bedroom, I noticed a soft blue glow in the darkness. Semias, shirtless and bleary-eyed, was sitting up in his bed. As soon as he saw me enter, he snapped his techband screen closed, and the light disappeared.

"Didn't think I'd find *you* awake," I said, sitting on my bed to remove my shoes.

"I—uh, suddenly felt really hungry. I was just checking the time."

I frowned. That didn't require opening the screen. Surely he knew by now that our communications were blocked. "I think we'll wait until everyone wakes up before we break out the pills."

"Sounds good." Semias lay back down and rolled over to face the wall. Either Semias was really tired or something strange was going on. He'd never passed up a chance to argue before.

"Vance!" Neb sat straight up in bed, and for a moment I thought he was going to come over and hug me. He seemed to think better of it and kept his blanket on. "They set you free! I knew they'd come to their senses."

"Don't get too excited. I'm on probation." The words felt sour in my mouth. They hadn't believed a single word of my testimony about Treena and the shooter. It didn't matter. I would discover why Treena had been targeted. Something told me that if I did, the mystery of her Rating would be revealed.

As always, I lay down on my right side, where I had full view of the room. Semias and Neb had gone back to sleep, and the bathroom door was closed tight. With a yawn, I allowed myself to drift into a fitful sleep.

o–●–o–●–o–●–o–o–●–o

"You can't pretend you're not hungry," Semias's distant voice said, waking me up with a start.

"Poor baby," Daymond whined.

There was a beeping sound as someone scanned their techband on the pill cupboard's lock, and then Poly appeared in the doorway. He tossed the pill container to Daymond, who twisted the tube open. Apparently Poly had asked Daymond to distribute breakfast rather than wake me up. That was completely fine with me. I pulled the pillow over my head and tried to drown out the light and noise.

There was some kind of crash followed by yelling. With a moan, I shoved the pillow away and sat up. There were nutrition pills scattered across the floor. The other guys stared wide-eyed at Daymond and Semias, who glared at each other over the mess. Treena had emerged from the bathroom and stood with her arms folded, frowning.

"That was totally you, man," Semias snapped, getting in Daymond's face. "You couldn't walk straight if someone drew a line on the ground."

"Nice try, Semias," Daymond said, "but I'm not stupid." He held the container out, and the guys started scooping up pills and dumping fistfuls back in. "I know what you're doing. When we count them, I bet there'll be some missing, and they'll magically appear in your pocket."

"Not so." Semias knelt and collected a few in his palm. "Don't blame your klutziness on me. See what a good boy I am? One for you," he said, handing a pill to Ross, who scowled, "and one for you." He gave one to Treena. She had come closer to help, kneeling a careful distance from Semias. I watched his hand carefully, making sure nothing disappeared down his sleeve. As the pill switched hands, though, I noticed something strange about it. Was it … brown?

She wrapped her hand around the pill and muttered a reluctant, "Thank you."

I stood.

Daymond slammed some pills into the container with a decisive whip of his hand. "I swear, if you ever trip me again, Semias, I'll break your leg. And maybe the other one too, just for fun."

Ross swallowed his pill, and Treena had just tilted her head back to down hers when I grabbed her hand.

"Wait." I swiped the pill out of her hand and sniffed it.

She stared at me. "What's wrong?"

I leaped to the floor and gathered up a few more, then held them up to the light. "Freeze. All of you. Don't touch the pills."

The other guys glanced at each other uncertainly, but they stood and backed away. Semias glared at me. "Why? You want them all to yourself, Vance?"

"This one's a different color than the others," I said. "Dark and coarse. It even smells different."

Poly shook his head from the doorway "Vance, it's good to have you back, but you're acting a little paranoid. They're just nutrition pills."

My fist was clenched tightly around the offending pill.

"Where did this pill come from?" I asked Semias.

"From the bottle," he sputtered.

"Then you wouldn't mind sampling it. Just to make sure it's safe."

"I—I already took one. Another would make me sick."

"You? Right. You'd take a dozen a day if you could. But no rush."

Semias glanced at Poly, who looked torn. "I didn't poison it, if that's what you're getting at."

"Good. You won't mind taking it, then."

"Vance," Poly said with a warning tone. "You're looking for trouble where there's none."

I whipped around. "Poly, Semias is on my team. With all due respect, let me handle this one."

Poly's jaw tightened, and his dark eyes seared into mine. I refused to drop my gaze. This was too important to give up on, even for a man I respected as much as Poly. Finally he nodded.

"Fates," Semias grumbled, but his voice seemed higher than usual. "I didn't do anything wrong. You're just jealous because I'm a high yellow."

His defensiveness only strengthened my resolve. "You're doing an awful lot of talking. How about we stuff that mouth with a poisoned pill and see what happens?"

"Shut up, Vance. I don't have to prove anything."

"I'm not leaving until you do."

"I won't take the stupid pill!"

"You'll do it, under your power or mine."

"You're crazy, man. Poly, you're seriously letting him get away with this?"

"Yes," I said firmly. "He is. You have three seconds. Three."

"I'm not. Taking. The pill."

"Two. Why? What'll happen?"

"I don't know." Semias's voice trembled slightly. "The commander only said—" He stopped, then gave a strangled gasp.

Everyone looked at him.

"The commander said what?" Poly growled.

Semias looked like a cornered rabbit. His eyes darted back and forth, his chin set in defiance.

Poly stepped forward and took the pill, then sniffed it. "Without a microscope it's hard to tell, but from the color and the coarseness of the leaves, I'd guess it's baneberry. Hard to detect, but it paralyzes the heart. Treena wouldn't have lasted an hour."

Everyone looked at Semias. His conviction seemed to waver, and then he finally broke. "The message said to slip it to Treena. But I didn't know it was poisoned, I swear. For all I knew, it just had extra caffeine or something."

For a few seconds the guys gaped at each other. Treena's face had turned a sickly shade of white.

"Semias," I said, "as long as I'm around, you will not succeed with that order."

"I can't believe it," Poly muttered, still staring at the pill.

Semias stood taller, glancing at Poly and then back at me. "I know it's horrible and all, but we all know EPIC is a tough job. We don't know why we do half the things we're ordered to do. It's not our place to question. If the commander wants her dead, he must have a good reason." He turned to face Treena. "Maybe your little trainee isn't what you think she is."

I took a step toward him, my veins pulsing with anger. "We are a division of law enforcement. We're not assassins, and we certainly don't murder each other, orders or not."

Team One must have felt the tension because several heads peeked in from the hallway. They watched us curiously, as if unsure whether to interrupt. Poly motioned for them to stay where they were.

I grabbed Semias's arms and wrenched them behind his back. He struggled for a moment but stopped when I locked his wrists. "Unfortunately, I can't let you roam free now. Not as long as you're willing to sell us out."

He gritted his teeth. "Treena isn't one of us. I'm telling you, there's something up with her."

"Wait." Treena's face had turned an angry red. "Let me talk to him for a second."

I shoved him to his knees so he couldn't hurt her, then took a step back. She bent over and got right in his face. "You said the commander told you to do it. Why?"

"I don't—He didn't tell me why. Just that the orders came from higher up."

There was a stunned silence. Higher up? There was only one person above a councilman.

"The empress," Neb breathed.

Daymond grunted. "Why would the empress be after you, Treena?"

She just shook her head, absently fingering the rock necklace that hung from her neck. "I don't know."

"When the commander doesn't hear back from Semias," Poly said, "he'll know the attack failed. He'll just send others. The question is, what do we do with Treena in the meantime?"

I put a hand on her slim shoulder. "Protect her. Despite what Semias says, she's still a member of our team. But I'll tell you one thing. If the commander and the empress are desperate enough to secretly murder one of us, it means no one is safe. We can't rest until we know what's behind this. From now on we implement a two-person watch, day and night—one from Team One, the other from Team Two. We'll figure out quickly who our teammates are and who can be too easily bought." I stared into Semias's eyes, and his gaze slid to the floor. I could feel Poly's glare from across the room. I'd never ordered his men around before. Hopefully he agreed that this was necessary.

"What about Semias?" Daymond asked.

"Unfortunately for him, he's stuck here. But that doesn't mean he's entitled to our trust. I think he's about to get some well-deserved rest."

"Rest?"

"Definitely." I felt a wicked smile spread across my face. "Chain him to his bed."

25

skipped breakfast. The thought of filling my stomach, even with a pill, made me sick. I'd been centimeters away from death, and Vance had saved me. Again. But this time it hadn't been a stranger that had tried to take my life, and it definitely couldn't be written off as an accident.

I was an anomaly in EPIC now. Instead of ignoring me like they had to this point, both EPIC teams stared at me with interest. I could just imagine the crazy stories they were attributing to my past. After several hours of training, I thought the whispers would never end. Vance seemed to sense my need for space and suggested an evening run.

We didn't talk much as we ran, and it was nearly dark by the time we got back, sore and weary from the events of the last forty-eight hours. Poly offered me a nutrition pill—perfectly normal and from a brand-new tube, he insisted—and I swallowed it with reluctance. It didn't kill me. I retired to the washroom, checking twice to make sure the door was locked.

Sleep eluded me for close to an hour. Every time I felt myself drifting, Semias's face came into view. *Maybe she's not what you think she is,* he'd said. If Semias believed it, perhaps it wouldn't be long before the others did as well. Curiosity could quickly turn to accusation, and tolerance to hostility. The empress wanted me dead. Why?

How had things gotten so complicated?

Two days, two murder attempts. I wasn't safe in EPIC anymore. Vance was kind to protect me, but we'd been lucky so far. Each failed attempt would raise the stakes. Besides, there was nothing holding me here any longer. My deal with the empress was most definitely off.

The white-hot anger simmering below the surface began to cool as doubt clutched at my mind. I had to leave. But where would I go? I wouldn't make it halfway home before they tracked me down and zapped me for not being where I was supposed to be.

My techband. If only I could get it off …

I thought back to Tali's offer. She'd been wearing hers. But what about the man whose disgusting fingers had tried to shove a pill down my throat? I forced myself to think back, to remember what the room looked like. His breath had been hot against my neck, his hairy arm wet with sweat …

No techband. He hadn't been wearing one that

day. Somehow Tali's group of smugglers could remove them. It was the only way for them to travel without punishment. And if they could do it, I could too. But how could I contact them? Surely they were long gone by now.

I took a deep breath and let it out slowly. A good night's sleep was all I needed. Hopefully my life would make sense in the morning.

o—●—o—●—o—●—o—●—o

It seemed sleep wasn't on the agenda because after another hour of restless thought, my techband buzzed. It read:

ALERT: NATIONAL TRANSMISSION AT 2330. PLEASE STAND BY.

"You've got to be kidding me," I heard someone say through the door.

I just sighed, washed my face to wake myself up, and opened the door just as someone turned on the bedroom lights. True to his word, Vance had posted two men by my door, Ross and one of Poly's guys—Kraddock, I think his name was. They'd pulled Semias's bed up against the wall and sat on it like a bench. Semias lay sprawled out on the floor, bonds still fastened behind his back, his face relaxed in sleep. He looked like a weary child several years younger than he really was. It was hard to believe he'd tried to kill me just hours earlier.

When I emerged, my guards sat taller and watched me cross the room. The only other person standing was Neb. He seemed to have taken it upon himself to wake the others. It wasn't going well. He grabbed a random shoulder and shook it, getting a halfhearted punch in return.

Vance sat on his still-made bed in his rumpled uniform, staring at nothing. I sat down next to him and leaned closer. "What's this broadcast about?"

"They haven't told me anything," he muttered.

"But you have a suspicion," I said. "It has something to do with our last mission."

"An opinion, nothing more. And I hope I'm wrong."

Someone yelped, and a pillow slammed into the wall beside us, pieces of cotton flying into the air. Vance grabbed it before it fell and tossed it to Neb, who whirled it at Ross's head. Ross snatched it out of the air and held it just out of reach, sending Neb hurling toward the floor.

Daymond growled. "Touch me again and I will ram this pillow down your throat."

"Give it a rest," Poly said. He stood in the doorway, still dressed and looking worried.

All too soon another message came over our techbands as they vibrated in unison. I flipped up the screen, hearing a series of clicks as everyone else did the same. It showed a poised woman, blonde hair pulled into a bun, her makeup displaying a perfect set of high cheekbones and arched eyebrows. Intricate eye tattoos framed her green Rating: 932.

"My dear citizens," the woman said calmly, flashing a white-toothed smile. "Today is an important day in the history of the New Order Republic of America. Tonight we wish to make an exciting announcement. May I introduce the Leadership Academy's top student and NORA's highest Level Three graduate, Dresden Wynn."

A startled gasp tore from my throat.

"Thank you, Cora," a familiar voice said, and the screen switched to Dresden. His face and hair were so overdone that he looked almost plastic, but it was him.

I couldn't believe it. My Dresden, announcing the latest news in front of the entire country! He'd done short segments in Olympus before, and that was a big deal for a student. Suddenly I felt a little light-headed. I pressed my eyelids together tightly and opened them, letting them focus again.

"We apologize for interrupting our citizens' nightly activities," Dresden continued, "but this is a timely message."

"Yes, Dresden," the woman said automatically, and the screen flashed back to her. Now I could see that they were sitting at a large table in some kind of studio—high up, it looked like, from the vast expanse of city below them. The studio had to be on the top floor of the steel Academy Building. "Last night the military had a great victory, and now our borders are that much safer."

"The *military*?" Neb snapped. "What about us?"

"Most people don't know about us," Daymond said.

"Safety is our first priority," Dresden said through his too-wide smile. "Which is the reason behind our most recent legislation, the new location law. As you know, each citizen is required to be at a specified location according to the schedule outlined on their techband. Failure to do so will trigger punishment mode. As most citizens have little or no experience with such punishment, we would like to offer you a simple demonstration."

"Eleven smugglers were recently captured near the border," Cora said. "Usually, such outlaws are arrested and sent to work camps, where they finish out their lives in heavy labor. But these are citizens who stepped far outside their allowed boundaries, engaged in illegal activity, and resisted arrest. They have been sentenced to maximum-level punishment."

I glanced at Vance, who looked as stunned as I felt. Eleven smugglers. There was only one group that could possibly be.

The two speakers disappeared, replaced by a darker screen. A group of people, arms locked in front of them, stood rigidly against a gray cement wall.

They all wore the latest techband model, a sleek silver color. I strained to see faces and groaned, realizing that I recognized nearly all of them. The man who'd given me the bruise stood close to the back of the group. And there was the first guy who'd jumped me, the one Tali had called Ben. NORA had slapped new techbands on them, apparently.

My heart beat a little faster, and I held the screen closer. None of them were girls. Tali had escaped. Wait. Was that—? A hat too large for the wearer's wiry frame rested over what looked like a young boy's face. I drew in a ragged breath. "No."

Vance jerked his eyes up from his screen, watching me with a serious expression.

No, it couldn't be! This wasn't happening. Tali had gotten away. She'd escaped before anyone else. I remembered how she'd bounded away with her bag of food after pretending to knock me out.

"Three," Cora said in an irritatingly smooth, false comforting voice.

It was my fault Tali was there. She'd spent her last moments of freedom trying to help me.

"Two."

"No!" I hit the call button on my techband and dialed Dresden's name, hoping to distract him long enough to stop this. Surely he could stop it! An error message appeared. With a growl, I slammed an angry fist onto the keys and felt a painful jolt.

"One."

Fates! Stop this now!

There was a sudden buzz, and the entire group stiffened, their eyes round in horror. Several gurgled, trying to scream, and others dropped instantly to the ground. Some thrashed around before they fell. Tali was the last one standing. She looked straight at the camera, right into the eyes of a watching nation. Her mouth was twisted in pain, but her gaze was clear and full of anger. Her body contorted as she fought to stay upright. Then her eyes rolled back into her head, and she collapsed.

An anguished cry tore from my throat.

"Thank you for your attention," Cora said, and suddenly the announcers were back. Cora looked composed, as if nothing had happened. Dresden's smile was frozen, his face a sickly off-white. His next words sounded hoarse. "Please—" He cleared his throat.

Cora jumped in. "Please consider this a reminder to be vigilant about your location at all times. You may return to your activities. As we align ourselves more closely to the high standards expected of us, we will be stretched and perfected in our collective quest to become the best citizens possible. Our obedience will make this nation a force greater than that which was built in the days of Rome." She smiled, suddenly looking a lot like the sanitizing-cream ad-board model, and then gave a quick nod. "Good night."

26

I stared at my empty screen for a long time after the broadcast ended. Four of those men I knew well from my childhood. I could have saved them.

I should have saved them.

It was one thing to send my clan members to work camps. It was a horrible life full of hard labor, but at least they were alive. This—electrocution of prisoners—went way beyond what I'd signed up for. This was murder. The Demander was using me now, messing with my mind. He would pay for this.

I buried the memories inside and focused on my men. Neb stared at the floor, his legs visibly shaking. The other guys weren't faring much better. Treena stood, dazed, and made her way slowly to the bathroom. Her strides were uneven, as if she were drunk or sleepwalking. The door shut softly behind her.

After a moment, Poly made his way over to me,

wearing a deep frown. "I never thought I'd see an execution televised nationally."

"It's happened before," Ross offered. "About forty-five years ago. This mentally disturbed woman who killed, like, seventeen people. Except they didn't use punishment mode in that case. Instead, they—"

"Not now, Ross," I said.

"The empress must be really worried about smugglers," Daymond said. "I bet every kid in the nation will be having nightmares tonight."

"Maybe it's good, though," Semias said. He sat casually on his bed.

"What's good?" I shot back. "Eleven less people to compete with?"

"Nah," Semias drawled. "I don't compete with outlaws. I mean that once all the smugglers are gone, or at least scared into leading honest lives, we can go home. The borders will be cleansed soon, and then our country. Any uprising the smugglers have started will be quashed. The commander won't need us anymore."

The other guys considered that, but I shook my head in disgust. "You're unbelievable."

Semias's hand dropped. "What's your problem, Vance?"

"My problem? My problem is that the outlands don't need *cleansing*, as you put it. If there's corruption and darkness anywhere in the world, it's here in your blasted Roman Republic."

Semias bristled, but it was Poly who spoke. "It may be hard for you to understand, Vance, but it comes down to this. First, we need fresh water. Ours is barely fit for human consumption—believe me, I've tested it. Second, our cities are bursting with new growth, and we'll need to expand soon. The only place to do that is outside the current border, and the only way to do that is to displace the settlers who live out there."

I pounded my fist into the wall. "You know better than anyone that this is not about land, and it's definitely not about the water. This is about the empress's little empire, Poly. It's not enough to rule a nation. She has to control everyone else, too. This New Rome she keeps talking about? It's a disease. The Romans tried to take over the world, and she won't be happy with anything less."

The room was silent.

Poly sighed, lowering his voice. "Vance, I'm sorry about the other night, but you have a different way of looking at things than the rest of us. Every country in the world—and in history—wants to expand its borders. Except that most of them just kill everyone in their path. At least the empress is giving her prisoners a better life."

"A better life." My voice was flat. "I thought you, of all people, would understand."

"Vance—"

"You've accepted it, haven't you? You're perfectly

content doing this forever."

"Of course not." Poly bristled. "We just haven't fulfilled our part yet, apparently."

"We fulfilled it *too* well. Now they're never letting us go." I turned to the others. "If you don't want to see the truth, fine. But next time you start to think we're out there saving lives, think about what you just saw."

I strode out before anyone could reply.

27

Tali was dead.

Death was for the elderly at the Olympus Sunset Clinic, patients who spent decades waiting to die. Death was for my grandparents and faceless soldiers and for history classes—not for my best friend. Tali was lying somewhere, pale and lifeless. How could she be so alive, so colorful and happy, and then just … gone?

I shifted my position on the cold, hard tile, feeling as dead inside as any corpse.

It's my fault.

I hadn't pushed the button, but I'd killed her all the same. Why hadn't I told her to run immediately? Why had I gotten myself captured in the first place so she'd need to save me? Worst of all, why hadn't I known the depth of my best friend's passion for freedom? The horrifying questions took root like a poisonous weed. Racking sobs threatened to escape me, but I gritted my teeth. I didn't deserve to mourn.

A gentle knock sounded at the washroom door. It barely registered.

After a moment, the knob turned and Vance poked his head in. I noticed his red-rimmed eyes and messy hair. "You forgot to lock the door."

I stared at him, trying to grasp the importance of his words. They slipped through my mind like water. He stepped in and pulled the door shut behind him.

"I saw your light was still on and thought I'd better check on you."

I leaned my head back against the wall and closed my eyes. "What time is it?"

"Three-thirty. The guys have been asleep for hours."

I didn't respond. There was a shuffling noise as he made his way over and then knelt in front of me. I forced my eyes open to see him staring at the ground.

"This tile is hard," he muttered.

"Try sleeping on it."

"Are you okay? I know that was hard to watch."

The real question was, would I ever be okay again? I'd just watched my best friend get electrocuted, and it was all because of me. No spy was worth this, no green Rating, and definitely no job as a Rater. Even a future with Dresden felt wrong in a world without Tali.

"My best friend died tonight." The words slipped out, cold and lifeless.

There was a sharp intake of breath. "Your friend?

One of the smugglers?"

"You didn't recognize her because she was dressed as a boy, but you met her at the Rating Ceremony." He should have arrested her then. She would have been sent to a work camp, but at least she'd still be alive.

Understanding registered in Vance's eyes, then pity. He pushed himself off the tile and sat beside me, staring at his hands as if unsure where to put them. His jaw was dark and rough from going days without shaving, and he smelled faintly of sweat and soap. He seemed to make a decision and reached up to wrap one arm around me, pulling me into his chest. I hesitated for a millisecond but allowed myself lean against him, soaking in what little comfort he could give. He reached up and wiped a wayward piece of hair away from my wet cheek, tucking it behind my ear.

His silent actions released the torrent of emotion. I sobbed into his shirt. It was soaked within seconds, but he just held me closer.

I don't know how much time passed, but eventually my mind took control again, and a shudder racked my body. There were no more tears left. The pain inside threatened to overwhelm me, and I had no desire to fight it.

Eventually he spoke. "I know this means absolutely nothing to you, but I'm sorry about your friend."

My throat hurt like there was a khel ball stuck in it. I pulled my knees to my chest and hugged them tight. I'd do anything—*anything*—to take it all back.

I'd worried for Tali's safety in Meridian. Now she was dead, and it was my fault. Self-loathing filled my stomach until I felt like screaming.

"She made her own choice. There's not a single smuggler who doesn't know the risk they're taking."

I considered that. "She knew exactly where she should be and what she wanted. Me? I don't know either one. I don't belong here, Vance. And yet I don't belong at home, either."

"Then run."

I jerked my head up.

His expression was intense, determined. "I'm serious. I've been meaning to speak to you about it. If NORA is trying to kill you, your only option is to run. You've seen the lengths the empress will go to for control."

I gave a bitter laugh, sounding hoarse. "And go where?"

"The smugglers. They're the only ones who can cut your techband off."

I blinked, causing fresh, hot tears to burn their way down my cheeks. "But there aren't any left at Meridian."

"That was only one hideout. There are four others like it."

A sick feeling swelled within my stomach. Four others. Vance shouldn't have known that. Not unless …

In a cautious tone, I asked, "Why would they help me?"

He hesitated. "Tell them about your friend. When they see your Rating, they'll believe you."

Suddenly it was clear. The evidence had been there all along, but I'd refused to see it. Vance's disappearing act on our base operation, his guilt at my injury, and his sudden determination to protect me. No matter what he pretended, Vance would always be an Integrant.

Vance watched the emotions playing out on my face. "What?"

I forced myself to pull away from him and felt his arm drop. Cold air replaced the warmth of his body. "You're the spy."

He blinked in surprise. "*The* spy?"

I didn't respond, watching his reaction closely.

Vance leaned back against the wall. "Ah. That's why you're here. And the reward was a high Rating with Bike Boy thrown in to sweeten the deal, I'm guessing."

"You make it sound so cold," I said, feeling a twinge of anger at his tone.

He shook his head in disbelief, pushing to his feet. "I'm no spy. The rebellion has been trying to recruit me since the beginning, but I refused."

"You mean the smugglers."

"No, the rebellion. It consists of smugglers, Integrants, and even lower citizens. NORA calls them smugglers for simplicity's sake—and because they don't want word to get out that there *is* a rebellion.

It's not about the food smuggling as much as the uprising that the empress is worried about. And she should be. They're planning something, Treena, and they've tried everything to pull me over. If there was a spy here, I would know about it."

He looked deep into my eyes, his expression so full of frustration and hurt, so *him*, that I somehow believed it. It wasn't logical, but I felt it deep inside. He was telling the truth, which meant my mission was a sham. "But—but if there's no spy, why did the empress send me here?"

"Remember that soldier who tried to kill you? I asked around, and a few others were given that same order. Something about *you* being a traitor."

"Me?"

"They're playing games with us, making us all suspect each other, using us as pawns. It's their way of making us think we're privileged. Flatter a weak mind like that, and they'll do anything for you. But I don't get why they tried to kill you. What would that accomplish?"

I shrugged and forced myself to my feet, wincing at the sudden tingling sensation in my numb legs.

He refused to drop the subject. "Treena, you said your dad was a traitor. Do you know what he did, exactly?"

"I don't know. I never met him, but his name is Jasper."

"Jasper." He felt the word on his tongue. "Isn't

that a type of stone?"

I stared at him. Something tickled the edge of my memory—something about rocks and names. But I couldn't remember, and the sudden lapse in conversation brought Tali's face back again. A lump formed in my throat.

"Go," he said. "If they want you killed, they won't miss next time. You have a chance if you go right now. I'll cover for you as long as I can."

"They'd know you helped me."

"It doesn't matter."

"But what about your family?"

"Let me worry about them."

I looked up, feeling sudden warmth at the realization that he was staring at me. Our faces were inches away now. His eyes were brown, with tiny flecks of gold and raw with pain. I wanted to reach up and smooth the unruly hair above his ears, stroke his unshaven jaw. My hand started to move on its own accord, but I made a fist instead.

Focus. I could do this. Even if the smugglers didn't accept me, I had a greater chance with them than I did here. Maybe I could offer them information in exchange for my life.

The thought made me frown. No. That would prove NORA right about me, and they were dead wrong. I was better than that. If I joined the smugglers—the rebellion—it would be despite my Rating, not because of it. It would be because I believed in their cause, not because I had nowhere else to go.

Haven't you ever been part of a cause worth dying for? Tali had asked.

"No," I said. "If the empress really wants me dead, I have to know why."

His shoulders sagged, but he didn't seem surprised. "They *will* kill you, Treena. I can't guarantee your safety here."

I didn't answer, and he leaned back with a frustrated sigh. We sat there for a moment in a silent deadlock.

"I'm not leaving EPIC," I said again, more firmly this time. "But I do need something."

"What, a bodyguard?" he asked with an exasperated tone.

I thought of Tali's smiling face and choppy dark hair. I checked the time. There was a salon four blocks away, and they would be opening soon. "Let's go for a run."

28

The morning heat was already unbearable. Fortunately, my neck was cooler than it had ever been. After an hour at the salon, my hair was now short and dark. Surprisingly, the lack of weight made my hair wavy and bouncy. No wonder Tali had liked this. I'd even gotten a pleased smile out of Vance, which I took as a good sign.

I felt my time ticking down, so I didn't dare try to sleep. Instead, I pulled each guy aside in turn for an interrogation. Vance stood nearby, arms folded, pretending not to listen. After the usual formalities, I told them I'd been sent to uncover a spy and watched their reaction.

Most of them were dumbfounded. A few laughed.

When it was Semias's turn, he just smirked. "Right. We all know that if there's a spy here, it's you."

"Thanks," I said, dismissing him. Vance had stood at his side, ready to subdue him at the slightest sign of aggression. The only person left was Poly, and I was already certain he wasn't a suspect. It seemed Vance was right. There was no traitor. Either the empress's information was wrong, or she'd sent me here to die. Neither conclusion made any sense.

It was during my shower that afternoon that my techband vibrated.

AMETRINE DOWELL.
YOU ARE COMMANDED
TO APPEAR IN THE
EMPRESS'S CHAMBERS
IMMEDIATELY.

I stared at the glowing letters, expecting to feel horror or nervousness. Instead, there was nothing. This was it, then. Would they execute me privately, in the seclusion of her chambers? Would Konnor be relieved that I wasn't staining the family name anymore? Would Dresden miss me at all?

I dressed slowly. When I opened the door, I sensed someone waiting outside.

"I was ordered to escort you," Vance said solemnly.

I didn't answer. I just passed him and made my way toward the hallway, feeling the cold more acutely than usual. Maybe it was best that everyone else had gone for a run, leaving us alone. Less awkward this way—no good-byes. I turned on the lights in the training room as we passed through, glancing around one last time. Remembering. The girl that had entered so long ago seemed like a distant memory. Vance was stiff, looking like he'd rather be anywhere but here. I knew the feeling.

I reached for the handle, but it wouldn't open. Vance's lock was still in place. He stood in silence for a moment before he finally spoke. "You can still run, you know. Just climb out the ventilation shaft."

"No, thanks."

"No, *thanks*?" He stared at me. "I'm not offering you a food pill or a new shirt, Treena. I'm trying to save your life. What's this about? Punishing yourself?"

"Take a good look at yourself, Vance," I shot back. "You spend every day arresting your own people and then beating yourself up over it. You keep trying to prove to the world that you're this horrible person, that you deserve this life. I don't think you should be lecturing me right now."

His eyes flashed with anger. "This is not about me. This is about you doing something stupid."

I yanked at the lock as I'd seen him do before, and the door clicked open. The air in the stairwell was cold and stale, but I strode into it and started climbing the stairs. Vance gave an exasperated sigh and followed.

We walked in silence for a few minutes. I had no idea what we'd find at the top. Guards? Monitors? The commander?

"Your Rating is wrong," he said. "Their precious Rating system says absolutely nothing about you and what you're capable of."

"So far, everything I've done has proven my number absolutely correct."

"Treena." His tone softened. "I don't know why that happened to you. But I do know one thing." He stopped on the step below me, and I whirled to face him. We were the same height now, and his expression was fierce. "You are the most loyal, most determined, and most fascinating girl I've ever met. No number could ever describe you."

The deadness inside me cracked, and the pain came flooding back. I felt like a five-year-old again. Falling, grasping for a handhold, for something to save me. "It doesn't matter now."

He gave me a long look. Then he sat down, right on the steps, easing me down next to him. I lay my head on his shoulder and let him pull me close. The warmth of his embrace felt completely and utterly right. For a long moment I allowed myself to forget about the past few days. There was no empress, no punishment mode, and no mission. There was just us. The world was cool and dark, and his touch sent my heart pumping as if it had just awakened from hibernation.

"When my dad died," Vance finally said as he began to gently stroke my hair, "I didn't handle it very well. I kept thinking if I'd just disobeyed his order and stayed with him he'd still be alive." He gave a bitter laugh. "I still think it sometimes."

"So that's why you punish yourself." I tried to

gain control of my voice. "But if you'd stayed, you would have died too."

"Dying isn't the worst thing to happen to someone," he continued thoughtfully. "Any coward can die. The hardest thing is being left behind and trying to make sense of a world without them."

Tali had joined the smugglers to make a difference, to leave a footprint on the world. I'd just wanted to slip into a quiet life, unnoticed. She was the one who deserved to live, not me. "It'll never be the same," I whispered.

"No, it won't," he agreed, still stroking my hair. It sent ripples of heat down my body. "Do you remember what I told you in our first training session?"

"Yeah. You told me to stop retreating and fight back instead."

He chuckled. "When you took on a dozen men at the warehouse, I thought I'd created a monster."

"I didn't do it for you," I said. He just hadn't known me very well yet. I'd never been one to run from a fight. But wasn't that exactly what I was doing? What would Tali do if she could see me now—beaten, helpless, and too guilt-ridden to think straight?

She'd slap me upside the head, that's what.

I tilted my head back and allowed myself to look up into Vance's eyes. They were so dark it was as if they were absorbing all the light that entered and saving it for some future purpose. His eyebrows were choppy, untrimmed, and his were lips chapped.

But somehow it worked. It was simply … him. No surgeries, no tallies of volunteer hours and checklists. Vance just took life one day at a time, keeping his family safe, trying to put the pieces back together. I could see it, the pain in his heart. It was something we shared now.

"When you see the empress," Vance whispered, "tell her I'm the spy."

I sat back, stunned. "What?"

"Tell her you found the traitor and fulfilled your mission. Maybe it'll make a difference."

I wasn't so sure about that. It hadn't stopped her so far. "I won't put my problems on you. You've spent the last two years acting as the commander's little slave, arresting people you probably knew well. I can't even imagine what two years of that must have been like. And you did it all to save your family."

He looked away quickly, as if my words had stabbed some part of him. He let out a long, frustrated breath. "I tell myself every day that they are the reason. I'm not so sure about that anymore."

I put a hand on his arm. "Is this about what the commander said? About you being willing to do anything to survive? Don't listen to him. He knows nothing about love and loyalty. What you did was brave."

He looked at my hand on his arm, and I wondered if I'd gone too far. But before I could pull it away, he grasped it with his other hand and squeezed.

"If either of us is brave, it's you," he said and gave a self-deprecating laugh. "You survived a week in the most dangerous military unit in NORA, with two kill orders and no weapon. Now you're going to meet with the person who wants you dead, and yet you're comforting me." His finger traced the line of my palm, sending tingles up my arm. "You don't deserve any of this. The least I can do is accept some of your punishment. Just tell her I'm the spy and let the chips fall where they may."

I didn't ask what chips were. A warm feeling spread through my chest until I thought I would burst. This was who he really was. The tumultuous battle within him seemed to have trickled away, leaving one gallant, vulnerable boy. A boy who saw me as something precious—who looked at me instead of at my Rating. His eyes stared at me questioningly, his usual confidence replaced with uncertainty.

"I think your first offer was better," I finally said. "Let's use the tunnel to escape."

"There's the Treena I know." He gave a tiny smile. "It feels good to finally choose sides, doesn't it?"

"Whose side are you on, then?"

As he looked into my eyes, I felt like he could see into my soul. His fingers brushed my cheek, then he cradled the side of my face in his hand, gently tilting my chin upward, and I felt his breath, felt the battle within him as well as I felt it in myself. But something pulled me toward him.

"Yours," he said. He slowly closed the distance between us.

And our lips met.

He was hesitant at first, just a soft brush of his lips on mine. Then the cool, damp air around us melted away in an instant. His strong arms went around me, pulling me closer, holding me tightly. His kiss became more insistent, and the pain and fear within me began to fade as I felt myself giving in. His chin was rough against my skin, but it only fueled the heat that pulsed through my racing heart.

It felt like hours, that brief moment of pure joy mixed with pain and longing. For the first time I saw past the rough exterior he hid behind to the soul beneath, and it was beautiful. It was a world I'd never known existed, communicated with perfect understanding.

And then there were footsteps overhead.

He pulled away, the sudden distance painful, his voice hoarse. "They're coming for you."

I tried to stand, but my legs weren't working right. The moment we'd just shared had made my thoughts fuzzy. "Do we still have time?"

The sound of pounding on the steps overhead got louder with each second. He jumped up, then grasped my hand to pull me to a standing position. The wistful look in his eyes told me enough. "Sounds like there are only three of them, Treena. I'll keep them occupied long enough for you to get away."

"Not a chance."

"You!" a woman's voice snapped. "Keep your hands up."

"Go," he hissed at me. "I'll catch up."

I took off running, taking the steps two at a time toward the bunker. There was a shout from above, and the pounding overhead intensified. I grabbed the rail and leaped down the last flight of stairs, landing hard on my feet, and then rushed to the door.

More shouting. They must have reached Vance. I pushed the door open and sprinted inside—only to run into a human wall.

Poly blocked my escape. He wore a gray shirt and training pants, his black hair tousled as if he'd just risen from bed. A deep frown lined his face. "Going somewhere?" he asked. "You were summoned, as I recall."

"I just—just—" I couldn't think of a single lie. All I could think about was the muffled sounds of fighting on the stairs. "Let me through! Please!"

Someone cried out in the stairwell, and I turned. Poly grabbed my shoulder, but I twisted out of his grip and tried to slide past him. He caught hold of my elbow and yanked me back. His grip nearly pulled my shoulder out of its socket, and I yelped with pain. In seconds, both of my hands were locked behind my back.

A woman ran inside and stopped when she saw us. "The girl is under arrest."

Poly shoved me forward. The movement sent an electric jolt down my arms. "I caught her running back inside. Do you need an EPIC escort?"

"No. There are others." She took my arm and guided me roughly toward the stairs. As we climbed the first stairwell, I glanced at Poly in the doorway. His face was emotionless, his arms folded. Apparently his loyalty to EPIC didn't extend past the empress's orders.

A minute later we rounded a stairwell to see her companions. They must have called for backup because there were five of them now, surrounding Vance, who knelt in the center, arms locked behind him. His face fell when he saw me. The monitor's grip on my arm loosened, and she yanked me forward. I caught myself on the rail just before my face hit the step.

"Careful," Vance growled.

"I'd say the same for you, EPIC leader," the lady said. "Both of you get moving."

29

pull you out of the gutter, give you a second chance," the empress said slowly, "and this is how you repay me?"

I'd expected to be shot down the moment I walked in. If not that, maybe arrested by a pair of waiting monitors. But her first words only confused me. I snuck a glance at Vance, who looked as surprised as I felt.

The empress sat on a chair that looked ridiculously similar to a medieval throne, golden and gaudy. Her tight-fitting silver robe, glittering with jewels, brushed the ground. After a moment, she stood and walked to the window, her hips swinging way more than seemed physically possible. The buildings outside were bright with the late-morning light. I couldn't see it, but I knew the streets were full of citizens riding their bicycles to work and school, unaware of the quiet battle taking place in the empress's chambers.

"Well? Don't you have anything to say, child?"

"I'm not sure what you're talking about, actually."

"Of course you are. You're a bright girl, so let's be honest with each other. I don't usually trust young reds with weapons and responsibility, so you owe me the truth, at the very least."

"What do you want me to say?"

She gave a dramatic sigh. "Did you, or did you not, allow a smuggler to go free because she was your friend?"

I blinked. Tali? "I—I, uh …"

Vance spoke up. "The smugglers jumped Treena. She was lucky to escape before they knocked her unconscious, and even then she distracted them for as long as she could. If it weren't for her, we would have caught half as many."

He was covering for me, making it sound like I knew what I was doing. But his words stabbed my heart. If it weren't for me, would some of those eleven smugglers be alive? Even if my best friend hadn't been one of them, hearing that nearly made my knees buckle in grief. I had been so, so selfish.

She took a step back and glanced at the tribune, who stood beside her throne. If she really was the person who wanted me dead, what was she waiting for?

The empress cleared her throat. "Despite this boy's outburst, I have several sources who claim Ametrine allowed her friend to go free without any attempt of arrest. What shall we do with you now, child? I certainly can't leave you in EPIC, and I can't send you home with that dreadful Rating and no assignment."

"Is it to be a work camp, then, Your Highness?" the tribune asked with a bored tone.

"Fair enough," she replied as if the idea hadn't occurred to her. "Ametrine, you will keep your Rating, as it suits you perfectly. Tribune, make sure she's assigned somewhere far from here and everything familiar to her. Now get her out of my sight." She waved her pointy finger away as if shooing away a pesky insect.

"Wait," I said. "What about the other matter?"

"Excuse me?"

"You said you'd order a Rating reconsideration."

"*If* you fulfilled your assignment, which you most definitely did not."

"I did."

Vance turned to me, but I held my ground.

"Really." A frown appeared on the woman's face as she looked at him. "You found the traitor? Tell me who it is, then."

The surprise in her voice told me everything I needed to know. There had never been a spy. My mission was a hoax.

I took a deep breath. "None of them." Vance jerked, but I spoke more quickly. "None of the EPIC guys are betraying you. In fact, they're the most loyal, hardworking guys I've ever met. The only spy there was me, working for you. Can I have my Rating reconsidered now?"

She threw her head back and laughed, a sound so fake it reminded me of Dresden's plastic smile. "Oh, that's funny. Really, girl. If we adjusted your Rating, it would only plummet."

"I'm willing to take the chance," I said.

"What are you *doing*?" Vance hissed.

The empress stood again and walked over to me, looking deeply into my eyes for the first time. Her indifference had been replaced with carefully masked uncertainty. "What are you trying to do, child? See how low you can sink into the depths of your society?"

"No," I said. "I just want justice."

She stared at me, and I lifted my chin. Her gaze hardened, and I knew she'd caught the double meaning of my words. The empress wanted me dead, and she knew that I knew. And even more important, I could see the desperation behind her stony expression. This woman would kill me before she let the Raters review my score. In that moment I knew I wasn't safe anywhere, not even in a work camp. No matter where they sent me, she'd win. Vance was right.

"Your Highness," the tribune said from the corner. "Pardon the reminder, but I do believe the law still requires a Rating adjustment in this case. This must occur before she leaves. It is simply the order of things—otherwise her Rating will not reflect what she has done."

Rather than arguing, the empress stalked to her throne and plopped into it. "Fine. Guards, put her in the political prison until we hear from the Raters."

The guards, two young, bulky soldiers with chiseled features, took my arms.

Vance's mouth was tight as he watched. He didn't believe the empress's act either.

"What of the EPIC soldier, Your Grace?" the tribune asked. "This report says he has a pattern of questionable behavior recently."

"This is the Integrant, yes?" She stood again and made her way over to him. "Hawking's son, if I recall. Denoux was rather insistent with this one."

"You murdered my dad," Vance said.

The guard's slap came so fast I barely saw it. Vance's head whipped to the side, then he slowly turned back toward the empress with hatred in his eyes.

"Increase the intensity of his cuffs," the empress ordered. "My instincts tell me there is still a traitor in your ranks, Integrant. Perhaps EPIC has outlived its usefulness after all."

"We've done nothing but enforce your laws." His voice sounded strained. "You know, laws—those inconvenient Standards that condemn murder. There are more direct ways than poisoned pills and assassins to get rid of innocent girls, you know."

The empress slapped him this time. It echoed

sharply against the white walls. Vance barely winced, but the guards must have upped the intensity of his cuffs even more because suddenly he arched his back and his face contorted in agony.

"He's stark mad," she said to the tribune. "Send him back. I have a surprise in store for him." She waved a hand in dismissal.

The guards yanked me backward then, and I would have fallen if they hadn't held on to my elbows so tightly. The last thing I saw before turning into the sterile white hallway was Vance, standing tall, head turned toward me, his face twisted in anguish.

And then he was out of sight.

30

Treena's gone," Poly guessed when he saw my face.

I just nodded. The other guys stood motionless, wanting to ask but unsure how.

"As in gone—" Neb said, "or dead?"

I slammed the door shut and slid the lock into place. "If she's not dead yet, it won't be long."

"But why were you escorted back?" Daymond asked, eyeing what was probably a red mark on my cheek. I scowled and rubbed my wrists, trying to get rid of the pins-and-needles feeling the cuffs had left behind. I'd hoped that my outburst would anger her enough that she'd send me to prison with Treena. It didn't seem like the empress to let a known enemy roam free. Something was definitely wrong here.

When I didn't answer, Neb spoke up. "Did Treena really let a smuggler slip through?"

I pushed away a stab of irritation. "She did her job, and she did it surrounded by enemies. She's done nothing to deserve what she's getting."

Semias pushed his way through the group to stand in front of me, arms folded. Someone had apparently freed him from his bonds now that Treena was gone. "She's a red, Vance. She played you with that innocent act."

"You know nothing about her."

"Oh, and you do? After the disgusting looks you've been giving each other and your secret talks in the washroom? I bet you know everything about her. And I mean *everything*."

"Shut up, Semias."

"Seriously? You guys really thought Vance was training her?" He snickered. "Running errands together, always picking her for his partner, protecting his prize. And those early morning workouts? Yeah, I'll give you one guess as to what exactly they were working out—"

My fist flew toward his mouth and would have smashed it in if Semias hadn't been ready. He stepped to the side and threw a punch at my nose, trying to catch his balance. I turned my head just in time, and his hand grazed off me. With a growl, I lunged.

"Vance!" Poly yelled. "That's enough!"

I landed on top of Semias, enraged, ready to pummel his face in. But he rotated midair and landed on his side, covering his head with an elbow. I jumped to one foot and kicked him in the ribs again and again, making him double over in pain. "Why were you supposed to kill her?" I shouted, putting all my weight behind the next kick.

"I … don't … know!" Semias managed to say.

"Stop this, *now*!" Poly was behind me now, grabbing my shoulders in an iron grip. Hot anger pulsed through my veins. I slipped one foot behind his and shot an elbow to Poly's nose. He grunted and released me.

Suddenly Neb was in my face. He positioned himself between me and Poly. Blood poured from Poly's nose, dripping down his chin and mixing messily with the dark hair on his bare chest. There was murder in his expression.

"Vance, please," Neb whispered. "You're upset. Just—just go take a break. Okay?"

Jessop and Tensom dropped to their knees beside Semias, who was still moaning on the floor. The rage I'd felt at his words pulsed hot in my ears.

Poly stepped forward and grabbed my collar, his other hand clasping his nose, blood dripping through his fingers. His voice was ice-cold. "If you ever touch me again, I will kill you. Understood?"

My breath shuddered as I struggled for control. "Yes, *sir.*"

"Hold on," Neb said. "What's that?"

The room stilled. A thumping noise rang from the direction of the training room door.

Footsteps, dozens of them, banged their way down the steps.

Poly stiffened, looking at me with heavy dread. There was only one reason for the soldiers to come down here. It made sense now why the empress had sent me back.

I also understood why the commander had stationed us here. I'd suspected it for a long time and installed the deadbolt for that very purpose. This was the perfect spot for us—cool, hidden from society, and far beneath the tranquility of the Council Building.

And above all, there was no escape.

"Weapons," Poly said sharply. "Now."

31

The prison cell was basically a large glass box with a metal sink jutting out from the wall and a tightly-made bed in the center. A hamster wheel would have completed the ensemble nicely. There was a tiny slit in the glass near the ceiling, barely wide enough for a hand to slip through. An oxygen vent.

The cool darkness didn't bother me, but the silence kept me on edge. I hadn't been truly alone in a long time, and it felt wrong. I sat on the bed, surprised at how hard it was, and pulled my legs in. My mind couldn't shake that last glimpse of Vance. I'd give anything to feel his embrace right now, to feel his fingers gently stroking my hair. Where was he now? Would I even see him again?

"Feeling sorry for yourself?" a muffled voice said.

I leapt to my feet, looking frantically around for the source of the voice. "Who's there?"

"Over here."

The man's voice came from the cell across the hall, but I couldn't see anyone. Then a flicker of movement came from the distant bed, and I realized there was someone under it. A head popped out, and he climbed out and stood. It was an older man with sagging features and peppered hair that didn't quite cover his 652 Rating. He wore a prisoner's uniform: a gold jumpsuit with a black stripe across the arm. By the condition of the uniform and its wearer, they'd both been living across the hall for a very long time.

"I prefer sleeping under the bed," the man said with a smile. "It's softer."

When I didn't answer, his eyes flicked to my forehead and took in my Rating. There was no reaction—no surprise, no disgust. He approached the glass.

"So what did you do? Trip a monitor? Steal a transport and go for a joyride?"

"I don't want to talk about it."

He sighed. "First visitor in three years, prettiest in six, and she won't talk about it. Figures."

He was trying to get me to smile, but it wouldn't work. The pain threatened to overwhelm me again. I put my head in my hands.

"It must've been pretty bad to end up here. This place is only for political prisoners—the ones the empress wants to keep a close eye on. Or the ones she doesn't want the people know about."

"Please," I begged. "Just leave me alone."

The man leaned against the glass, making his palms turn white. "Fine. When a lady says please, I obey." He turned away and headed for a chair in the corner. "But," he called over his shoulder, "whatever you did, I guarantee it's not half as bad as my indiscretions."

I wanted to collapse on the bed and let sleep capture my aching mind, but I knew I couldn't sleep. I sighed. "Sorry. I'm just not in a talking mood right now. But if you are, I'll listen."

The man returned to the window and stood there, staring at me for an uncomfortable minute. Finally he said, "What did you say your name was?"

"I didn't. It's Treena."

"Nice to meet you, Treena. You look as if you carry the weight of the world on those shoulders." It almost set me off again, but I bit my lip. Hard. He chuckled bitterly. "I suppose we are in prison, eh? Not a place for counting butterflies."

A bell rang somewhere overhead, and he stepped back like a robot. There were footsteps down the hall, and a guard appeared. It was the woman who had escorted me earlier. She opened a hatch to the strange man's cell—I hadn't noticed the hatch before—and placed something in it, then she closed it again. It opened from the inside so the prisoner could remove it. He popped the object into his mouth and swallowed.

The guard turned to me. "Your nutrition pill is still being prepared," she said simply, then left.

"Ooh, you really ticked off the empress," the man

said when the footsteps disappeared.

"Why do you think that?" I asked.

"Just do yourself a favor and don't take the pill when it comes."

The realization hit. "You think it's poisoned?"

"Whenever a pill is 'being prepared,' the prisoner drops dead in his cell. I've seen it happen. It's the cleanest way to kill someone."

I sat on the bed, stunned. A poisoned pill again. Why would the empress have me killed so secretly when she could have ordered an execution earlier? It made no sense at all.

"How long do I have?" I asked.

"They usually do it around midnight. Easier to dispose of the bodies."

Midnight. I had a few hours, then. "So the empress wants me dead, but she doesn't want people to know about it."

"Probably. You must have a very interesting story to tell, young lady."

I gave him a sideways look. "How long have you been down here?"

"Almost twelve years," the man said. "I wasn't always this chatty. I suppose you could say I've been saving up words."

Twelve years? The horror must have been evident in my expression because he laughed.

"They won't kill me. Sometimes I wish they'd just get on with it, but they can't. The empress is still in love with me."

If I had been stunned before, now I was horrified. Was this where they put the crazy people? Or maybe his captivity had caused his insanity. Twelve years in prison could definitely make a man believe the empress was his girlfriend.

His mood quickly became somber. "I know. It sounds insane. Maybe this cell has rotted my mind. But I swear to you, the empress and I were in love once." His expression softened. "She even nominated me the Ratings councilman."

I raised an eyebrow. "You were her lover *and* Ratings councilman?"

He snickered. "*Were* is the right word. As soon as we stopped seeing eye to eye—which was all about her eye, apparently—she tossed me in here like a piece of refuse. Appointed some idiot to my post and forgot about our years together." He shook his head. "It's what I get for leaving my wife and child for the empress. It only took a few years for the fates to return the favor."

The information whizzed through my head at a breakneck pace. "That's quite a sad story," I said, hardly feeling sad at all. The man really did deserve what he'd received. And yet there was something about him that felt strangely important.

"Sir," I said slowly. "What's your name again?"

"Jasper," he replied.

I nearly fell off the bed, catching myself just in

time. "J-J-Jasper?" I stammered.

He seemed alarmed at my sudden shock. "Have you heard of me? Do they talk about my work with the Ratings?"

He left his wife and child ...

"Was your wife's name Lanah?" I asked quietly.

The color drained from his face. It was all the answer I needed.

"Ametrine," he whispered.

32

It was strange, talking to my biological father while awaiting death. He told me of my mother, how she'd been young and beautiful when they'd met and married. He'd been a top-ten graduate, just like Dresden, and he'd graduated from the Leadership Academy's technology department.

"I helped design the first techband," he said proudly. "Took me from the academy to councilman's assistant in one year." I told him about the empress's new punishment law, and his smile faded. "She promised she'd never use punishment mode as a weapon. Should've known she'd break that promise, too."

We fell into a thoughtful silence. It was ironic that I'd survived Semias's poisoned pill only to die here, the same way, in the same prison as my biological dad. A part of me wished I could get to know him a little better, to find out more about my parents and my past.

No, you don't, I told myself. *He abandoned you.*

"What do you think of the Rating system now?" I asked cautiously. "After living down here for so long, I mean."

He gave a deep sigh. For a moment I wasn't sure he'd heard me. Then he said, "I think it's the most sophisticated and chilling system of control known to man."

I thought of the empress and the diamonds embedded in her forehead. I thought about Dresden's record, about my mom's struggle for a green Rating, and about Vance and his clan. I thought about the tower and how it felt to dangle from the top, terrified of the hard pavement eighty-two floors below.

"I knew it back then, too," he continued. "Even as a councilman I still had my doubts. I know it's why she threw me down here. We both knew that my ambitions were different from hers. I don't know what's worse—that I doubted my own nation's government or upheld a system I didn't believe in."

"I'm not sure I really want to know this," I said slowly, "but how did your relationship with the empress come about?"

I learned they'd been paired up at the academy and that Jasper had just finished a round of testing on the new techband. She was young and intelligent, one of the top graduates of her year. He skipped over much of that part, his face coloring a bit. I thought about my mother, a young newlywed in medical school then, and glared at him.

"It's not something I'd expect you to understand," he said, noting the look on my face. He paused, suddenly very interested in a loose string on his sleeve. "How is your mother, anyway?"

"Lanah remarried," I said, the bitterness creeping back into my voice. "Her husband has his sights set on becoming the new Integration councilman."

"Really. That's incredibly ironic."

"He's an egotistical jerk. But she can't have another divorce on her record without taking a huge hit on her score, so she refuses to leave him."

"I'm truly sorry to hear that," he said. "She deserves so much better. I hope she can forgive me someday."

My mind floated back to the night she'd given me his stone. She'd defended him. He was right. She deserved a different life.

I fingered my stone necklace. Its giver was right in front of me now. I could finally ask him the meaning behind the gift. But something held me back. I didn't need to ask what his intended message had been because it didn't matter. What mattered was the meaning I brought to it. This stone had probably started out as a rough, angled chunk of rock and been sanded and polished over time.

"Are you really sorry?" I asked.

His eyes glanced up in confusion. "Of course. I feel awful."

"You realize that your stupidity has affected many people?" I asked, suddenly sounding a lot like my dad. Well, my stepfather.

"Yes, I know. Especially you. I'm so sorry, Ametrine."

"If you're truly sorry, you need to get us out of here." My mind was forming a plan. I just hoped it wasn't too late.

He gave me a puzzled look. "Don't you think I would have escaped by now if I could?"

"There must be a way," I said stubbornly. "You're a scientist. Is there a way to break the glass?"

Jasper shook his head. "I've tried a hundred times. It's coated with an unbreakable substance called LiquiPlas. It was developed by my mentor at the academy. It won't shatter, no matter the force raised against it, and it's completely heatproof."

"What about the slot at the top?" I gestured to the air hole. "Wouldn't that weaken the glass somehow?"

"Tried that, too. Stacked the bed and the chair and tried to climb up. It didn't work, and the guards bolted the furniture to the floor after that."

I sighed. There had to be a way or I was dead.

Dead.

A surge of excitement rushed through my veins. *That's it.*

"How long after taking the pill did those prisoners die?" I asked, trying not to shudder.

"It was instant," he said. "They starved them all

day, so the pill took effect immediately."

"Did the guard wait around until they fell to the floor and then remove them?"

I saw the flicker of realization in his eyes. "Yes. She usually waited until they collapsed, then she called for a guard to remove the body."

"It's worth a try," I said.

He swallowed. "But if you fail—"

"What else can they do?" I asked bitterly.

He paused thoughtfully. "I don't like it, but you're right. It's your only chance."

It was only a few minutes before a set of footprints echoed down the hall. Jasper ran to his bed and sat on it, feigning disinterest. I forced myself to ignore the surveillance cameras placed around the corners, hoping they hadn't been monitoring our conversation. It was the same woman, a small package in her hand. She opened the hatch and sent it through the glass. I picked it up.

"May I get a drink to wash it down?" I asked.

She gestured to the sink on the wall behind me. "Just hurry up."

I grabbed the plastic cup by the handle and filled it with water, then pretended to put the pill into my mouth, gulping the first mouthful of water down quickly. The pill disappeared down my sleeve, just as Tali had once shown me. *Thank you, Tali.*

Jasper had said the poison worked immediately, but he hadn't said how. Was I supposed to convulse, roll my eyes and froth at the mouth, or simply drop to the floor?

Option three seemed to require the least acting. I dropped the half-full cup on the floor and made my legs give, hitting the ground much harder than expected. The impact jarred my head painfully, swirling my thoughts around until I thought maybe I had taken the pill after all.

But a few seconds later a woman's voice said, "She's down." Then there was a click and a squeak as a door swung open on the opposite wall.

One.

The woman walked over to me, pausing overhead.

Two.

She tapped me with her foot. I forced myself to stay still. My lungs ached for air, but I didn't dare make a single movement.

Three.

I struck right as she started to kneel, my leg sweeping out and taking her down in one swift motion. She shrieked as she hit the ground. My other leg whacked her face, effectively putting an end to the scream as my hands reached up for a chokehold. Before my mind even realized what had happened, her head was crooked inside my elbow, her eyes pleading, her breath completely cut off. If I ever saw Vance again, I'd have to thank him for the training.

I squeezed a little harder. Her eyes widened and a squeak escaped her throat. A few more seconds and she would black out. I almost didn't notice the slight movement from below, but Jasper yelled, "Look out!"

My leg lifted just in time to smash her moving hand and stunner to the floor. It clattered on the concrete and cracked, sliding to a stop a meter away.

The sound made the woman strain for a second, then her eyes rolled back and her body relaxed. I waited for a moment, making sure she was really unconscious, and then examined the stunner. It was cracked, but hopefully it still worked.

"Where did you learn that?" my father asked, his eyes wide.

I gave him a grim smile. "A great teacher."

"The lock is a techband scanner," he said. "Hurry, drag her over here."

I stood and pulled her arm. She didn't move. I yanked harder and almost fell over.

"You can knock her out with some crazy move, but you're not strong enough to drag her two meters?" he asked incredulously.

"At least it's not a big, burly guy," I said, picking up her leg. Pulling as hard as I could on her arm and leg finally made her body budge, and a minute later I was close enough to scan her techband. It sprung the door right open. We both gave a sigh of relief.

He stepped out tentatively, a warm glow on his face. "Thank you."

It wasn't a moment too soon. Footsteps sounded down the hall. And voices.

"There's two of them," he whispered.

"Can you handle one if I take the other?" I whispered.

"Uh …"

"Just poke him in the eye or smash his nose or even kick him in the crotch. Just keep him from signaling anyone or we're dead."

He nodded and we backed into the shadows as the men trotted in.

The guard, a short, squat man in his later years, aimed his stunner, but it was too late. Remembering another trick Vance had taught me, I leaped on him from behind and forcefully clapped his ears with my cupped hands. I could almost hear the pop of his eardrums. With a howl, the man covered his ears. I grabbed the broken stunner out of my pocket and aimed it at his head, punching the trigger.

Nothing happened.

Out of the corner of my eye, I saw the other man raise his techband to his lips and step away from Jasper, who now lay twisted on the floor. Closing the distance, I tackled the guy to the ground. He threw me off and reached for his stunner, but I punched him flat in the nose. His hands immediately cupped around his injury.

Meanwhile the shorter guard, looking a bit disoriented, had pulled his stunner out and started toward me. Blood trickled down from both his ears onto his crisp white uniform, and he eyed me with a

269

cold, controlled gaze. I leaped at him, but he dodged out of the way. I sent a quick kick toward his crotch. He blocked it easily, then aimed the stunner at my face.

I ducked just before he fired, then leaped back and executed a perfect sweep. The guy went down like a lead weight. The man crumpled to the floor, trying to catch himself with one hand while aiming the stunner with the other. My next kick connected with his wrist and sent the stunner flying. He groaned, but he didn't get up.

"Are you okay?" I asked Jasper, who was still on the ground.

"Just … can't … breathe," he gasped.

"Can you stand?" I said, watching the short guard bring his techband slowly to his lips. I ran to where the stunner had fallen, grabbed it, and aimed at his head. "Put it down."

He obeyed, but the call was already in progress. "Reply, Captain," a voice on the other end ordered.

"End your call," I told him. "Now."

He moved his arm slowly to his face, but instead of hitting the End button, he spoke. "Red alert. Prisoners have escaped—" I pulled the trigger, but his leg shot out and kicked the stunner out of my hand at the last second. I started after it but thought better of it when the man raised his techband to his lips again. *I'm sorry, but you leave me no choice,* I thought, and kicked at the techband with all my strength.

The screen shattered. Suddenly the guard stiffened and started to gasp. He curled into fetal position, an anguished wail escaping his lips.

Jasper had crawled along the floor, grabbed the man's stunner, and made his way over just as the guard went limp. Jasper yanked at the techband, muttering something about "newer version." Then he pulled back, eyeing me with a horrified look. "He's gone."

I stared at him, stunned. "I didn't mean—I'm sorry—"

"What did you think would happen?"

"I just thought he'd go unconscious," I mumbled. "That's what happened last time."

"Last time? You do this often?" He shook his head incredulously. "The intensity of punishment mode depends on the force transmitted to the techband, Ametrine."

"Huh?"

"The harder you hit it, the worse the punishment."

"Oh." Another death. The harder I tried, the more people I hurt. Perhaps the prison truly was the best place for me. I reached over and closed the man's sightless eyes, hoping he didn't have children waiting for him to come home.

"The others will be here any second," Jasper said. "This way."

33

Jasper didn't speak again until he had navigated us through the maze of white marble hallways. I wanted to ask him how he knew where to go after being locked up for twelve years. But the expression on his face was so determined that I clamped my mouth shut and followed.

As we came around a corner we heard footsteps. He flattened himself against a wall, motioning for me to do the same behind him. We had a working stunner now, but it wouldn't do us much good against a group. Luckily the soldiers turned the other direction, and we continued on. After two more corners, I finally whispered, "Where are we going?"

"To get my things," he said under his breath. "We have to hurry. They'll discover those guards any second, and then they'll start tracking our techbands."

I stared at him in surprise, wondering what was so important, but I had no alternative other than to follow him down a dark flight of stairs into what looked like a storage room.

"How do you know what's in here?" I asked, covering my mouth and nose. The dust was nearly overpowering. He flipped the light on. It was definitely a storage room—an old, disgusting one that had long been forgotten.

"This is where they put my belongings. I'm sure of it." He started sorting through a few objects, tossing them onto the floor to get to the items near the back of the room. I just stood there. We had just escaped prison, the empress wanted me dead, and he was sorting through the storage room for his stuff? Maybe he really had gone a little loopy in his cell.

Without turning, he said, "Ametrine, help me out, would you? It's a tin canister about ten centimeters high. It'll be near the back."

"You can't be serious."

He stopped shuffling and pulled his head out. "Unless I find that can, we won't make it to the doors."

"Why not? We were almost there before you pulled us in here."

His mouth was set in a firm line. "There's a set of band clippers with my stuff. I have to get your techband off before they trigger it."

The blood drained from my face. "Oh."

"I locked everything in that canister and hid it before they arrested me. Never thought I'd be using my trusty band clippers on my own daughter, though."

The last part was muffled as he shoved his head back into the shelving.

I started clawing at the boxes stacked neatly against the wall. There was a thin layer of dust everywhere, making my nose itch and forcing me to sneeze. I looked around with a critical eye, trying to forget his warning about my techband. How did he even know the tool was here? Maybe they had discarded the can after all. Or maybe they'd opened it somehow and found his tools.

I considered stunning him and dragging him down the hall myself. But then I gave a start. In the far corner there was a pile of old-fashioned wooden shelves. Real wood was too precious a resource these days to use for storage. That was a good sign—they had to be old. It seemed as good a place to start as any.

The surface was dry and brittle when I touched it, a piece tearing away in my hands. Perfect—rotting wood. I began at the top layer and looked through every box. It was all junk.

"Why aren't you worried about your own techband?" I asked, trying to keep my mind off the danger we were in.

"Mine is different than yours," his muffled voice floated back. "Vallorah never updated mine or hers to the newer version with punishment mode."

So the empress doesn't have punishment mode either. I filed that information away, heaving the last dusty box to the floor. The top two shelves of the massive unit had collapsed, dumping their contents onto the bottom shelves. I couldn't get to the junk without lifting the shelves out of the way. I pushed upward. It was surprisingly heavy and refused to budge.

"Look at this," I said.

He trotted over and felt the wood. "We stopped using wood shelving during my tenure," he murmured. "Good thinking, Ametrine. On three." He took hold of one side, and I grabbed the other. "One—

Suddenly my techband vibrated. I glanced at it in surprise, the words making me freeze.

WARNING: PUNISHMENT MODE ACTIVATED.

34

Jasper—" I began, my voice shaking, but I didn't get the chance to finish. One second I was standing there, my hand on the soft wood, the next I was writhing on the floor. Pain. It was like nothing I'd ever experienced before. The world was aflame with a white-hot, smoldering heat. It seared through every vein, every organ, every inch of my insides. I could almost smell the charred flesh. Someone was screaming.

I felt hands on me, felt tugging at my techband. The pain was a part of me, overcoming my mind. I felt my sanity slipping into the darkness. Somewhere in my consciousness there was a yell and a crash, then a feeling of pressure on my wrist.

And then everything went black.

Vance was crying. His tears dripped onto my face,

and sobs racked his body as he held my shoulders. I ached to comfort him, to tell him everything was all right. I wanted him to know that he wasn't alone anymore. But my body felt wrong. I was hearing things as if I were removed from everything, like hearing a conversation through a wall.

And then the pain hit. It slammed into me like a hammer, and I wanted to curl into a ball. But my body wouldn't move. All I could get out was a whimper.

The sniffling stopped. "Ametrine?"

It wasn't Vance. It was Jasper. The memory came flooding back and I gasped. The storage room. Punishment mode.

Was I dead?

My eyes fluttered open, but the room was dim. My biological father let out a breath, holding me tightly to his chest. "Thank the fates."

"Jasper?" I croaked. Even that small movement of my jaw hurt.

"I'm right here. It's all right."

I strained to remember, but the memory of the pain made me sink deeper into his arms. "What …"

"What happened? A miracle," he said, his voice strained. "They triggered punishment mode. I tried to disable your techband without the tool, but it didn't work. Then I caught sight of my tool container under the shelf we were about to lift."

I tried to sit up to see, but I still couldn't move. I caught a glimpse of the corner of a heavy wooden object on the floor next to me. The shelf. It lay on its side, its contents scattered across the floor.

He gave a grim smile, his mouth tight, understanding my glance. His eyes were red and swollen. "Adrenaline is an amazing thing."

Jasper had saved me. He'd left us for another woman and a career, but he'd saved my life. Twice now, actually. I couldn't sit up—even the thought made me wince—so I just studied him. Dark hair— the same color as mine. Deep brown eyes. A softness in his expression that made me warm inside. My stepfather had never looked at me this way, as if I were a treasure worth risking everything for.

I'd only seen that look in the eyes of one other person. And it wasn't Dresden.

"Help … me up," I said, my voice raspy.

He looked like he was about to argue but then sighed and stood, lifting me in his arms as if I were a child. "You're too weak," he grunted. "And so small. Are you sure you're sixteen years old?"

"Where …" I asked, letting myself slump in his arms.

"If we can manage to get out of here, we'll go underground. Hopefully we can find a medic."

"Your techband," I protested.

"I cut it off, don't worry. They can't track us now." He motioned to his bare wrist. "That'll only buy us a few more minutes, though. Once they figure it out, they'll send patrols and check security feeds."

"Wait. One more thing."

"What's that?"

Jasper wasn't going to like this, but I had to know. And something deep inside told me there would never be another chance. "Take me ... to the monitoring room."

He belted out a laugh. "Right. I'm going to carry you, practically unarmed and helpless, into the highest security room in the nation, where all our enemies are frantically trying to find you so they can take your life. Not a chance."

"Need to know ... the truth," I said. His gaze flickered to my forehead, and understanding dawned. He seemed to know what I wanted.

"The monitoring room is too dangerous," he finally said. "But I know somewhere else that has back-door access to the system. We'll have to be quick."

○—●○—●○—●○—●○—●○

My wrist felt strangely naked. I started to rub it but recoiled in pain. The flesh was a fiery red, burned to the point of blistering. I tried to push the pain aside, forcing myself to think of other things. It was hard.

Jasper had ditched his prison uniform for a spare he'd found among his belongings. The cut looked too bulky, and the color was a little faded, but it would work. He stashed our techbands under the broken pallet. Hopefully the empress was expecting us to escape, not make our way deeper into the maze of white hallways.

It was strangely silent. I tried not to imagine the troops of monitors waiting for us at the exits.

Finally we came to a door. It was just like every other door we'd passed. The plaque next to the doorway read, "Maintenance." It was locked. A sophisticated identification lock covered the top of the knob.

"That wasn't there before," he said.

"Just knock, then stun whoever opens the door," I suggested. My voice was getting stronger by the minute, but my body was still extremely weak and shaky.

He cocked his head as if listening. A sound drifted through the door. Singing?

A knowing smile spread across his face. "Actually, that's not a bad idea."

"You can put me down now. I'll be fine."

He set me down gently just around the corner. As soon as my feet touched the ground, needles of pain shot up my legs. I bit my lip to keep from crying out.

"Be right back," he said.

I watched around the corner as he straightened and tapped lightly. We waited for a moment, ears strained for any sign of intruders. After a minute, he knocked more loudly. Still nothing.

"On lockdown, probably," I heard him mutter. But then the door opened.

"Jasper?" a voice boomed.

His shoulders relaxed. "Kert? Is that really you?"

"You gotta be kidding me. Shoulda known you were the escaped prisoner. Who else would do it with such flair?"

"Kert, I need to get inside and look something up. I won't leave a trace, I promise."

The man hesitated. "I have a wife and kids now. I really don't want to end up where you've been."

"No one will even know I was here. I've got a kid too." Jasper jogged over to me and started to pick me up, but I waved him away, struggling to take a step. He put a gentle hand around my waist and helped me make my way to the doorway.

"Who's this?" the thick man in the doorway asked. "A red?"

"My daughter. They triggered punishment mode on her."

Doubt crossed the chubby man's expression as he realized the depth of trouble we were in. But he stepped back to let us pass. The room was large, several floors high, with a huge glass screen in the center. The screen glowed white, with blue lines outlining the floor plan of the entire building. Different sections were coded with different colors—I assumed, machinery. The room that surrounded the screen was cluttered in contrast. Between this room and the storage room, the sanitized, marble-white image I'd always had of government buildings was now completely shattered.

"I'm the only one on duty right now," Kert said as we scanned the room. "But they're searching for you, probably floor by floor. You don't have much time."

"Then we'd better hurry." My father guided me to a chair and stood in front of the screen.

"What are you doing there, ol' buddy?" asked Kert, concern apparent in his voice.

"Don't worry. I'm not changing anything. I just need to check something." His fingers flew across the screen. "Thank the fates they haven't changed much."

"We still use your system," Kert said proudly.

I leaned far to the right to view the screen better. It went dark for a moment until he completed his sequence with a decisive tap. Suddenly it lit up and said, "Welcome, Jasper."

Kert nodded in approval. "A back door. Very clever."

"I knew it'd come in handy someday." Jasper's hands flew across the keys again. The screen paused for a second, then loaded several paragraphs of text. I strained to see.

Name: Ametrine Dowell
Rating: 440
Implant Level: Red
Age: 16
Mother: Lanah Dowell
Father: Konnor Dowell

"Konnor Dowell," Jasper said with a bitter tone. "It's like I never existed."

After that, it listed my entire record. I half

realized that my mouth was open, but I kept reading, completely fascinated. I'd always known they knew *everything*, but … they knew everything. My free-time activities, my missed questions in school, my hairstyle preferences, my khel goals at each game. It was interesting and horrifying at the same time. There was nothing to explain my Rating score, though.

Jasper gave me an approving look. "Squeaky clean. You're right to question all this. There's something wrong here." He typed in something else, and the screen scrolled down. His eyes narrowed.

"What is it?" I asked.

"A handicap," he said. "See that icon?"

"But I'm fine," I said.

He shook his head. "No, I mean they applied a handicap to your record. That explains the low score. Even though you're a nearly perfect citizen, it emphasizes your misdeeds and gives them more weight. We used to use handicaps for—" He stopped, suddenly self-conscious. "Well, it wasn't right, I'll admit it. But we would apply one or two to the individuals we knew shouldn't advance in their Ratings."

My eyes widened. "Shouldn't advance?"

"Don't look at me like that. It wasn't my idea, and none of them were contenders for the throne anyway. Just citizens who stirred up trouble and needed to stay out of the way, is all."

Kert snorted. "Somewhat like you, I'd imagine."

"Except that we never used more than two

handicaps," Jasper said, a puzzled expression on his face, his eyes still darting across the screen. "Any more than two and it would seem suspicious."

"How many do I have?" I asked, still confused.

"Six," he said.

Kert gave a strangled gasp. "Six?" we both exclaimed.

"Six." My father's voice was solemn. "We don't have much time. But I have a theory." He turned to me, his eyes serious. "Let's see what your Rating would be without the handicaps."

He typed in something else. The screen paused again, longer this time, and for a moment I was afraid that an alarm would go off or something. Kert leaned over my shoulder, his hot breath on my cheek.

The screen flashed. I saw it before Jasper could say anything.

Ametrine Dowell. Temporary Rating Score: 979

"Holy fates," Kert breathed. "That's higher than the empress."

I didn't realize I'd sat down again, but my legs shook uncontrollably even in the chair. 979. That was the highest score I'd ever heard of. If the calculations were correct, that put me above the highest Rated person in the entire republic.

It made me … the successor.

PART THREE

35

That ... that can't be right," I said.

"Is that possible?" Kert asked. "I mean, no offense, but a brand-new graduate? It's never happened before."

"Vallorah was only eighteen when she ascended," my father said. "It's the numbers that matter, not the age." He pulled up another screen. "Let me check one thing, though. Kert, can you pull up a list of the top ten Ratings right now, and then a list of the top ten over the last three years?"

Kert gave him a funny look, but he complied, and they sat back to study the screen. I scanned its contents. Names and numbers, all unfamiliar. Many of the names had scores higher than mine. "I'm not the highest. See that?"

"Just as I thought," Jasper said. "Look." He pointed.

"Deceased," Kert read.

"Every person above you, Ametrine, has died in the last three years. Everyone except Vallorah."

"Fates," Kert breathed. "The empress has been killing off her competition."

I looked from face to face, my vision fuzzy, trying to comprehend the situation. I wasn't a red after all. Far from it. It made sense now why she'd been so reluctant to allow the Rating reconsideration. The last thing she wanted was for the Raters to look deeper into my score. Not before she could kill me, anyway.

"There's got to be a way to reset this," Jasper murmured. He stared hard at the screen, as if trying to change the numbers with his mind. "The nation needs to know that you're the rightful ruler, and they need to find out quickly. If only I had my old system back, without the updates."

A light on the side of the screen suddenly flashed, and the men froze.

"Uh-oh," Kert said. "The lift just stopped at our floor."

There was a soft buzz of vibration. I reached automatically for my techband before remembering it was gone. Kert flipped his techband screen open and angled it so we could see.

"Attention all personnel. Security alert lockdown still in place," my father read. "Suspects: Ametrine Dowell, age sixteen. Jasper Frederick, age forty-three. Detain immediately if seen. Considered armed and dangerous." He glanced at me. "So much for our escape."

Heavy footsteps filled the hallway right outside the door. The soldiers had come straight here. I looked around, frantic, but the equipment lined the walls. There wasn't a single place to hide.

Jasper pulled out the stunner I'd given him, but then his shoulders slumped. It was cracked.

I'd grabbed the wrong stunner.

The door burst open. A team of silver-clad soldiers filed in, their stunners trained on us, helmets covering their faces. We stood and threw our hands upward in surrender. Jasper stepped in front of me, protecting me from their view. Then the leading figure dropped his hand and pulled off his helmet.

36

I aimed my stunner at the first person I saw. A man, short and round, leaped up with his hands stretched to the sky. Another guy stood beside him, and a smaller figure hid behind them. A face peeked out and I exhaled in relief. Treena. She looked deathly pale and unsteady, but it was her. She was alive.

I lowered my weapon and pulled the helmet off. Her horrified expression turned into one of relief as she stumbled toward me. "Vance!"

I caught her in an embrace, then gave her companions a questioning look.

"They initiated punishment mode on her," the graying man said. "I was able to cut the band off at the last moment."

"And she's walking around?" I said incredulously.

"Just a little zap," she said with a weak smile. "How in the fates did you get away? And how did you find me?"

"The empress pretended to give me another chance. Instead, she sent a contingent down to exterminate us."

Her hand flew to her mouth. "The ventilation shaft?"

"Yeah. I took everyone who would come with me." Once the unit had blown through the door, the fight hadn't lasted long. Poly had ordered his team to surrender. The last thing I'd seen before escaping was a masked soldier gunning Poly down. My throat tightened.

"I can't believe it. Why would they—" Her voice trailed off and her face paled. "Because of me, right? The empress did this because of me!"

"Don't start. It had nothing to do with you. She's been looking for an opportunity, and I gave it to her."

She shook her head slowly. "You saw this coming. I thought you were just paranoid, with your special lock and the escape route."

"If there's one thing I learned from my father, it's to be prepared for anything. Can you lean on me?"

"I'll try." She wrapped an arm around my waist and turned to face the two men still standing near a tall glass screen in the center of the room.

The older man had a strange look on his face. "The teacher?"

"Yep," she said.

The graying man stepped closer to confront me head-on. "But that doesn't explain how you found us, soldier."

"A hunch, really." I smiled down at Treena. "Our techbands have been lighting up with alerts about your escape. I knew you'd never leave without answers; we scoured the building for you, pretending to be on alert. Ross used to work here and suggested we try the maintenance room. It's the only place besides the monitoring room where you can access personal records."

"And I was right," Ross said proudly. "About time you guys started listening to me."

"I'm enjoyin' the reunion so far. Really touching," the other guy said, "but please get outta here. After someone stuns me already, 'cause they can't know I helped you. This ain't the best job in the world, but I'd like to keep it."

"Right." The older guy made a couple of quick keystrokes, then shut down the screen. "Thanks, friend."

"Anytime." They clasped hands. "Well, actually, please don't come back. It's bad for my tough-guy, tech-geek image, you know."

The graying man smiled and stepped back. "Hopefully I'll see you again soon." He swiped the gun out of Neb's hand before he could react and checked the setting. Then, with a practiced hand, he pulled the trigger. His friend collapsed to the ground. "May we meet again in better circumstances." He gave the gun back to a surprised Neb. "Let's go. But put Treena in the middle of the pack, boys. And give her a decent stunner, for fate's sake."

I raised an eyebrow, and Treena gave me a half smile. "My dad," she said. "I'll explain later."

o—●o—●o—●o—●o—●o—●o

We didn't have much time. Once the bodies in the bunker were identified and NORA realized we weren't there, my group and I would be in big trouble. I had no doubt the empress would trigger our techbands as soon as she could. The only thing we had going for us was the fact that we were in the last place she'd expect   in the heart of enemy territory.

We made our way to the other end of the building, grouped in a pack of sweaty and nervous soldiers. Each hallway, each door was identical to the last. The office numbers were all that changed. I shook my head in disgust. It seemed NORA architects liked their government buildings just like their citizens.

Jasper insisted on staying near the front, mumbling something about repaying a debt. I had my arm around Treena's waist. Despite the chalky color of her face and the way she winced with each step, she insisted on walking. At least she was alive. After maximum punishment mode, that was a miracle in itself.

"So where are we headed now?" Neb asked.

It was a good question. We'd already jammed all four lifts, which left two exits. Both led to stairwells and then to the ground floor, which was heavily monitored. I could only imagine how many soldiers were stationed there, all armed and aiming at the doors.

But we couldn't wander inside much longer, either. With Treena and her dad in the group, our cover was blown. We had minutes left, if not seconds.

"I have an idea," Treena said. She pulled away from me and leaned against the wall, looking like she would fall over any second. The rest of us flattened against the same wall, watching warily. We hadn't run into any other patrols yet, but it was bound to happen soon. "They'll be expecting us to escape underground, since that's what we're familiar with, or maybe to fight our way out on the ground floor."

"What other option is there?" Daymond whispered.

"The exact opposite of what they expect," I said, a realization dawning. "Brilliant, Treena."

"What?" Jasper asked.

"We go up," Treena said.

They stared at her like she'd just sprouted horns. Daymond shook his head. "That's crazy. We might as well turn ourselves in right now."

"There are wing suits in the choppers," I reminded him. "We can use them to leap off the building. Their stunners won't work well from that range, and their long-range artillery isn't accurate enough. They'll have to chase us by transport. With the darkness, it may buy us enough time to escape."

The hallway was silent, the guys motionless. For a moment it seemed like time stood still. The first person to move, surprisingly, was Jasper. "Actually, that's not a bad idea," he muttered.

"I say we climb out a window," Ross said, "and descend down the outside. They're probably just gathered at the exits and not around the entire building."

"That's a huge risk," I said, "and we don't have the right equipment. Besides, they'll be expecting that."

The group was quiet again. Finally Daymond spoke up. "I say we try Treena's plan."

I nodded. "Everyone who agrees, show it."

Daymond and Jasper put a fist to their chests. Ross stared at the floor. "I'd feel much better climbing down the outside."

"It's your choice," Treena said. "Thank you for coming to help me. I really appreciate that."

Ross looked at me. I shrugged. "EPIC is disbanded. I'm not your leader anymore. But if you really want to try it, use the north side. The alley has fewer lights and less room for soldiers, so you may have a chance. Just don't jump until you hear them following us."

"I'll go with Ross," Neb said, giving me a level stare. "We'll split their attention and gunfire."

I grasped his shoulder, both worried and relieved at the offer. "It's been a pleasure. You are both excellent soldiers. I hope you can find a better life out there."

"We'll see you again soon," Neb said, a look of fierce determination on his face.

"If you survive," Ross said.

"Wait! Don't go yet," Jasper exclaimed, and we

turned to him in surprise. "There's one more thing we need to do." He reached into his uniform's deep pockets and pulled out his tool. It looked like a pair of scissors but had a strange vibration to it, almost like it was electric. He held it up triumphantly.

I knew what it was immediately—a techband cutter. The only way to remove a band without setting it off. I'd seen them before, but only the highest of officials were allowed to touch the things. They were extremely dangerous. If he didn't know what he was doing, he'd set it off instead of removing it. I held my arm out. "Test it on me first."

Jasper raised the tool, a look of intense concentration on his face. I winced internally when he sliced though the metal, but before I knew it, the techband had been cut clean off. I caught it before it fell to the ground.

"Who's next?" Treena's father asked.

37

Our trip to the roof was a blur. We jogged—or stumbled, in my case—up the empty stairs and swung the door open slowly. Vance peeked out first, then signaled that the roof was clear. My mind was foggy, and I was shaking so badly I could barely walk. Was it the effects of the techband, or was it something else entirely? I let myself consider what we were about to do, and the anxiety nearly overcame me. Jump. Off a building. On purpose.

My mind went back to that fateful first day as an EPIC team member. This building had seemed so stately and grand, and I'd felt so small. My biggest worry then was failing a mission that had never truly existed in the first place.

But now I knew the truth. I was the successor. The empress knew that, and she wanted me dead. If I gave up now, she would succeed.

The question was, how would I tell Vance? It

wasn't like I could say, "Thanks for your help. Oh, and by the way, I'm supposed to take the empress's place." I couldn't bear the disappointment I knew I would see in his eyes. Would he be disgusted? Would he refuse to help?

Of course not. Vance wasn't like that. Ratings didn't matter to him, so this new revelation wouldn't change a thing.

I'll tell him later, I promised myself. A surge of determination overcame my nervousness, and I straightened and followed the others.

It was dark and cool outside. Two shiny choppers sat in their places, probably the same ones we'd used before. Daymond touched the first one gently, as if caressing a loved one he'd never see again. I touched his arm. "Are you okay?"

He pulled away. "I'm fine."

I tried again. "Thanks, Daymond, for coming back for me. It means a lot."

"The empress has to learn that she can't just kill people off." He pounded his chest with a fist. "Especially *this* person."

Jasper pulled on the door. It slid open, unlocked. "The fates are with us. I'll grab the packs. You guys watch that exit." He disappeared into the chopper.

Vance looked annoyed. He opened his mouth, then shut it, cocking his head.

I heard it too—a banging noise coming from the door we'd just come through. Vance had propped it closed, but it didn't lock from the outside.

"Fates!" Daymond cursed. "Jasper, hurry with those packs!"

"We don't have time," Vance said, and gave me a shove toward the door. "Get in, quick. Day, you too."

We leaped inside, startling my father, who had made a pile of supplies on the floor. Vance jumped in behind us and slammed the door shut just in time. A shot hit the side of the chopper, making the entire thing vibrate, and then more shots. I stood as close to the center as I could without stepping on the pile of suits, trying to keep away from the sides. The deadly sound waves from a dozen stunners rocked the chopper in one continuous round. The vehicle shuddered and moaned, and I resisted the urge to cover my ears.

"Day, you remember how to fly?" Vance shouted over the noise.

Daymond glared at Vance. "Don't even think about it. I never finished my training. I could kill us all!"

"We're dead anyway. We have no choice." Vance gestured to the steady flow of monitors and soldiers emerging from the building. They surrounded us.

Daymond's eyes were wide and panicked. "I can't—I don't—it's probably locked. It won't even let us turn the engine on, much less lift off."

"Don't know till we try," Vance insisted and shoved him toward the pilot seat. Daymond sat and stared at the instruments like they were poisonous.

I glanced out the window again. The black-clad figures were still coming, and the buzzing only increased. How long could the chopper withstand the attack? Could the technology even work when being blasted like this? We had bought ourselves a few more seconds, but by the barrage of fire around us, we had to assume their stunners were on fatal mode.

"Yes!" Daymond shouted in triumph, and suddenly the chopper roared to life. The engine sounded more strained than usual, but hopefully it would be enough. The chopper gave a lurch as we left the ground.

The buzzing's intensity increased as the guards below made a last desperate attempt to ground us. The engine gave a strained whine. Daymond's reluctance had been replaced with a focused intensity. He guided the instruments and raised us higher and higher until we were nearly out of range and the engine's noise returned to its normal noise level. Then we started forward. With a sigh of relief, I glanced out the window. My father sat beside me and handed over a headset.

In the copilot's seat, Vance put his on also. "We're not out of this yet. We'll try to land somewhere safe, but I'm assuming they'll send jets after us, so we need to be prepared. Have you ever jumped before, Jasper?"

My father nodded. "Once, but that was from a private plane."

"Parachute?"

"Yep."

Vance looked troubled. "I don't think that's a good idea this time. Even if we drop you low, it'll take too long to reach the ground. You'll be an easy target."

The chopper made a sharp turn, throwing us all to the right, and I snapped my seat belt into place. The radio on the dashboard came to life. "Chopper 502, you are ordered to land immediately. Violation of these orders will bring you under fire. Over."

Daymond started to reply, but Vance gripped his shoulder and gave a slight shake of his head. Better not to respond at all.

"If we can't use parachutes, what are you suggesting, Vance?" I asked. My voice sounded too high.

"We could wait until the last possible second to deploy the chute," Jasper said. "That, combined with the darkness, might be enough."

Vance shook his head. "It'll be too dark to see the ground. You'd end up a pancake."

"A pancake?" Jasper repeated.

Vance's lips turned upward for a second, and then he was all business again. "Never mind. We'll use wing suits."

Jasper leaned forward. "From this height? That would be suicide."

"How do they work?" I asked, a new wave of nervousness washing over me. The adrenaline pulsed like a drug through my veins.

"Have you ever seen a flying squirrel?" Vance asked. At my blank look, he sighed. "A wing suit has fabric between your legs and attached to your arms so you have a little control over direction and speed. It's tricky to control, but you'll still have a small chute to help you land."

"Wing suits are for small jumps," Jasper snapped. "We'd never survive a leap from this high. It's way too dangerous."

"I've done it before. Not from this high, of course, and it was hard to adjust the airflow even then. But I think it's possible."

"Let me get this straight," Jasper said. "It's too dark to see the ground, but it's not too dark to go flying at breakneck speeds through the air in a wing suit. Above a city. With absolutely no experience and no margin for error."

"We'll drop you as far from city limits as we can," Vance said. "Less chance of running into buildings. Trust me. I wouldn't suggest this if there was any other way."

"In that case," Jasper said, eyeing me with a careful look that said, *I hope you know what you're doing with this guy,* "you'd better give us some basics—and quick."

Vance stood, grabbing a handle to steady himself as the chopper lurched, and then began his demonstration. I watched through a shaky haze of growing terror. He showed us how to leap out the door, arms tucked and feet together. Then he showed us how to spread our arms and legs and lean forward or backward to control airflow. Last, he demonstrated how to deploy the small landing chute on our backpacks.

Jasper rummaged through the supplies and retrieved the suits. He pulled out the smallest one, although—no surprise—it was still far too big. When I stood to put it on, my legs buckled and I nearly toppled over. My adrenaline was wearing off, leaving behind the annoying prickles that reminded me what my body had been through today. It would be awhile before it worked right again. Assuming I survived this at all.

"You okay?" Vance asked.

"Fine. Just the angle." I sat and shoved my legs into the suit. From the look on Vance's face, he didn't believe me.

Once outfitted, I instinctively tried to check the time on my wrist before remembering it was gone. It had probably been ten minutes or so since boarding, but it felt like decades. I left my seat belt unbuckled and leaned back to look through the window but saw mostly blackness. The roads were barely lit since the only people who used them at night were monitors. With so many buildings outlined far beneath us, I could almost pretend it was Olympus and not the suburbs of Aiguille.

My stomach lurched at the thought, and suddenly I was five again, feeling my palms sweating, silently pleading with my father not to let go. I could almost feel his grip loosen, about to send me plummeting to the ground. Almost. The metal floor of the chopper was solid, and it brought me back to reality. I wasn't at the top of the tower but in a helicopter. I was safe.

Except that my father—a different father—really was about to send me flying toward the ground, and my life depended on it.

"Are you okay, Ametrine?" Jasper asked. My breath came fast now, and sweat dripped down my neck. He took my hand and clasped it tightly, but I pulled away. His hands were sweaty too.

"No sign of pursuers so far," Vance's voice said over the feed. He sat in the copilot's seat again. I took a deep breath and forced myself to think. If we weren't being followed, there wouldn't be cause to jump. Maybe they didn't know where we were, or perhaps NORA thought we weren't worth destroying a perfectly good chopper.

Just as I settled back in my seat, a light started flashing on the instrument panel.

Vance turned to look at us, dread filling his expression. A new wave of terror swept through my exhausted body. I couldn't move. This was for real.

Jasper stood and unlatched the side door. As he yanked it open, the sound suddenly became deafening, and the cold wind began whipping my short hair painfully into my eyes. My father stood there for a moment, staring out, then came back to check my pack's straps again. I wondered if he really knew how tight it should be, or if he was just reassuring himself. After a quick check of his own gear, he stood like stone, holding on to the rail as the wind whipped violently through the chopper.

I stood next to him and looked out at the deep blackness. Suddenly a hand gripped my arm. I turned. Vance had climbed back over the seat. His eyes were unreadable in the darkness, but his face held such a look of tenderness that I wanted to melt. He pulled me in for a quick hug. My body shook so badly that I could barely return his embrace. A feeling of foreboding settled on me, and I looked at him again, pushing my hair back so I could see him better. After a second, I realized what was wrong.

Vance wasn't wearing any gear.

He wrapped his fingers in my hair and pulled my face to his. Our first kiss had been gentle and slow. This time Vance pressed his lips to mine in fierce desperation. His other hand pressed against my back, pulling my body against his, and an intense heat burned through my body.

There was only one reason he wouldn't be wearing a pack.

I pulled away, feeling his hand untangle itself from my hair, and glanced at Daymond. He wore a pack as well.

"It's time," my father yelled into my ear, motioning for me to put on my helmet.

"I'm not going until you put on gear!" I shouted
to Vance.

He shook his head. "Later," he said simply and
pulled the eye guard down onto my face.

"You'd better jump," I shouted to Vance, hoping
he could hear. He didn't respond.

"Ready?" Jasper exclaimed.

"Don't be an idiot, Vance!" I screamed above the
noise. He just looked at me, a hint of sorrow in his
eyes.

"Ready?" Jasper yelled again, a hint of hysteria in
his voice.

I wasn't. I tried to give Vance one last look, but
my father grabbed my arm.

"Let's go!"

38

Jasper had a firm grip on my arm, and before I knew it, a rush of air left me breathless. My lungs burned, longing for air. A blanket of darkness opened up below me. Time seemed to freeze. This was really happening. I was falling, plummeting toward the unforgiving ground, feeling it grow closer with each second. It felt like my nightmares.

Except this time it wasn't a dream. And I couldn't see anything.

The feeling of being utterly helpless in gravity's clutches made me freeze in fear. I couldn't see Jasper anymore, but there was a faint light on the ground below. I made it my anchor. With a mighty heave, I threw my arms out, fingers splayed in the wind, and kept my legs apart in what I hoped was a flying-squirrel position, but I was shooting forward as fast as downward, and the light soon disappeared behind me. So much for that.

The ground came into view not because I was close to it but because the land was darker than the sky. My father's falling form, a faint spot of light against the drab landscape beneath us, was several yards in front of me. I leaned forward, reaching toward him, and my body sped faster until we were nearly even with each other. His helmet hid his expression, but he tried to motion something with his fingers. I spread my arms and legs out, feeling the fabric grow more taut, and tried to understand what he was trying to say. He held up three fingers, then two, then one.

Were we that close to the ground already? One hand clawed desperately at the pack above my shoulder, making me lurch sideways, but it came free when I yanked it. A whoosh of cloth behind me told me it had worked. A second later a huge force sucked me momentarily upward into the sky. It was so strong that I felt breathless for several seconds, and then I was quickly drifting downward again. It took a while for me to realize I was laughing—a hysterical, uncontrollable laugh.

As I looked over, I saw Jasper touch down first. Then I saw the ground approach—much quicker than I'd anticipated—and put my legs down just in time. I was so numb from the cold descent that my legs collapsed when they hit the ground. I lay there, shaking and laughing, feeling the fire in my veins and the dry coolness in my lungs. Jasper was lying on the ground too, his breathing heavy. It took a moment for me to free myself of the parachute, then I stumbled over to my father. He stared at the sky.

"That was incredible!" I yelled, although my voice sounded hoarse.

He nodded, still distracted.

"You all right?" I asked.

He let out a deep, shaky breath. "I think I'll leave the death-defying drops to you and your crazy friend from now on."

I threw my head upward, searching the night sky. The chopper's lights were nowhere to be seen. I didn't see any jets, but then again, they were probably designed for invisibility. I hoped Vance and Daymond wouldn't be far behind us. There was something about Vance's good-bye that bothered me, and I couldn't tear my eyes away from the sky. Was it the desperation in his embrace or the hopelessness in his eyes?

Vance, you'd better jump.

"Ametrine," Jasper said urgently. "I think we'd better head for—"

Suddenly an explosion rocked the night sky. The blast lit the clouds above like fireworks. The inferno fell like a fiery hand, tendrils of hot flame and smoke flashing brilliantly in the darkness, and then it was swallowed up in black.

I gasped, unable to rip my gaze away. My legs gave way as I sank onto the packed earth. Whatever strength had held me up seemed to seep into the ground beneath me.

"Ametrine, I'm sorry."

"Don't say that," I snapped, still scanning for movement. If he'd jumped in time, he would be landing about now.

"There's nothing left but chopper parts. We've got to go before the jet sees us, Ametrine. They probably have night vision."

I barely heard the words. Vance had known he wouldn't make it out. He'd probably waited until the very last second, getting Daymond out before himself. It sounded like the kind of stupid, idiotic kind of thing he would do.

Jasper grabbed my arm to pull me up. A surge of red-hot anger spread through my chest, and I leaped to my feet, giving him a hard look. "Don't touch me!"

He recoiled. "Look, I'm sorry, but they obviously didn't make it. It's time to go."

"Then go. That's what you're good at, right?"

He took a step backward. "I know you're upset, but I'm just trying to help."

"No matter what you do, it doesn't make up for a lifetime."

My father stared at me, his expression pained and frustrated. "I can never make up for that. But I can protect you here, now."

The anger was already dissipating, leaving behind a bone-deep exhaustion I'd never experienced before. I let his reply slide and tore my gaze away to stare at the sky. There was no evidence of the explosion now.

The distant stars shone more brightly than I'd ever seen before, and the air held a defiant chill. There were no dark figures in wing suits swooping in to join us. A distant hum made me pause. Definitely an aircraft. My father was probably right about the night vision—it was time to go.

"He made it out," I said. "I'm sure he did."

My father's voice was strained. "It's always possible. He seemed—seems—like a survivor."

He started to wrap an arm around my waist, but I shook myself free. I could walk. I couldn't think, but I could make my feet move. It gave me something to focus on. *Forward. Right, then left. Avoid the tumbleweeds and rocks. Focus on survival. Get back to the city and don't get caught.*

Above all, don't think about Vance.

Jasper decided to call in a favor from an old friend who lived just outside the city. I'd never realized how cool it could get at night, even in the desert. I found myself shivering after the first hour. I gripped my necklace for comfort. It was warm from the heat of my body. I remembered how gently Vance had cradled it in his rough hands, listening patiently to my theories about its colors and what they meant—things that probably sounded ridiculously silly to a guy who was just trying to keep himself and his family alive.

Alive. The thought made me choke, and Jasper

gave me a questioning look. I just shook my head.

For an older man, Jasper was extremely alert. Twice a spotlight appeared overhead, the chopper slow and deafening, and we hid behind scraggly trees and an old, half-standing structure. We both knew that once it was light, they'd find our trail and follow on foot. Frankly, I didn't care very much right then—whether they put me in prison or shot me, at least it meant a little rest.

We reached our destination shortly after sunrise. "Wait here," my father said. The house had a small patch of green lawn—not shiny like the plastic ones I was used to but *real*. The homeowners had probably wasted their entire water allowance on it. Either that, or houses on the outskirts had more lenience about their water supply. "What is this place?"

"My good friend lives here. Or, at least, he used to. If I'm not back in ten minutes, run and find shelter."

Sitting and waiting sounded heavenly, but I knew once I sat, I'd never get back up. I still saw the desert floor beneath my eyelids when I blinked. "Not a chance. I'm going with you."

"Are you always this stubborn?"

"Yep."

He sighed. "All right, but stay behind me."

After a long trek up the front walk, Jasper knocked on the door. There was no answer.

"Are you sure this is the right house? It's been twelve years," I said.

"Actually, it's been thirteen. I came to visit before I was thrown into prison. Vallorah had started acting strangely, and I came to Mills for advice." He shook his head grimly. "Mills wasn't married himself. I don't know why I thought that was a good idea."

"You and the empress stayed together for a long time, considering her position," I said, trying not to be weirded out by the turn in conversation.

"She was different then. She changed a lot in those last years—got more self-centered and power hungry. More obsessed with the Romans. She said that building an empire, making NORA the New Rome, was the key to her immortality."

The door opened suddenly, making me jump. It was a woman, a yellow—695. She had light brown hair, which was strange enough, but her eyes were startlingly falcon-like. "Yes?"

"Are you the wife of Mills?" Jasper asked.

"He doesn't live here," she said and started to close the door.

My father threw his hand out and caught it. "Please, I really need to find him."

"It's extremely important," I added.

"Hold on," she said, staring at my face. "You're that girl, aren't you?"

"What girl?" I asked.

The woman flipped up the screen on her techband and typed something. Then she held it up so we could see. There, in full color, was my photo. It

311

said, "Ametrine Dowell, age sixteen. Rating: 440. Extremely dangerous. Report immediately if seen."

"Was this alert local or national?" I asked.

"Definitely national," the woman said. "We woke up to it this morning. They've repeated the message every thirty minutes."

My father cleared his throat. "Sorry to bother you, ma'am," he said. "Sounds like we'd better get going. Any chance you'd consider forgetting about this visit?"

She stared at him, squinting hard. "You look familiar too, but not from the news alert. Who are you?"

"I'd rather not say—"

"Oh!" She clapped her hands together. "I remember. You were the Ratings councilman way back, before the empress threw you behind bars. Never thought we'd see you again."

Panic spread across Jasper's face. "Come on, Treena. We're going."

The lady's hard expression softened just a bit. A tiny bit. "Don't worry. We've made it our business to know these things. Come inside. I suppose it's worth finding out if you're friend or foe."

39

Forgive me, Mills, but we've had a new development. Two refugees have come asking for you." She held the small rectangular device closer to her face, even though he could probably see her fine, and lowered her voice. "One appears to be the wanted girl."

"Are you sure?" a gnarled voice asked. I peeked over her shoulder and examined the graying man's face on the little screen. The skin beneath his eyes sagged, but his eyes were clear and sharp. Surprisingly, he had no Rating. His forehead was as clean as a child's. Had he managed to remove his implant, or had he evaded implantation altogether?

"She looks like her and has the 440 Rating. And her hair is dark."

"That means nothing. Anyone can dye their hair."

This was taking forever. I swiped the device out of her hand and glared at him. "The empress tried to kill me."

Surprise swept over his expression, and then amusement. "Well then, you have my attention. What's your name again?"

"Ametrine Dowell. This is my father." I tilted the screen sideways.

If Mills was surprised before, he was dumbfounded now. "Jasper! We thought you were dead."

"So you're leading the rebellion now?" My father chuckled. "Do your followers know about your interesting past?"

A pause. "That's irrelevant."

"Whatever you say. Where are you, exactly?"

"That I can't tell you, sorry. Protocol and all that." Mills smiled, but it didn't touch his eyes. "But I'm where I can do the most good, and they won't find me anytime soon. The question is, what are you doing in my house?"

My father quickly told his story, his eyes flitting to me when he talked about Lanah and then his years in prison. Then he switched to my Rating, and Mills sat a little straighter. "Are you telling me that this girl—this child—is the successor?"

"That's exactly what I'm saying," Jasper said.

There was an unnatural brightness to the old man's eyes, but his words were carefully controlled. "And she just happens to be your daughter. That sounds a little convenient, don't you think?"

"She earned it all by herself, before I even found her."

"No one is going to believe it. I hardly believe it myself."

"Wait," I said. "What do you mean by 'no one'?"

"The rebellion," Mills said matter-of-factly. "If this is true—which I doubt, to be honest—it could change everything. We've been waiting for something like this."

"No." I shook my head. "You won't tell a soul without my permission. I'm tired of being chased by people who want me dead."

"She already sounds like a leader," Mills said, watching me with a tight smile. "That's a good sign."

My father sighed. "You have a point, Ametrine. I shouldn't have assumed you'd want to join the rebellion. What is it you want?"

I shook my head. "Do you really want to know? Because it sounds like you have my whole life planned out for me already. Just like NORA, just like Konnor, just like everyone else I've ever known."

"What are your options?" Jasper whispered. "You don't want to be used. That's understandable. But look at it this way—you're getting the throne, and they're getting a leader who can change things. Everybody wins."

I ground my teeth in frustration. They weren't getting it. My Rating had been the most important thing to me for so long. It had taken Vance and EPIC to pull me out and help me see life for what it was. Now that I was free, the rebellion was trying to pull me back in again—into the center, no less. "I don't know what I want. But I know that I have no desire to become empress."

Silence. Jasper sat back in his chair with a heavy sigh.

"Ametrine," Mills said carefully. "The empress tried to have you killed. Do you really think you're the only one? She's abused her power for years, destroyed families, and taken away what people have rightfully earned. The system may have worked initially, but now it's so corrupt it's beyond repair. We're not asking you to fix everything by yourself. In fact, you don't need to do much at all. What we need is a face to unite behind, a symbol of hope to inspire those who want change."

"You want me to become a giant target," I said. "Everyone in the country will recognize me as a rebel."

"Or a hero," Mills said.

"I'm sorry if I was too pushy, Ametrine," Jasper said. "This really is your decision, and I'll support you no matter what. But I want you to understand what Mills is proposing here. This will be very dangerous. In addition to the entire country being on alert, you'll be exposed to patriots wanting to sell you out. We'll do our best to protect you, but the bigger this gets, the harder Vallorah will try to take you down."

Haven't you ever had a cause worth dying for? Tali's voice echoed in my mind.

I hadn't, but she had. And she'd paid the ultimate price for it. If I disappeared now and left the rebellion to itself, Tali's death would mean nothing. I fingered the hair I'd cut and dyed in her honor, twisting it around my forefinger.

The empress had meddled in my life long enough. She'd taken Vance's father and his clan, his family, and finally his life. She'd taken Tali. And she'd taken my future and wanted desperately to extinguish me as well. I was sick of running.

If you're attacked, they think they can beat you, Vance had said. *They won't expect you to fight back.*

"Okay," I said. "But three conditions. First, we do it my way. I have an idea, but it means we'll have to hit her hard, and soon, before she knows I'm alive. Second, I'm the one who decides my future if we win. And third," I leaned forward, "do *not* talk about me when I'm sitting right here. Keep me involved and informed of every conversation or count me out. Got it?"

Jasper covered a pleased smile, but Mills frowned. "I suppose we can agree to your conditions, assuming that you really are who you say you are. We'll have to verify that. But I'd like to know more about this plan of yours. I've been gathering loyal followers since you were crawling, girl, and I'm not just turning them over to you."

"I think you mean, Your *Highness*," Jasper said with a chuckle. "Ametrine, welcome to the rebellion."

o—●—o—●—o—●—o—●—o—●—o

Securing a transport with the tracking device removed was a little tricky, but the next morning, I stood outside the academy doors once again. Keri, the woman who had helped us contact Mills, closed the door and climbed back into the vehicle, keeping a wary eye on me. She hadn't approved of Mills's decision to include me in their plans, but apparently she wasn't high enough in the decision-making scale to express her opinion. I wasn't sure if she was here as my bodyguard or simply my guard.

I'd acted confident in my plan before, but now I felt sick. Dresden and I knew each other so well. Even in the beginning, when it was just studying and playing khel, we couldn't bear to be apart. And yet I stood here, staring at the building that housed his future, and wondered how well I really knew him. Was he the same tender, laughing Dresden I'd always known? Could I trust him with my secret, or would he turn me in?

That was ridiculous. Dresden was happy here, but he would never turn me in. I just had to pretend like nothing had changed—even though everything had.

It didn't take long to find him. All I did was wait by the doors and watch for a crowd trailing a tall, confident figure. I fell in line with them, hoping the wig Keri had provided would help me blend in. It fell thick in the front, hiding my Rating without being too obvious. Luckily, no one seemed to notice me at all. Even the security girl was distracted. Very distracted. She stared at Dresden in awe as we passed.

"Professor Geldon? Yeah, he wouldn't notice me if I slapped him in the face," a guy beside him was saying, striding quickly to stay in step with the taller Dresden.

Dresden laughed, a familiar sound. "He only told me congratulations. I'm sure he says that to everyone. Besides, Jacque, if you slapped him, I'm sure he'd have something to say."

The girl next to him broke into a fit of obnoxious laughter. If anyone was going to be slapped, I wanted it to be her. Forcing my hands to my sides, I used the moment to whisper. "Dresden." He didn't hear me at first. I tried again, touching his arm. "Dresden."

His eyes flitted to mine, then widened. His expression was mixed. Surprise. Confusion. Then something else. Was it … horror?

"I wondered if you could help me with my homework," I said, adjusting my stolen uniform self-consciously. "Do you have a second?"

"Ah, yeah. Of course." He turned to his friends, who watched him with varying degrees of disappointment. "I'll catch up in a minute."

"Treena," he began when his friends left. "You have *got* to stop showing up here, especially now that the entire country is looking for you! Do you realize—"

"They tried to kill me."

He took a step back. "W—what?"

"Shh," I said, lowering my voice. There were people everywhere, but no one was close enough to be listening. Hopefully. Dresden just stared at me as if I were a stranger. "I need your help."

He sighed, then eased me forward until we turned the corner. "I saw the broadcast. What in the fates did you do? Fail your assignment?"

"You could say that. Is there somewhere we can talk?"

"I know just the place. Follow me but keep your head down. Your Rating is a dead giveaway."

No problem there. I kept my eyes on the shiny metal floor as he led me down the hall. A couple of turns later, we arrived at a gray door. Dresden tried the knob, then yanked hard. It clicked open to reveal a small, dark room. "A custodial closet?" I asked.

"The only place in the building that isn't monitored," he said, closing the door behind us. "We won't have much time, though. Tell me everything."

The story spilled out. I told him about Tali, my father, and my real Rating, leaving out any mention of Vance. It was hard not to think about him; it was like trying to distract myself from a gaping wound in my body. I'd been waiting so long for a moment like this with Dresden. And here I was, thinking about someone else.

It was too dark to see his reaction, but I could sense

his doubt. "You, the successor? Come on. You're a fugitive."

"And now I know why. She's been killing off her competition. The empress has tried three times to take me out, and if they catch me again, she'll succeed."

He was silent for a moment. "That's a pretty serious claim. How do you know she's behind the deaths?"

"When we hacked into the system and checked my score, Jasper noticed it. It's too convenient to be a coincidence. It's no mistake, Dresden."

"You really are …"

I nodded, even though he couldn't see me in the darkness.

"That's why your Rating was so weird. The empress was just protecting her position. Of course."

"You make it sound like a game," I said. "She tried to have me killed."

He sat back against the wall. "Although if she'd been smarter, the empress would've set your Rating lower, like in the 800s. Nobody would have noticed. I don't understand why she'd make you a red." He chuckled. "I just can't believe it. I never thought you could—I mean, wow."

That made me pause. He never thought I could what? "That's where you come in, Dres. I need you to steal a camera for me."

"You want me to do *what*?"

"Sounds crazy, doesn't it."

"Crazy? I have a better chance of making it rain. No, not rain. Snow. In the sweltering heat of summer."

"Dres, I know you can do it. You can figure out a way."

He took a deep breath. "Do you realize what you're asking?"

"Yeah. I'm sorry."

He was quiet for a long time. I could almost feel him wrestling with it, feel his mind weighing the risks and the benefits. Calculating. I shifted uncomfortably on the floor.

"You're joining the rebellion, then," he finally said. "Smugglers and the Integrants and all that. They'll help you get the throne."

"I don't know about the throne part, but there are other citizens too. The empress has made a lot of people angry."

"You can't honestly think this is possible."

I felt a twinge of irritation. If I said no, would he still help? Then I thought of his friends and the doting females, and I felt even worse. I was asking him for something that I couldn't even give him in return.

I was asking for his loyalty.

"I don't know if it's possible," I said honestly.

"Treena, the last couple of weeks have been hard. I feel like a different person here. Everyone knows who I am, and they watch me, you know? I feel like I can't be myself, or they'll discover who I really am— just a dumb kid from Olympus."

I opened my mouth to argue, but stopped. He was right to question this. If I'd been in his position, there was no way I would have agreed to it. "Go on," I finally said.

"But you're the one who got me here. You helped me with my coursework, my language, even my posture." I smiled at that. His posture had been atrocious in Level Two. "And now you're asking for a big favor. I should be jumping at the chance to pay you back."

"You don't owe me anything."

"I'm not done," he said quickly. "It's just that this feels like such an impossible task, and if we fail— well, I'd be in prison at the very least. And I feel guilty for even thinking that."

"I know."

"But none of that should matter. Everything here seems so fake when you're out risking your life every day so we can be together." I felt his grip tighten on my hand as his other arm pulled me in close. I leaned against him, trying to relax, breathing in his natural scent. It was the same but different. Stiffer somehow, like he'd been using overscented soap.

"It's fine," I said, unsure how to respond.

"The girls here are so annoying," he said with a chuckle. "They just want to climb the ladder. You know, use me as a rung to get somewhere else." He stopped. "But you're different. You cared about me even before I got my Rating."

I nodded, feeling the guilt rise to my throat like bile. Was he testing me? Trying to figure out where I stood? Could he sense that something was different between us?

Dresden pulled his arm back and I sat up, then I felt him ease closer. He stroked my face in the darkness, his fingers leaving a hot trail of betrayal. I was trembling. He pulled me closer, entwining his fingers in my hair. "What have they done to you?" he murmured.

And then he leaned in, slowly, as he'd done a thousand times before. I nearly pulled away, but his lips brushed mine. The gentleness of his lips made my eyes burn, and a tear trickled down one cheek before I could stop it. He tightened his hold until I could barely breathe.

I'm such a traitor.

"I'm so sorry," he said between kisses, his breath warm on my lips. "You deserve so much more."

I betrayed you, Dresden. I fell for someone else—I don't deserve you at all.

He pulled away, probably mistaking my reluctance as concern about our situation. The light on his techband flickered on as he checked the time. "I've gotta go. If this is going to work, they can't suspect anything."

I blinked. "Really? You'll do it?"

"I want you, Treena. You're more important than any of this. If it means we can be together, I'll do it.

Assuming I haven't already lost you."

I paused. He couldn't know about me and Vance, could he? Pain shot through my body at the thought of Vance. I couldn't imagine being with anyone else. But he was gone, and it made no sense to reject Dresden's help now. I pushed away my emotions and hardened my heart a little more. "Of course not. Thanks, Dres. You have no idea how much this means to me."

He pulled me into his arms again, and I tried not to stiffen. "I think I do."

40

P lease whisper," my father said, his own voice definitely louder than a whisper. He was speaking to a group of twenty block leaders standing uncomfortably packed together in the small showroom of a shoe store where a screen flickered in front of them. But the arguing continued as if he hadn't spoken.

It was the second night of briefing, and Dresden's camera had already been put to good use. We'd shown a recording of my father's confession to a dozen groups so far. I had expected Mills to send out the information to his followers quickly, but apparently the empress's new location law made communication much more difficult. Their solution was to show the recording to the neighborhood heads in each area and allow them to spread the word.

And since Jasper, Keri, and I were among the few who couldn't be punished—Keri's techband had no punishment mode, either—we were the chosen emissaries.

No, that wasn't it. They wanted to show me off. I was their showpiece, their crowning jewel. It was just a nice convenience that I couldn't be zapped.

Zapped. The memory the word conjured up made me cringe. Everything reminded me of Vance now. Certain faces in the crowd, a whiff of pine, a head of dark, messy hair. My mind knew that if he were alive, he'd be here; my heart refused to accept that he was gone.

Focus, Treena. I forced myself to look around, taking in the anxious faces of reds and yellows, all standing around nervously because there was nowhere to sit. The racks of shoes had been pushed to the walls, and any chairs or benches had been removed to make room for more people. It was unbearably hot. More so for me because of the protective vest I wore under my uniform.

"Just start it already," an older man spoke up, his voice carrying above the others. He was in the middle of the pack and probably sweating horribly by now. I was in the corner by the door and could barely breathe the air was so stale.

"The time has finally come," Jasper began. "The empress and the Council have overstepped their bounds and begun attacking their own people. And now we finally have proof. Remember, this information is absolutely classified and top secret.

Everyone involved is receiving the same information."

He nodded to me, and I hit the Start key on the glass screen. His face filled the screen and he began telling his story. Since I'd seen it several times, I let my mind wander. Dresden had looked grim when delivering the camera to our meeting place yesterday, his usual smile hidden by a deep concern. I think he knew there was no going back now. If something happened to him, it would be my fault.

The crowd was starting to react now. The recording only specified that the successor was female, not who it was—at Jasper's insistence they'd find out later, once they had committed—so they didn't seem to notice me. But they did keep staring at Jasper. Their faces showed cynicism at first, sometimes disdain. After the first minute, though, their reactions weren't as pronounced. A couple of the women shook their heads. A man coughed. Finally it ended, and there wasn't a sound.

The older man in the middle was the first to speak. "All right, we agree that the empress has to go. Everyone knows she's a weasely little rat messing with people's lives. But what's the plan? The recording didn't tell us."

"Wait," a woman said. "If anyone doesn't want to be a part of this, they should leave. Right now."

My father nodded. "Actually, that's what I was about to say. If you stay, your participation will be expected. For obvious reasons, I'd recommend that those who would like to leave do so now."

I expected several to leave, like in the first group, but no one did. The woman's jaw was firmly set. Finally Jasper spoke again. "Thank you. If you could please file out of the room and make your way upstairs, Mills will explain the plan there." He opened the door and stood aside for the crowd to file past.

I watched them carefully as the room emptied. One man, his hair slicked back to reveal a yellow Rating, held back. Finally the crowd was gone, and it was just the three of us.

"Did you have a question, sir?" my father asked, making his way over to the man. The stranger's face darkened at his approach. My heart sank when I saw the glint of metal in the man's hand.

"Wait!" I shouted, but it was too late. The man leaped forward, grabbing my father's shoulder with one hand and plunging the knife deep into his stomach.

My father gasped, a horrified expression frozen on his face as he fell to the ground.

"No!" I closed the space in two steps. The man was aiming the bloody knife for a second thrust. As it fell, I redirected the knife back toward the attacker's thigh. It sank deep. He gave a sharp intake of breath and bent over, clasping his leg. I swept his other leg, throwing him roughly to the floor, and yanked the knife out. The man's startled yelp instantly ceased as I aimed the bloody knife at his throat. "Don't. Move."

His eyes were wide and full of pain, but he froze.

Rage pulsed through my body, along with a strong desire to hurt him back, to tear from him what he'd torn from my father. Instead, I asked, "Why?"

His chin lifted a little. "The empress rewards loyalty."

I glanced at the Jasper on the floor. His face was turned toward me, losing color by the second.

"Someone help!" I shouted. "Is anyone there?"

The footsteps stopped in the doorway, and there was an exclamation of surprise. Then everyone in the building swarmed us and time seemed to move in slow motion—Keri letting out a horrified gasp, and someone else checking his breathing. A group of men with grim expressions surrounding the man who had probably murdered my father, rolling him onto his stomach and locking his hands together.

A soft hand brushed my shoulder. "You can put that down now, sweetie." I realized that I still held the weapon and that I was shaking. It clattered to the floor as I sank down.

The man examining my father frowned and stood. "He's breathing, but it's faint. He needs a doctor."

"He's a fugitive," I said. "They'll kill him."

"He's at the brink already, love," an older lady said.

"My brother runs a red hospital out of his house," a man spoke up. "He'll have some blood in storage. Someone help me carry him. You, there."

With that, my father's slumped body disappeared

down the road. Keri and a couple of men tied up the attacker and led him out. He glared at me as he left. I just avoided his gaze. What he'd done was unforgivable, but I did understand his reasoning—he'd been desperate for a higher Rating, willing to sink to anything to get it. I had been that way once, and I hated myself for it.

The next group of people waited outside the open door, shifting uncertainly and wondering what they had just gotten themselves into. I stood mechanically, ignoring the blood on my uniform, and forced myself to usher them into the viewing room. There was lots of whispering, but I didn't care. My father's face was frozen on the glass screen, ready to be replayed.

With a sinking feeling in my heart, I realized that all of this wouldn't be enough. The Rating system was too powerful. Greens were too comfortable with their lives to take a chance. Yellows wanted to become greens, so they'd do whatever it took. And reds? They were too dangerous, too unreliable to be taken seriously. We were going about this all wrong.

Mills wanted a face for the people to unite behind. Well, he was about to get it.

"I want to say a few words before I play this video for you," I said to the waiting group. They shuffled their feet and seemed ready to bolt, but they were listening. I reached into the bag I'd left in the corner and pulled out the camera, turning it on and handing it to a girl close to my age. "Just keep that on me."

"Got it," she said.

I turned to the camera and spoke loudly. "I know I'm young and small. You're probably wondering why you're listening to a teenage girl. Up until a week ago I was just like you—going about my life, following the rules, and trying to make the best of things. But something happened."

It was quiet now, the shifting and movement completely gone. Keri had stepped back into the room and was leaning against the doorway. Good. I wanted her to hear this too.

"The Rating I earned was taken from me," I continued. "The empress tried to have me murdered to cover it up." There were a few gasps and whispers, but I plunged on. "We also have evidence that she has staged the deaths of multiple others she felt threatened her position. My father once called the Rating system a sophisticated and chilling method of control. I would have argued with him once." I paused. "Now, after what I've experienced, I know he's absolutely right."

"We agree," another said. "But what can we do about it?"

I paused. "Get rid of the Rating system."

There was silence, then murmuring.

"So this meeting is about overthrowing the Ratings?" someone said, the skepticism in his voice heavy.

"That's blasphemous," a man said. A green. One

of only a handful who had dared come. "I'm not surprised about the empress, but the Rating system is the foundation of our nation. The system works when the ruler follows the laws."

"The system fosters competition," I said. "Initially the kinder, more society-minded citizens were supposed to be rewarded. Now we're killing each other, threatening one another, scrambling for the slightest edge over our friends and family. It just isn't working anymore. Now, I understand your desire to protect your families. As you just saw, the Rating system is a powerful tool in the empress's hands. Our plan is risky and dangerous. It's probably downright crazy, actually. But if it works, your children will grow up without fear of pain and punishment in a world where a leader serves her people without using, manipulating, or murdering them. A world where everyone has an equal chance of succeeding."

"We've heard all this before," someone said. "The empress herself said such things when she was crowned, and look at her now."

"Is this really possible?" a woman asked.

"I don't know," I admitted.

The voices came fast now, and I simply listened.

"The leaders are always the same," a balding man with a huge nose said. "They promise change, then cave to whatever the Council wants. Our situation never improves, regardless of who rules."

"If we're to risk our lives over this, we have to

know what the outcome will be," a younger woman said in a quiet voice.

Baldie humphed. "We all know what the outcome will be. Not a thing. These rebels will take everything and give us back nothing."

The quiet woman spoke more loudly now. "But if we don't try, we'll never know."

"True," a tall, slender man said thoughtfully.

"And what if, by some miracle, we do succeed? Fates!" Baldie was yelling now. If the neighbors didn't hear, it would be a miracle. "Don't you people remember your history? Look what happened to Old America. Our life here isn't perfect, but at least it's better than that."

"For you, maybe. You're a high yellow!"

The room exploded with noise, some yelling questions and others shouting at their neighbors. I hit Play on the screen again and slipped out the door before anyone could see the emotions struggling to the surface.

A world without numbers, I thought. For a moment I listened to the voice on the recording and mourned the thought of losing the father I'd barely begun to know—and all because of the stupid Rating system. I'd caused quite a stir in there and hadn't even known what I was about to present before I'd done it. But if someone had asked me to take it back, I wouldn't. The empress was a huge problem, but the Rating system was what enabled her abuse of power. In that moment, a world without numbers was the closest thing to perfection I'd ever imagined. Determination flared up within, and for the first time in a very long while, I felt what Tali had described. If there was a cause worth dying for, this was it. She'd fought the system in her own, small way, but I had a chance to make a real difference. I was the only person in NORA who had the potential to change the system completely. Maybe that was her final message—choose to fight, and never give in.

"I'll do it, Tali," I whispered. "Better late than never."

o—●o—●o—●o—o—●o—●o

I couldn't sleep that night. The smugglers had added a couple of bedrolls to the attic for us, but looking at Jasper's empty bed was too painful. They hadn't let me visit him last night. "He's in surgery," they said. "Come back tomorrow." But the look they gave me was one of pity, and I knew. They didn't expect him to make it.

It shouldn't have bothered me that much. He'd thrown away his chance to participate in my life already. It wasn't like I needed him now. For some reason it was hard to convince myself of that.

When the first rays of light finally came through the tiny round window, I sat up. Dust particles floated slowly in the sunlight, a colorless glitter of lazy specks. It reminded me of the dome at the Block in Olympus.

Except that the cold white building hadn't been filled with the song of birds. The sound was so ridiculously happy, so carefree. What did these birds eat, anyway? Surely whatever bugs they ate didn't live in plastic grass. And yet, here they all were, defying order in their own way.

I tried not to think about the second phase of the plan that would occur tonight. My legs felt restless and cramped. I missed my early morning workouts. This was probably as good a time as any to do some training. It was what Vance would have done.

Stop it, I thought. I had to stop torturing myself with recurring thoughts of him.

It felt so good to stretch my muscles. I put my hands to the floor, breathing in deeply, forcing my brain to turn off for a while. A few stretches with my arms and I felt like a new person. In the quiet of the morning and with the approval of the birds just outside the small window, I decided to practice the kata Vance had taught me.

A sweep step to the right, with a block and a punch to my invisible assailant's jaw. I lifted my leg in a kick to his head, then brought an elbow down into his chest to send him toward the ground. I could almost feel Vance beside me as he had been at our daily training sessions, directing my wrist to make a straight line, my skin tingling at the roughness of his fingers against mine. It was almost as if I could smell the wildness of his essence when I did this.

Stop it.

Right kick to the groin, sweep of the leg, hammer punch to the nose. I was working up a sweat now. The floor beneath my feet creaked, but I barely noticed, completely lost in the movements. It was a couple of minutes before I noticed the figure at the top of the stairs.

"Look behind you at the back kick," a familiar voice said.

My heart leaped in my throat. I turned, and there he was, an easy smile on his face. I pushed down the thousands of emotions that hit me then, forcing myself not to run into his arms. Instead, I stepped slowly toward him. "I did look. You're just underestimating my peripheral vision."

"Ah. So you see invisible men, but not real ones," Vance countered. His hair was tousled and unkempt, and his uniform was wrinkled, but he was clean-shaven.

"If I see a real man, I'll let you know."

He smirked, ready to retort, but my restraint finally burst. I leaped toward him and let him catch me in his arms, allowing myself to melt into his chest. As he pulled back to look at me, his smile disappeared, and he softly tucked a wayward piece of hair behind my ear. "Sounds like you've had a rough couple of days."

I pulled away. "You mind telling me where you've been?"

He raised an eyebrow, his mouth twitching. "Why?

Were you worried?"

"You idiotic piece of slimy—"

"It was a simple question," he said, his tone light, but he watched me carefully. "Were you worried?"

I looked away, the fight draining out of me. "Of course! I thought you—you know …"

"Got blown up?" His words were playful, but his expression was grim.

"I saw the explosion," I said quietly.

"Got out just in time. Daymond wouldn't jump until I put a pack on, and he yelled something about kicking the fates out of the empress for him, then shoved me out the door. He probably tried to maneuver the chopper away from us before impact to give us more time."

I tried to imagine Daymond, with his thick arms, shoving Vance out the door. I would have loved to see that. "Not Daymond."

"It was his choice. He knew what he was doing." His words were certain and sure, but his lips pulled into a frown. Daymond's death had obviously affected him more than he wanted me to know. "Your dad survived the surgery, by the way. I checked on him on my way here. He'll have a rough recovery, but they say he'll probably make it."

I let out a long breath, feeling my shoulders sag. "Thank you."

There was a long silence neither of us wanted to break. Finally he spoke. "So. I'm gone for three days, and suddenly you're overthrowing an empire. I wouldn't expect anything less from you."

I shrugged. "It hasn't happened yet."

"I heard about your recording and the support you've helped gather. Mills's followers seem to really like you. Very impressive."

"Not really. They wanted a change, and I'm just a means to get there."

"You sound bitter about that."

"Vance, I thought you were dead."

His smile faded. "It doesn't look like you ever needed me here."

"You went to find your family?"

His hesitation was all the answer I needed. I watched his face closely, looking for something. The soul I'd caught a glimpse of before was locked away again under those dark, unreadable eyes, but there seemed to be a crack in the wall—a tiny trickle of uncertainty. He looked away. "Yes."

"Did you find them? Are they all right?"

He nodded. "I smuggled them out. They're headed where no one can ever use them again."

"Why did you come back?" I asked softly.

He didn't answer, but we both knew. Our eyes met again, and he seemed to be looking for something in mine. The hardness of the man gave way to the boy. He looked at me with a searching, pleading expression. I felt myself falling, totally and completely—like jumping out of a chopper but without the wing suit.

I'd never felt this way with Dresden.

A flash of clarity brought me back to reality. Dresden. We'd gotten back together … hadn't we? He was helping me, risking everything for me. For us.

Vance watched me carefully. "It's Bike Boy, isn't it? He's your contact at the academy."

"Yeah." It was barely a whisper.

He pulled away, letting out a deep, frustrated breath. "Is he really what you want?"

"No." The answer slipped out before I realized it, and I took a deep breath. "He was once, but now—I don't know. Now that you're here, it complicates things."

His expression darkened. "I tend to do that, complicate *things*."

"I didn't mean it that way, Vance. A week ago I had it all figured out, and then I met you, and what I've always wanted suddenly seemed so stupid. And now they're trying to force me back into that dream, with Dresden again, and that's not what I want anymore."

"What do you want?" He threw his hands in the air. "Don't think about it—just say it. Tell me exactly what you want, because frankly, nobody else is asking."

"I'm not—I don't—"

"You know what I want?" He gripped my shoulders. "I want us to run away. Right now. Leave all this nonsense about attacking the palace behind, and let all those mindless citizens go on with their dreary lives. You don't have to fight for them, Treena. Mills showed me how to get my family out, but I couldn't leave without you."

My mouth worked soundlessly, as if my brain and my lips were disconnected. Vance could have escaped, and yet he came back for me. He wanted me. Vance was alive, and he wanted me to leave with him. I tried to process his words, but it was all too incredible to believe.

It was as if someone held a precious jewel in front of me, one that I'd never dreamed I could actually own, and my arms were tied so I couldn't take it. After all this, there was no way I could abandon my people now. I couldn't let Tali's death and Jasper's sacrifice mean nothing, not when I had the opportunity to change things. "I can't."

"Yes, you can. The system is rigged against you— you couldn't succeed, even with half the nation on your side. Mills only has a few hundred followers, Treena. You're going up against the empress, the commander, and hundreds of thousands of soldiers. There's only one way this can end." His expression was pleading now, and I felt a stab of pain somewhere between my heart and my stomach. "Please. Come with me. They'll figure things out when we're gone, maybe come up with a better plan that actually has a chance."

I sighed. "I know it sounds crazy, but I have to do this. I can't spend the rest of my life wondering."

Wondering if I could do it. Wondering what happened to my mom, to Konnor and his ambitions, to Jasper in the hospital. To the people I had abandoned. "I wish you could understand. I do care about you, and I want to be with you. But I can't run away, not yet."

He folded his arms and nodded as if he'd expected that answer. I could almost feel him slide his protective wall back into place. When he spoke, it was the voice of a stranger. "Fair enough." He turned and put his hand on the stair rail, but paused. "I also came to deliver a message, in case you decided to stay. It's from my clan."

"Your clan? You met with them?"

"The few that I could find. Most are scattered, but there are about eighty who have managed to congregate. They've set up a communication system using the smugglers. It took some talking, but they agreed to help you ascend. On two conditions."

"If I let them go home," I replied.

He nodded.

"Of course. If we succeed, they're free to go. Not just your clan but anyone who wants to leave. What's the second condition?"

Vance watched me for a moment, his expression hard. "That I can't tell you. It's a condition for me, not for you, and nothing you'd care about anyway."

I longed to throw my arms around him, to tell him that all I wanted was him, that I would follow him anywhere. That my world had died with him when the chopper exploded. But something told me that would only make this harder. The thought of him leaving and never coming back made me scramble to say something, anything. "Don't leave. Please."

His expression slipped, just a little, and exposed the pain beneath, but he covered it quickly. "My window of opportunity is rapidly closing. It's now or never."

"Your clan needs you. I need you."

"Believe me, no one knows better what my clan needs. I'll think of a way to get them out, and we'll find a better place to settle, far away from NORA's grasp."

A realization dawned. "You're next in line with your dad gone, aren't you?"

"Would have been." The look of naked pain on his face was enough to break down my defenses and send me running into his arms. "I really do hope you win, Treena. Be careful." He whirled and stormed downstairs.

Then it was quiet again, except for the annoying sound of birdsong in the plastic trees.

41

I stopped by the Red hospital later that day, which was basically a small house with a converted second floor. They let me in but told me to keep it quick. Jasper lay flat in bed, shirtless and pale, a sheet tucked up under his arms. His eyes were closed. I sat softly on the chair at his bedside, unsure whether to wake him. In case things went badly for me tonight, I wanted to say one last good-bye. Instead, I sat and studied the man I would have called Dad.

He still had a thick head of chestnut-brown hair, although it was graying at the edges. The skin crinkled at the corners of his eyes. This man had chosen to abandon me and my mother. We shared the same DNA, but nothing about our lives was the same. Now that I'd found him, it seemed the fates were determined to keep us apart again. Even if he lived, I probably wouldn't survive the night. It was strange, how rational that thought was. Or maybe I was just numb at this point.

Jasper's hand suddenly grasped mine, and I nearly jumped in surprise. His head turned a bit to look at me. "Hi, Ametrine." His voice was barely a whisper.

"Hi. How are you feeling?"

"Fantastic." A twinkle in his eye told me that he still had his humor at least. He took a painful breath. "The protest?"

"Tonight. Mills said nighttime meant less civilian casualties. I need to get ready soon, actually. I just wanted to check on you first." *How can I lead an army by myself? Why did you have to get hurt?*

"Your ... stone." He was looking at my necklace. I usually kept it hidden under my uniform, but the top collar of my uniform was unzipped just enough that he could see it. "She gave it—to you."

"Shh, don't talk," I said, grasping the stone with my other hand. "Yes, Lanah gave it to me on my Rating Day—the day my life turned upside down."

His face grew serious, and then he struggled to speak. "Not ... just ... your Rating."

"Jasper, it's okay. You don't have to speak."

He spat the words out more forcefully. "Your Rating. Not just because ... you're the successor."

I paused. "What do you mean?"

He took a moment to gather his strength. When he finally spoke, it was a whisper. "Your stone. It's ametrine."

I didn't understand at first. "My stone?"

"Yes." He stared at me as if hoping I would understand.

"Wait. Lanah said you *wanted* me to be named Ametrine. After this stone?"

His lips curved upward in a soft smile.

"Is that because you're named after a stone too?"

Jasper's smile widened. And then I knew. The realization hit me like a punch to the gut. It was true—Peak's posterity were all named after stones. Tali's mother had been right after all. "You're a descendent of Richard Peak."

He let his breath out slowly and gave a slight nod. "So are … you."

I sat back. It didn't change anything, but it was a stunning realization just the same. I had accused Jasper of selfishness and abandonment, and here he was, trying to help me understand our family's legacy. "You left us because the empress offered you power, right? Because she was young and beautiful. Or was there more to it than that?"

He just watched, as if waiting.

"There's got to be more. Is it what she would have done to us, if you refused?" The look in my father's eyes was something I'd never forget. It was a mixture of pain, sorrow, and relief. He didn't have to say it. "She would've sought Lanah out, taken out the competition. Just like she's doing to me now."

"Yes."

Of course. *I thought he loved me,* my mom had

said. *I guess I was wrong.* But he had loved her, and sacrificed a lot for her. She just didn't know it.

How long had he wanted me to understand this? How long had he beaten himself up over it? And I'd blamed him for my low Rating. It wasn't him at all.

It was all her. The empress. The imposter. What we were doing was right. She had destroyed my family. She'd caused hundreds of deaths and separated families, all in the name of her little empire. But there was something she didn't know. A Peak had started the Rating system, and a Peak would remove it.

"I love you, Ametrine." His eyes glistened with unspoken emotion.

"I love you too, Dad," I said, realizing that it was absolutely true.

42

I cursed and retreated back into the shadows. A slow-moving vehicle hummed by, and the sidewalk went bright for a moment, then dark again. The entire monitor force seemed to be patrolling tonight, complicating my grand escape. I'd be miles past the wall by now on any other night. If Mills thought his protest tonight was a secret, he was a fool.

Wishing I could stretch my legs, I arched my back and looked up. Despite the streetlights, the sky was a deep black. Not a star in sight. I wondered how many citizens had even seen the stars in their lifetime. They'd probably never felt the need to gaze upward, had never weighed their singular insignificance against the magnitude of the universe.

Treena had, on our early morning walk. She would have loved my favorite stargazing spot up Lightning Creek trail, overlooking what had once been a fertile green valley. That would never happen now.

She made her choice. It's her loss, not mine.

When the patrol vehicle was out of sight, I turned back to my escape plan. I'd been here dozens of times, but the massive wall was still daunting. Eleven feet thick and thirty feet tall, the metal slab extended the entire length of NORA's eastern border. During the day, it reflected the hot sun like a giant mirror. Even now, in the cool part of night, it probably radiated heat. The electricity buzzing through the metal was deafening in the silence of a sleeping city.

Citizens thought it was to keep outlanders out. It was probably the other way around.

I pulled into the shadows again, letting out a long, frustrated breath. I hadn't planned past this point. Any citizen trying to escape over the wall would be punished with their techband. Since I didn't have one anymore, that wasn't an issue, but I still had to deal with the electricity. There had to be a weakness, some way to disable the current and climb over. And I had to do it soon, before my clan realized I was escaping.

Laughter echoed through the empty streets. I carefully stuck my head out from behind the corner, just enough to watch the border wall guards shuffle off, replaced by two new ones—a heavy-set man and a tall, athletic-looking woman. I squinted as they took their positions. The soft glow of the light behind them illuminated what I'd never noticed in the daylight. A door. It was nearly invisible, but the shadows revealed some kind of handhold that looked like a doorknob in the surface of the wall's metal.

I crouched, then shuffled around the corner, ducking behind a parked vehicle just as another patrol transport came by. Its headlights illuminated much of the road, making the shadows contort and rotate, and then it turned down the next darkened street.

The female guard swatted at her partner. "Quit looking so nervous. It took me forever to convince Blare to put us together. Just act natural."

The man beside her grunted. "Not too hard considering nobody's even told me what's going on."

"Oh, quit pouting. I only know the plan because Mills needed exact coordinates for his stupid missile. I'm the only one on the force who was qualified."

I'd started to creep closer, but at the mention of Mills, I froze midstep.

"He really has one, then? I thought he was just pretending," the man said.

"Far as I know. Not sure if it still works, though. I guess it doesn't matter whether it's seventy years old or brand-new—you shoot it, and it'll explode somewhere."

"Hopefully not in his face."

"Why not? We've already been paid."

More laughter. Without realizing it, I had retreated back to the parked transport. A missile? Mills's plan didn't involve a missile, and even if it did, why would the border guards know about it?

"What I don't understand," her partner said, "is

why he hasn't shot it yet. What could he be waiting for? Every second, the chances are higher that he'll be detected."

"That's the genius of it. Mills sent some kind of distraction, something sure to draw the empress out. Probably the whole Council, too. In one strike he'll take out both branches of government. 'Like fish in a barrel,' he said."

The man paused. "Fish in a barrel? What's that supposed to mean?"

"No idea. Must be an Integrant thing."

I sat against the cold metal of the vehicle, anger burning through my body, hot and thick. Mills was an Integrant. Or rather, he was an outlander, and probably far outside the borders right now. That would explain why the guy refused to appear in person at meetings. How convenient that we had agreed to run his rebellion for him. All he had to do was sit back and orchestrate it all, with no risk to himself. Brilliant, actually. He'd throw the whole country into chaos by taking out the entire government at once. And its successor.

Treena.

"So when are we supposed to let him back in?" the man asked. "When the missile strikes?"

"Shh! Here comes another patrol. You don't want to get thrown in prison tonight, believe me."

"Hey, you're the one who brought it up."

I couldn't understand the rest of what they said. My breathing came hard and fast, and rage muddled my thoughts. Treena. She thought she was saving people, making peace. Mills obviously had other plans for her and the hundreds of innocent citizens supporting her. A lot of people would die tonight.

But both sides hated me—NORA's citizens because I was a red and an outlander, my clan because I had changed sides. I didn't belong in either world. If I was going to escape, the chaos that would ensue tonight would be the perfect cover. I could overpower the guards in seconds and escape out the door to freedom.

Keep them safe, my father had said. His last words. Well, I'd done that, practically selling my soul to NORA for two years and then making that stupid agreement with Mills—he'd arranged for my family to be smuggled out yesterday. They were already outside the wall somewhere, waiting for me to join them and start a new life. If we went far enough east, no one would ever find us. We could survive on our own.

If I stayed, I knew what my clan would do. In a small settlement where people depended on each other so much, treason was unforgiveable. I'd be executed.

Keep them safe.

Them.

My memory was clear, the words unforgettable. Dad hadn't said to keep my family safe. He had said to keep "them" safe. Was he referring to his people or his family? If it was the clan, I had failed miserably.

Even if I hadn't spent the past two years rounding them up, I had just talked the remainder of my clan into joining the rebellion. They would be arriving at the square any minute, completely unaware that a missile was aimed in their direction. What was left of our clan would be decimated.

Keep them safe.

I had once asked Dad what it was like to be the clan leader. He gave me a thoughtful expression, set his book down on his lap, and said, "A leader doesn't just order people around, Vance. He gives himself to his people, sacrifices his wants for the needs of everyone. My grandfather died serving in the Old American War. When the dust died down, my father built this settlement and welcomed any who wanted to join us in peace. I'm proud to call myself a Hawking, and you'll make an even better leader someday."

That future had been torn from me. NORA had nearly succeeded in taking who I was, but they couldn't alter my DNA. If Dad was here now, there was no question what he would choose.

I crept away, waiting for the sound of footsteps and shouting behind me, but the night was still. The square was over twelve miles away.

Once I turned the corner, I took off running.

43

This was the stupidest thing I'd ever done.

I adjusted my sequin-lined uniform dress as we walked, chilled by the cool night air and incredibly self-conscious. Mills had insisted I look the part of the successor tonight. I felt ridiculous. He'd placed me at the head of our mob—although the 230 worried faces behind me looked more like a death march than a mob—and insisted I make myself visible to unite the people. It wasn't going so well.

We'd started at the store, shouting "Treason" to wake up the neighbors. Now, several kilometers later, our chanting had become a bit more subdued. Even our whispers echoed sharply against the hard surfaces of the roads and buildings. Mills had said our march would impassion and ignite the people, but nobody came out as we passed. Instead, we'd grown accustomed to the sound of locks being shoved into place. We were on our own.

A twelve-year-old boy marched behind me, unable to suppress a grin. He'd bounced along the entire way so far, excited to be a part of the excitement. To the other side of me was a gray-haired woman, and it was obviously painful for her to walk. She should have been relaxing in a comfortable chair, safe at home, rather than facing an uncertain future.

I glanced behind us, eyeing the patrol vehicle that had been tailing us for two kilometers now. Not only were we breaking curfew, but we were obviously headed for the palace. Why weren't they confronting us? That worried me even more. Mills's brilliant plan to "peaceably protest" now felt like a death wish, and dread permeated every muscle of my body.

We came to an intersection with a blinking light. I paused, then chuckled and marched through. What was a traffic law at this point? I was breaking pretty much every law possible, and there was no going back now. My followers had cut their bands off tonight with Jasper's tool. That alone ensured a work-camp sentence at the very least, and at the most—well, I didn't want to think about that. I rubbed my wrist again, wondering if I would ever get used to the exposed skin.

Another patrol vehicle pulled up and flanked us on the other side, and then another. They matched our speed like shiny escorts. Adrenaline pulsed through my body, and the chanting behind me was replaced by murmuring. We were only two blocks away now.

I'd ridden this way in a transport on my first day in the city, gaping and nervous at the adventure that had awaited me. It seemed ages ago.

"Everyone get ready," I announced, although there was nothing to left to do. We had no weapons, no way to defend ourselves except to show that we were peaceful. That was critical, Mills had said. We were victims, not attackers. Someone waited at the square with Dresden's camera, ready to capture our grand entrance and show the nation our struggle for justice. Everyone nodded at my words and steeled themselves, and a girl my age moved to stand beside me. She was about the same height as Tali.

Please, I thought silently. *Don't let me lead these brave people to their deaths.*

When we turned into the square, I stumbled to an abrupt stop. There they were—hundreds and hundreds of soldiers and monitors. The city had gathered its forces to protect the palace, just as Mills had predicted. Every single person was armed and had their weapons aimed straight at us. I glanced around but didn't see any camera.

"Close in behind them," a deep voice growled from within the enemy lines. The soldiers obeyed, and soon we were completely cut off from escape.

"Drop your weapons and put your hands in the air," a voice said, the echo from the amplifiers bouncing across the hardness of the stone square. "Now."

"We have no weapons," I said. My voice wobbled, and I cleared my throat. "We come in peace to protest the empress's illegal occupation of the throne."

A figure emerged. A dozen guards surrounded him, so it was hard to tell who it was until he stopped in front of me. It was the commander himself, looking as fresh as if it were the middle of the day.

"You are all under arrest," he said, his voice carrying easily over the stunned silence of the group. "Those who put their weapons on the ground now will be treated less harshly than those who don't. The rest of you—put your hands on the backs of your heads."

Clattering sounds echoed across the square as several rebels dropped stunners on the ground and raised their arms. They had just made me a liar. I completely understood, though. If I'd owned an illegal weapon, I probably would have brought it too. Not that it would make any difference now.

"That's what I thought," Denoux said. He motioned his soldiers forward, and an entire contingent broke off from the main group. They immediately kicked our stunners out of the way and started securing cuffs.

"Where's the camera?" someone whispered behind me. "They're supposed to be broadcasting this, right?"

A quick glance at our captors told me all I needed to know. There was no broadcast, nor was there a camera. The citizens would never know what had gone on here tonight. I'd just walked everyone right into a trap.

Mills had pored over every detail of our protest. There was no way he hadn't anticipated this. So why hadn't he warned us or given us a backup plan? Maybe he would descend at the last second in a dramatic rescue.

I thought back to that first time I'd met Mills, when Jasper had said something about his questionable past. If he was really working for NORA and wanted to crush the rebellion, this was a great way to do it. Fates. I'd fallen right into his hands.

"We're dead!" a woman exclaimed. "It's all over now."

"Mills will come through for us," a man said confidently. "We just have to play along."

"You're a fool. We're alone."

"Who's the fool? This was all a setup, and you walked into it same as anybody else."

The voices rose in pitch and intensity until I couldn't understand them anymore. A few of them decided to fight back and stormed the soldiers. They just ended up in an unconscious heap on the ground. One guy in his fifties took down three soldiers with his fists before he was clubbed. He lay motionless on his stomach, a puddle of dark liquid pooling around his head. The guard who had done it simply stepped over him to the next person.

Rough hands grabbed me from behind and yanked my arms down, and then there was the all-too-familiar feel of steel on my wrists. Luckily, there was no techband to connect it to, which meant I could still move without pain. I considered fighting back for a moment. But then something shoved me forward so hard I tripped and landed on my knees with a startled yelp.

"Wait," Denoux said. "Bring me that one."

The guard lifted me up by the back of the collar like an unruly kitten, then practically dragged me over to the commander, who looked puzzled for a moment. When he saw my face, recognition finally dawned. "The wanted girl. I assumed you'd be involved somehow. An interesting outfit for such a night, don't you think?"

I couldn't agree more, but I met his gaze. "The empress is the one breaking laws, not us. You have no right to treat us this way."

"No right? Bringing an army to the palace gates, especially at this time of night, breaks a multitude of laws. If you had applied to plead your case with the Council at their next meeting, you may have had a chance—"

"And I would have been arrested," I cut in, "and then silently executed. You know it's true."

The haughty amusement in his face was now a cold, dark glare. People probably didn't interrupt him often. "You thought this would bring about a different outcome?" He chuckled and turned to the man on his right. "Take her to the political prison, and inform

Her Majesty that the girl has been captured."

"What about the rest of them, sir?"

"Run the food test to find out which ones are confirmed smugglers. The rest can go to the work camps."

"Yes, sir." The soldier put his fist over his heart and strode toward me. He gripped the back of my neck and shoved me just like the first guard had, but I managed to stay up this time.

"Commander!"

Denoux turned as a runner shoved his way through the crowd. It was one of the empress's personal guards, a stone-faced guy with wide shoulders. He pulled up in front of Denoux. "Her Majesty orders that the girl be delivered to the gates. She wants to speak to her."

I should have been terrified, or at least scared, but my mind was simply numb. Empty.

All our hard work and I was right back at the beginning, in the empress's hands. Would she execute me publicly like Tali, to make a statement? Or would she lead me to the shadows and do it in secret?

The commander gave an exasperated sigh and nodded. Each soldier took an elbow and guided me through the chaos of prisoners and soldiers, monitors and gate security guards.

The gate looked like rod iron, but I could tell by a soft buzz that it was electrified. It opened automatically when we reached it, swinging outward, and I gazed up at the palace. Such a beautiful building to be at the center of so much strife. Hundreds of lights shone on its surface, which gave off a strange orange hue.

"Should've known it would be you," the empress said. It took a second to see her through the shadows, but there she was, leaning casually against the guard post. "I could sense a certain rebellion in you, a stubbornness, on that day we met. Although I never thought your treason was quite this … extreme."

"Forgive me for not dying," I spat. "I'm sure three failed murder attempts can get pretty inconvenient."

"Higher positions require tougher choices, and that's something you'll never understand."

"Because you'll finish the job yourself?"

"Not necessarily." She motioned for someone to join her. Two bulky guards stepped forward, supporting someone between them. The figure was incredibly skinny and shook as if barely able to stand. A gray sack covered the face and neck. The empress put one manicured hand on the person's shoulder. "There's something I want you to do, and this prisoner is why you're about to cooperate." She whipped off the sack. The prisoner blinked at the sudden light.

I felt my knees buckle as I stood there, gaping. Her body was broken and shaky, her head bald, and her face bruised almost beyond recognition. She looked exhausted, scarcely able to hold herself up. But I'd know my friend anywhere. "Tali?"

"Hi, Treen," her hollow voice said.

This wasn't happening. I'd watched her die that night, and then dozens of times afterward in my dreams—stumbling forward, glaring at the camera, the fire of rebellion in her eyes. There was only a spark of it now, but it was there. She could hardly hold her head up to meet my gaze.

Of course. The Raters knew everything, so they would know Taliyah was my best friend. The empress had turned down the intensity of Tali's punishment a bit, allowed her to suffer nearly to death, then stopped punishment mode when she'd blacked out. It did explain how she'd lasted longer than her friends on the broadcast. But it didn't explain what the point of it all was.

"You tortured her." My voice shook with barely controlled rage.

"Insurance," the empress said. "A backup plan. I knew she may come in handy if my assassins failed."

I felt my eyes widen at her bluntness. She was surrounded by guards and didn't seem to care what they overheard. Her mouth curved into a smile. "Oh yes, they know, Ametrine. They're loyal to me. You don't think I'm the first ruler determined to secure the throne, do you? Some reports say Emperor Ashford executed sixty-one people he deemed a threat to his position."

My mind raced, processing every horrible word. How many people had this woman killed? I didn't stand a chance against such brutality. I had to buy myself some time. "There's one thing I don't understand. Why make me a red and have me killed? You could have easily given me one handicap, or even two. Nobody would have suspected a thing, and I wouldn't have been a threat."

Her lips pursed as she considered the question. "Someone I loved once betrayed me, and it made me realize how much hurting you would hurt him."

"My father."

"Jasper. At first he was just a brilliant coworker with advantageous bloodlines. I knew we could be powerful together. And we were." Her expression was strangely vulnerable, but it soon turned sour. "I thought it was real until I caught him looking at his wife's image one day. He didn't know I was there, but the look on his face was so gentle, so tender, that I knew what we had was a lie. All those years—gone in an instant."

"So you threw him in prison, then tried to destroy his daughter?"

"Being empress is a tough job, Ametrine," she snapped. "Since you'll never experience it, I'll enlighten you. Imagine dedicating your life to a group of people who admire you but then plot to overthrow you at the same time. With every bow, people scheme how to take your place. Your own friends and family members see you as competition." She was so close she looked down on me now, a towering statue of disapproval. "You can't even trust those who profess to love you. No, empress is not a title for the weak, and definitely not one for a teenage girl fresh out of Level Three school. So I'll tell you how this goes. You will announce on a national broadcast that you lied, that any claim you had to the throne was fabricated, and then accept punishment. You will also turn over any other smugglers you've been hiding."

I glanced at Tali. Her head was still down, her body tense. I knew she was hanging on every word. "You'll kill me either way, so why would I agree to that?"

"Your little friend here. She's a resilient one, but she's been through a lot the past few days. It won't take much more to break her." The empress grabbed Tali's hair, tipping her head back. Tali gasped.

It sent a painful ache through me down to my toes. She was alive, but barely. Tali was in this position because of me, and rescuing her was finally in my power. I'd wished for the opportunity to save her a hundred times. It seemed the fates had a very twisted sense of humor.

The empress held Tali in front of me like a prize, but it was about much more than threats. Giving up meant selling out the hundreds of people who had supported me, those who hoped for a better life and had made a stand. Hundreds of families waited silently in their homes tonight, waiting for fathers, mothers, sons, and daughters to come home. Those people believed that I could change their children's futures. What kind of leader would I be if I gave in so easily? Was one person's life worth the suffering of hundreds, even if it was Tali?

This was the type of decision an empress made, I realized. The worth of human life, one against hundreds, number against number. This was the very decision Vance had faced when the commander had offered him a deal—his family for his clan.

I was no better because there was no way I could turn Tali over to the empress. If it meant her safety, I'd arrest the rebels myself, one by one.

Tali's eyes met mine, narrow and determined. Her expression seemed to say, "Don't you dare."

I fingered my necklace, familiar and comforting. Purple and gold, two colors in one stone. I thought of Vance, with one foot in each world and yet living in neither. My father, Jasper, protecting his family in his own way. My mother, turning away and burying her problems. There was a time to run and a time to fight.

Tali gave an imperceptible shake of her head. I could almost hear the words in my mind.

Let me fight.

I settled my gaze on the empress. My stare seemed to unnerve her, and a flicker of uncertainty in her eyes gave me my chance. I thought of Vance and the father he'd lost. I thought of Jasper and the years this woman had taken away from us. I thought of her cold new punishment law, the poison pills, the lies and manipulation. I gathered all the anger within me at her injustices, at all the pain she'd caused, and my body began to tremble with rage.

At my expression, the empress took a step backward. I leaped and hooked her leg with mine, toppling us both. The empress lay on the ground, lips parted in a silent gasp, her dress twisted in a very unladylike fashion.

The guards were only a split second behind. One aimed his stunner at me, but Tali lowered her head and barreled toward him, hitting him right in the gut. He threw his arms around her and they tumbled to the ground together, Tali biting and kicking for all she was worth. I stepped aside just as a huge blast whipped by, and the other guard who'd tried to stun me growled. I didn't wait for him to aim again—I rolled toward the empress.

"No!" she snapped, scrambling backward to get the footing to stand, and then she winced and glanced down at her ankle. I followed Tali's lead and knocked her back down with my head.

There was a shout from somewhere and the sound of heavy footsteps headed toward us. I didn't have much time. Both guards aimed their stunners at me, and I rolled closer to the empress to discourage them from shooting. She took that opportunity to wrap both hands around my throat and situated herself above me on her knees.

"Look what you've turned me into!" she growled. "You've ruined everything."

Pain crushed my windpipe, and I saw black spots flashing across the empress's crazed expression. I had a matter of seconds left. I heard Tali grunt, and then a guard shouted something, but my mind was swimming. *Think, Treena.*

The empress's techband caught my eye, silver and glittering in jewels like her uniform. If only I could get punishment mode to work.

She leaned forward, closer, and began to whisper. "You should have taken my deal. I had a much better death planned for you, but this will do. Good-bye, child."

No. It's still time to fight.

I gathered all the strength my weakened body contained, and with a mighty heave, bucked my hips upward. It unbalanced her enough that she broke contact. Just as she sat up, I swung my legs around and kicked. My foot connected with her forehead.

A strangled scream came from the empress as her hands shot to her head, and then she started to convulse. It took a few seconds for me to realize what I'd done. The implant. It was electronically connected to her techband. The band itself didn't have punishment mode, but apparently her implant did.

The guards, who had been waiting uncertainly for a chance to attack, now watched in horror as the empress thrashed on the ground, writhing and kicking like a madwoman. Then she curled up on her side, let out a long, quiet breath, and was still.

I coughed, sucking air, and stared at the empress in horror. Her chest didn't rise.

"Hands up," the guard said with a look of fear and aimed the stunner at me. I raised my arms, too numb to fight. Tali lay on her back several meters away. I held my breath, but then she turned her head and looked at me. A tired grin spread across her battered face, and I smiled back.

It was then that the world exploded.

44

I swiped a bike and sped through the city, but I was still far away when the missile shot overhead and disappeared into the distance. The explosion rocked the ground underfoot. I could almost hear the buildings around me rattling on their foundations. The streetlights flickered and died. I swore and pedaled faster.

Before long the air was heavy with dust. If it had been daylight, the sky would probably be solid gray. A fit of coughing forced me to stop and tear part of my sleeve to use as a mask. Citizens lined the streets in their nightclothes, their faces lined with worry. They looked toward the square, as if wanting to investigate but afraid of what they would find. I tried without success to shove my way through the crowds. Finally I gave up and ditched the bike, sprinting as fast as the crowd of spectators would allow me to.

I finally rounded the corner to the square, my

lungs desperate for air. Smoke and dust rained on the still mounds of what looked like thousands of bodies of both civilians and soldiers. It was all too familiar. A gray-and-black sky, an eerie silence. My stomach lurched when I saw a woman, half her body blown away, try to push herself up with a groan. The sounds of soft moaning and sobbing filled the darkness. The only color was the red-orange flames scattered amidst the black-gray sky. Fire. It was always fire.

I was too late. If I hadn't tried to run, I could have done something.

No. If I hadn't run, I'd be one of these dead bodies. At least now I had a chance to look for Treena. I tried to force myself forward, but my feet seemed cemented in place. There probably wasn't much left of her. Maybe it was better not to know, not to add her to the charred bodies that haunted my dreams.

"Help me," a teenage boy mumbled and reached out his hand. He was pinned under a chunk of concrete, a different shade of black than the rest of the carnage around us. I clasped his hand and tried to pull. It was no use. The concrete was too heavy.

I glanced around for help and noticed a group of people standing between two buildings. They seemed frozen in place.

"Hey!" I shouted to them, then tore the cloth off my face. "Come help me!"

A man stepped out, and then two women. They took notice of the injured boy and trotted over. I waved to the rest of the group, but they hesitated before following. As they emerged, the group surveyed the damage, their faces registering a range of shock and horror. Some turned and hurried away. Others sank to their knees, their fists grasping shards of glass and dusty broken pieces of metal and rock.

The man reached me, shadows from the firelight flickering across his face, and I realized who it was. Anton. The women didn't look familiar, but a few of the others did. The remnants of my clan were here, alive. A wave of relief swept over me.

"You take that side," I told them and motioned to the concrete slab. "On three."

We counted and gave a mighty heave. The cement didn't lift at first, but with enough pressure to the corner, it finally gave and fell to the side. Anton jumped out of the way as it crashed to the ground and cracked apart. The teenage boy moaned, and one of the women knelt to examine him.

"We need to help," I told Anton. "The city won't recover from this for a while. They probably drew in their entire monitor force, and now there's nobody left to help the survivors. They'll have to send in forces from other cities. So right now, we're it."

"Or we can run while they're distracted," Rutner's son Gavis said.

"You can," I agreed. "But you won't, will you?"

Most of them didn't look at me, but a couple of them shook their heads and picked their way through the debris, covering their noses and mouths with their hands. Soon the square began to wake up with shouts of "Over here!" and "Help me lift this!"

Anton stood with hands in his pockets, staring at the ground. "I thought you'd run, Hawking."

"I almost did. But I couldn't abandon the clan again."

"It'll take more than lifting some cement to convince them of that."

"I know. But it's a start. I need your help, Anton. Will you split the volunteers into groups? Send each group to cover a different corner of the square and work toward the middle. Move the survivors over there, by the road, so they're ready to transport when the emergency workers arrive. I'll be back in a minute." I turned and began making my way through the wreckage, half-expecting Anton to try to arrest me. Instead, he stared after me in disbelief.

It was impossible to tell who was who in the darkness. Each body was covered in gray dust and dirt broken up only by the dark blood splattered everywhere. "Treena!" I shouted, my voice echoing through the heavy air. "Can you hear me?" There was nothing but the groans of the injured, and more hands reached to me as I passed.

An elderly woman sat on an overturned piece of stone, head in her hands. "They took her through the palace gates." A fit of coughing racked her body, and she turned away.

"Thanks." I waded through the mess and past what had once been an impenetrable stone wall. The missile had struck the southwest wing of the palace, exposing several floors, which looked like my sisters' dollhouse. Thick black smoke billowed from the inside. The fire cast a menacing glow on the wreckage. Most of the damage was centered where the palace's flower garden had been, and now it was a charred, smoking crater. The rebels in the square would have been safe if not for the tall buildings that had come down around them.

I stared at the palace in dismay. They took her inside, most likely. But where? Had she made it to the other end of the building before the missile hit?

Before I made it to the main doors, a pile of bodies caught my eye. Several pairs of legs, mangled and lumped together, lay heaped up against the front wall. Through the dust, I saw the navy-blue corner of a palace guard's uniform. I rushed over and started turning over bodies. Guard. Another guard. And then there was skin and a slender leg partly covered by sequined cloth. I shoved the rest of the bodies aside, and there she was, curled up in a ball like a cat. She lay still as death, her face pale beneath the streaks of black and matted blood in her hair.

"Treena," I said quickly. "Can you hear me?" I took her hand and discovered it was still warm and soft. I felt the side of her slim neck for a pulse. Weak, but it was there. I put my ear to her mouth and felt her breath against my cheek.

"You are the luckiest girl alive," I muttered. I lifted her and cradled her head against my chest. She didn't even stir. Treena was alive, but she needed immediate medical attention. She'd get it if I had to carry her across the city to the hospital myself.

"I said I'd protect you," I told her. "I've never failed to deliver on a promise so many times in my life."

My foot caught on something and I nearly tripped. Steadying Treena in my arms, I glanced downward. It was a body covered in gray debris and twisted unnaturally. The head was bald and bloody. The face was bruised, although some of the bruises were in various stages of healing, and thick dark eyelashes framed the feminine features. She looked familiar, although I couldn't place her. The strangest thing, though, was her expression. Her lips curved upward in a peaceful smile, her eyes softly closed in death.

I made my way back through the entrance, wondering how my father had felt as he died. I had to believe he'd felt a measure of peace amidst his violent end, knowing he was protecting those he loved.

The square was filled with volunteers now. Anton had taken charge, directing groups this way and that. The area near the street was nearly full of survivors already, some sitting and others spread out across the concrete. An emergency transport pulled up, its bright lights stabbing through the gray haze. I smiled to see

Integrants and NORA citizens working together, calling out to one another and checking each body for signs of life. Reds, yellows, and greens, together as equals. Today it wasn't about the numbers or even the place we'd come from. Today, it was about people.

Maybe there was hope for us after all.

45

I was floating in the air when the chopper was hit. It burst into flame and fell past me, a burning skeleton of metal, its blades still spinning wildly. Dresden sat in the driver's seat, his body charred, his head turned toward me as the tangled mess descended around me. Vance stood in the door, the wind whipping his messy hair. He watched me, his expression sad, and I ached to pull him close and lose myself in his arms. But before I could move, he jumped. As he fell past me, arms outstretched, I felt that something was wrong. Then I saw it. He had no wing suit or chute.

I woke up screaming.

"Shh, Ametrine, it's all right," a familiar voice whispered. He put a comforting hand on my arm.

My breath came fast as I took everything in. "Dad?"

"I'm here. You're safe, but you had some bleeding on your brain. Lie back down and take it easy."

Safe? What a strange thing to say. I was in a large, brightly lit room with white walls and bright tile floors. I racked my brain but couldn't remember much. My dad held my arm in a firm grip. He sat in a wheelchair and pain creased his eyes, but the only emotion I saw was concern.

It started to come back. The empress. Had I really killed her? It seemed surreal now, even though I hadn't meant to take her life. An explosion. Images flew rapidly through my mind now, and I winced. Tali's grim smile. I pushed it all away.

"You're up, then?" I croaked. My throat hurt like the fates.

He chuckled. "If this counts as up, then, yes. I'm more worried about you. It was a little scary there for a while."

I took a quick inventory of my body. My muscles ached, and I could feel the sting of a hundred cuts and bruises, but I could move everything with no problem. My head hurt, though, a deep and sore ache that tinged my vision. "What was the explosion?"

Dad swallowed hard, and his grip on my arm tightened. "I'm so sorry, Ametrine. I had no idea Mills would betray us. We were the best of friends once, and I assumed we could trust him, but it seems he had another agenda in mind. He ordered you to draw out the empress, then tried to blast you all to the fates. Maybe he thought destroying the entire government and its successor would bring NORA to its knees." His face darkened. "Except that he murdered hundreds of people in the process. He played us all for fools."

Hundreds. All those people, mothers and fathers, sons and daughters, who had entrusted their lives and their futures to me. Gone in a second. If the empress hadn't drawn me away from the group, I would have died with them. It would've been fitting. Instead, they were dead and I was still alive. I thought back to that awful confrontation with the empress. "Wait. What about Tali, my friend? Is she here too?"

He hesitated, then slowly shook his head.

Pain gripped my heart like a hand squeezing it. My best friend was gone once again, and this time she wasn't coming back. I remembered the intensity of her gaze, the communication that had passed between us. The smile that said we'd done the right thing. At least she'd died on her own terms this time.

She'd definitely gone out fighting.

"Have you seen Vance?" I asked quietly. "He was supposed to back us up with his clan, but I never saw any of them."

He sat back in surprise. "You don't know? I guess you wouldn't."

"Know what?"

"The Integrants arrived late and saved dozens of lives. Vance is the one who brought you to the hospital two days ago. He wouldn't leave your side until Dresden sent him away this morning. His entire clan has been officially extradited."

Each piece of information felt like an anvil to the head. I put a hand to my eyes and took a deep breath. "Extradited? You mean kicked out of the country?"

"Exactly. Although I wouldn't call say 'kicked out,' exactly. They got what they wanted."

"But you said Dresden sent him away. Isn't Dres at the academy?"

Dad's face tightened in anger. He spoke carefully. "That's something your stepdad and Dresden need to explain to you. They're on their way now."

Someone tapped on the door, firm and sharp. Dad's anger was quickly masked, and he wheeled himself backward. "Perfect timing. Come in."

The door opened to reveal a tired but smiling Dresden. His uniform looked freshly laundered, his hair immaculate. His grin revealed a row of too-white teeth.

"Hi, Dres."

"Hey, Treen. You look great."

"You look awful," I said. He grinned wider and hurried across the room to take Dad's place at my side. I caught a whiff of clean soap smell.

"That's so much better," he said, brushing his fingers against my forehead.

I recoiled from his touch. "What are you doing?"

"979," Dresden said. "It switched over this morning, while you were still out. I can't begin to tell you how much better you look now. It finally reflects who you are."

I reached up to my forehead, feeling the slight impression of the implant beneath the skin. *Who I am.* But if I didn't know that, how could the Raters? How could a computer network know who I was, even? What kind of girl would blindly obey the laws, then organize a rebellion against the palace? Which girl was it that kissed Dresden, then turned around and kissed Vance? I lived in two different worlds, with two different guys, and now I didn't know where I was anymore. "I don't want to be Rated, Dres."

He blinked. "What?"

"I'm serious. I don't want to be a green or a red or a walking number. I just want people to look at me and see *me*." Like Vance did. Like the Integrants did. "And I want others to have the same right."

"Unfortunately," Konnor said from the doorway, "the Standards don't allow for exceptions, even at the top. Especially there." He wore the uniform of a councilman, deep silver with six stripes on the arm. His nose was bandaged in heavy white gauze and tape, his face littered with red cuts.

"You were at the square," I said.

"Of course. I had just been appointed to the Council. We were celebrating my appointment when you pulled your little stunt." His eyes darkened, and I felt a chill. "None of us suffered more than a broken bone. Once the bomb hit, however, the guards took us into hiding for our safety."

I stared at him. A flicker of doubt crossed his

expression, but he hid it quickly behind a composed smile. He was lying. He had known I was in danger, and he'd chosen to hide.

"So I'm empress, then?" I asked. "Because I have some serious changes to make, and there's no time to lose."

The room went silent. Dad, who still sat in his wheelchair, could have bored a hole in my stepfather with his accusing gaze. Konnor and Dresden exchanged looks, and I could tell they were debating who should speak next. Dresden cleared his throat and stepped closer to me, taking my hand. "Treen, your dad—I mean, your stepdad—signed away your right to the throne."

"What?" I jerked my hand away.

"You were in a coma," Konnor said. "We didn't know if you'd ever wake up, and the nation needed a leader. And we all know that politics aren't your thing anyway."

I stared at Konnor, dumbfounded. It was as if he were dangling me over the edge of the tower all over again. No, more like he'd shoved me off. My stomach rushed upward, and I tasted bile.

"Mr. Dowell did what was best for you, your family, and the country," Dresden continued, only half talking to me now. "He convinced the Council to appoint me in your place, Treen. I'm honored that he would choose me."

"Your boyfriend is number four, technically,"

Konnor said, "but the other two ahead of him are on the verge of retirement anyway. It didn't take much for the Council to approve. He's an announcer and a social icon, so everyone is familiar with him already. He's young enough to learn. And he has the Council to guide him in the right direction, of course."

There wasn't enough air in the entire room. It was as if the weight of their words pushed down on my chest, heavy and foreboding.

"This way," Dresden said, "you can move into the palace with me when it's finished. The smoke and fire damage was too bad to salvage much, so I'm making it bigger and fancier than ever before. Our union will strengthen the throne, Treena. We'll be the most powerful couple NORA's ever seen."

I searched Dresden's face. He eyed my Rating again, his smile too controlled. Would he ever look into my eyes again without seeing my number? Could we ever be like before as long as my Rating was higher than his?

I knew the answer. I'd known it for a long time now. Being with Dresden, even in a palace, would be like living in a dark, damp prison after I'd experienced flying.

Lanah stepped into the room and gave me a soft smile. When Konnor frowned at her entrance, her gaze shifted to the floor. He'd probably told her to wait outside until he sent for her. They wouldn't want her in the room while they broke the news to me, of course. Jasper glanced from her to Konnor, and then back again, his expression closed.

"Say something, Treena," Dresden said. He was all confidence in front of my parents, but I knew he wouldn't leave until the biggest threat to his sovereignty was quashed. If I challenged Dresden's authority, it would be me against NORA. I couldn't do that again. I didn't want to do it again.

"You're exactly what the citizens would expect," I finally said.

Dresden's shoulders visibly relaxed. "I'm glad you feel that way. I'll let you rest now. They're converting a section of the Council Building to an apartment, so I'm going to oversee the preparations. That's where we'll live until the palace is rebuilt." He squeezed my shoulder. "Then there's the war council, and a million other things to do today."

"Wait. War council?"

"Of course." Dresden shrugged. "After that attack on the palace? You didn't think we'd let that slide, did you? As of today, Integrants are considered the enemy. Any of them caught inside our borders will be shot. The empress shouldn't have allowed them to set foot here in the first place."

"But—but it wasn't the Integrants who attacked!"

"To the people it was, Treen. It's easier to peg something like this on a group than an individual. That way, if you never find that one person, someone still pays the price. I'm just doing what my people demand. As of today, we're at war with those who live outside our borders, since it's clear now that we can't coexist." He lifted my hand to his lips and gave it a peck, as if we'd been discussing or haircuts or shoe brands. "Get better soon."

"Take care, Treena," Konnor said with a smirk as he turned to follow Dresden. He'd never called me by my nickname before. Maybe he felt he could be nice now that he'd taken everything possible from me.

"Be alert," Dresden said quietly to someone just outside the door. "And ask your boss why her techband hasn't arrived yet. There's no excuse for this kind of delay." His footsteps disappeared down the hall.

A guard. Of course. Dresden had probably insisted on that, since it wouldn't do to lose his greatest claim to power. He'd keep me rigidly within reach yet far enough away that he got the glory and made the decisions. He'd never agree to change the system that had gotten him there. He probably hadn't even stolen the camera, I realized bitterly. He'd probably hired someone to take the risk for him, knowing all the while that he could step in as the hero when the time was right.

"Love you, sweetheart," Lanah said, and then her gaze fell on Jasper. Her eyes went wide in surprise. He sat rigidly in his wheelchair, looking very much like a guilty child. The blood drained from her face, and she staggered out the door. Jasper stared at the empty doorway.

"She wasn't expecting to see you," I said.

"Obviously."

"I want to be alone now."

He sighed and turned his attention back to me. "I'm sorry about the way this turned out. It's not the way I wanted it either. After all we've done, all the sacrifices we've made—well, let me just say that I hope you can forgive me someday. I used you every bit as much as Mills did, and I had no right. For what it's worth, you would have made a fantastic empress."

"Thanks, but please go. I need some time."

He hesitated, then wheeled himself out. "She's sleeping now," he said to the guard. "Make sure she's not disturbed." The door closed.

I forced myself to sit up, and the headache returned full force. Sleep was the last thing I wanted right now. A neatly folded uniform sat on the side table. I unfolded it, noting the silver bands on both arms. What rank that was, I had no idea.

A strange weight toppled out onto the sheet. Curious, I dropped the uniform and felt around. My fingers closed on a cold, round object. My stone. The silver thread was gone, but I'd know it anywhere. Part purple, part gold. Tiny specks from within reflected against the light. Purple for NORA, but gold for something else. *Someone else.*

Suddenly I knew exactly who had placed it here and why.

I dressed quickly. The door wasn't an option. I put

Rebecca Rode

the stone in my pocket and lifted the window open slowly. Warm outside air brushed my hair aside, and the window made a tiny squeak. I watched the door, but the guard didn't rush in. Taking a deep breath, I put my head out the window and looked downward. My room was seven or eight stories up, and the evening shadows now darkened the empty street below. To my right, only two meters away, was a fire escape. I wanted to laugh with relief.

Placing one leg over the windowsill, I eased myself out and sat on the edge. The city spread out before me like a blanket of buildings, all painted a soft orange by the afternoon sunlight. It was nearly the same sight I'd seen at the top of the tower all those years ago. Fortunately, I was a very different person now.

There was only one place to go now. It would be a difficult and dangerous journey, but it was where I belonged.

"I'm coming, Vance," I said, and took a leap toward the brightness of the sun.

46

I met my captors just past the wall.

Supposedly my mom and sisters were waiting at the largest of the potential settlement locations, a hidden meadow near Millennium Peak, with a creek and dark, rich soil for crops. It meant food and water, but if they thought they were safe there, they'd be disappointed. I knew better than anyone how easily NORA could find us if they ever decided to. And I wasn't entirely convinced they wouldn't. Either way, it was time to fulfill the second part of my bargain.

Anton had weaseled his way into the role of enforcer again. It was as if the missile attack had never happened. He sat casually on a rock, surrounded by ten thugs. They had thick facial hair, most caked with years' worth of dirt and grime. The men stood as I approached, their backs loaded heavily with travel gear. A couple of them shot murderous looks in my direction.

"You actually came," Anton said.

I shrugged. "Where would I go?"

"Back to your girlfriend. Or did you dump her because she lost the throne? Well, you're here, so put your arms up."

I resisted the urge to punch him in the nose and raised my hands. Four of the men aimed their stunners at my chest.

Anton stepped forward and cuffed my hands in front of me. Since I had no techband, these were simple chain cuffs, thin but sufficiently sturdy. It wouldn't take long to get out of them. If necessary.

"His rights," one of the men muttered. "Ain't we supposed to arrest him proper-like?"

Another man spat, leaving a trickle of wetness on his gray beard. "Nah, he knows plenty about that. He's arrested hundreds of innocent people, my wife and son among them."

"Vance Hawking has no rights," Anton announced, his voice cold. "He's a traitor and a spy, and he can't be trusted, no matter what he pretends. He'll answer for his crimes as soon as we get back." He yanked on my bonds, making me stumble. I'd been wrong about the cuffs. They didn't use an electric punishment, but they'd been sharpened on the inside so that the metal bit into my wrists whenever I pulled against them. I took a reluctant step forward, and Anton grinned. "See? Good little pup. Maybe we'll make something decent out of you yet."

The group turned to leave, and I allowed myself one last look at the border wall, the sunlight reflecting almost painfully off its metal surface. A few concrete and steel buildings peered over it, and the sound of bicycle traffic hummed from the other side. If it weren't for Anton's group, I would have enjoyed the solitude of nine days' travel before seeing another person. It seemed my last days of freedom had been taken from me, along with everything else that mattered.

I pushed away the thought that followed. Treena had her boyfriend, her Rating, and everything she'd ever wanted. My family was safe, my clan was gathering again, and they'd choose a new leader to protect them and decide my fate. Soon everything would be as it should.

"Your girlfriend was a pretty one," Anton said. "If she wasn't already taken, I might take a crack at her myself." He yanked sharply on the chain. The metal bit into my wrists and I stumbled to my knees, ignoring the cold laughter of my escorts. With a growl, I jumped quickly to my feet and straightened to face Anton. His eyes widened slightly. After a moment he swallowed hard and looked away, keeping the chain slack this time. "All right, then. Time to go."

The men shuffled away, giving me plenty of space to walk in the center. I had nine days of travel to plan my defense, to explain why I'd sacrificed their families for my own. Nine days of Anton's comments and traveling and forcing Treena out of my head for good. Nine days of climbing ever higher, watching the trees close in and wondering whether I faced mercy or justice. I would kneel for now.

But whatever my fate, they would not see me kneel long.

I was a Hawking.

ACKNOWLEDGMENTS

Call me strange, but I always enjoy reading the Acknowledgments section of books. It's amazing many people are involved in the birth of a good story. Now that I'm on the other side of the page, I'd be ungrateful not to shine the spotlight on the amazing friends, family, and professionals who helped *Numbers Game* see the light.

I had many victims—er, volunteers—who stepped forward to beta read over the three years (and six drafts) it took to get this book finished. I'd like to thank Ashlei King, Geneen Jacobson, Sally Johnson, Melanie Auman, Randy Roberts (of YouTube fame), Kristina Roberts, the ever-encouraging Brad and Gayle Myler, and Scott and Lisa McDougle, who refused to let me set it away for long.

It's an honor to be a member of two critique groups, and it's an even greater honor that they tolerated my pleas for readings (sometimes multiple times) and yet still like me. At least, they haven't kicked me out yet. These wonderful professionals and friends include Adrienne Monson, Karyn Patterson, Ruth Craddock, Mary King, Karen Pellett, Rachelle Monson, Jen

Greyson, Kara Bosshardt, and the talented Roxy Haynie, whose beautiful writing style I will always covet. I'd also like to thank the lovely Cindy Hogan, whose expert advice will always be cherished, as well as Cindy Anderson and Susan Tietjen. Special thanks to Angela Woiwode, who gave me no less than fifteen manuscript pages of advice at one point. (It took a year and several tissue boxes, but I finally finished her revisions and it was a much stronger story. Thanks, Angela!)

I'm also grateful for my fabulous cover designer, Clarissa Yeo of Yocla Designs, and for the chapter graphics by my talented cousin, Corey Egbert. A big thank-you to Cindy C. Bennett for her beautiful formatting and her patience with my tricky ideas and timeline, as well as to Eschler Editing. Heidi Brockbank and Sabine Berlin tore the story apart and showed me how to put it back together, and I'm so glad they did. And finally, thanks to my Facebook pals, iWriteNetwork, Author's Think Tank, and Master Koda for being my sounding board on cover designs, formatters and a dozen other things. We live in an amazing age where help is just seconds away, and at the very least, it's good to know I'm not alone.

And finally, a giant hug to my family members for their unwavering support and love, and especially to my husband and children, who took Mac n' Cheese, hundreds of "Just a minute" replies, and endless hours of post-dinner Netflix in stride. You are everything to me.

ABOUT THE AUTHOR

REBECCA RODE is an award-winning author, journalist, and mother of four. She is the author of the inspirational book, *How to Have Peace When You're Falling to Pieces*, and writes for Deseret News, KSL.com, FamilyShare, and Provo Daily Herald. However, her true love is writing for teenagers. She enjoys traveling, reading, and martial arts, and she has a ridiculous addiction to chocolate-banana shakes. Learn more at www.AuthorRebeccaRode.com.

Find her online!
www.facebook.com/AuthorRebeccaRode
Twitter: @RebeccaRode

Get free stuff and find out first about Rebecca's hot new releases! Sign up at http://eepurl.com/bdwUKL or visit www.AuthorRebeccaRode.com.

If you enjoyed *Numbers Game*, please leave a quick review. It only takes a minute, and reviews are very helpful in spreading the word. Thank you!

DISCUSSION QUESTIONS FOR NUMBERS GAME

1. In NORA, a person's Rating is based on appearance, athleticism, intelligence, social class, and obedience. Do you feel that these are accurate indicators of a person's worth? Why or why not?

2. When NORA citizens look at each other, they immediately focus on the number they see. Do you believe we tend to label people by the same standards today? Why or why not?

3. Lanah tells Treena that there's a time to run and a time to fight. Have you ever run from a problem and wish you hadn't? What should you have done instead?

4. Treena thinks she knows what she wants in a guy, but meeting Vance changes her mind. Why? What qualities does he have that are not recognized by NORA Raters?

5. There are several instances where a character

must decide between family and loyalty to a group, such as clan or country. Have you ever been faced with such a choice? If not, what do you think you would choose?

6. The empress, Vallorah, will do anything to keep her position and status. Has she always been that way, or does she change over time? Why?

7. Treena believes that Jasper left to protect her and her mother. Do you believe it? Why or why not? Do you think he was successful in keeping his family safe from the empress?

8. Tali says she wants to go down fighting. Is there a cause you would give your life for? Why or why not?

9. Treena has a fear of falling because of a traumatic experience in her childhood. Does she overcome this? Why or why not?

10. Treena is given a stone that she wears as a necklace. What does it represent to her at first? How does the symbol change over time?

11. Vance associates fire with painful memories. How is fire symbolic in his life? Do you have an object, smell, taste, or sight that reminds you of a painful memory? A happy memory?

12. Treena and Vance both want something completely different in the beginning than

they want at the end. What makes that change? How have your dreams changed since you were a child?

13.   The number two appears often in Numbers Game—the story is told by two characters who are torn between two worlds. Can you think of other instances where the number two comes up? What does this number symbolize, and why is it significant?

Rebecca Rode is available for school visits and book club discussions. Email her at AuthorRebeccaRode@gmail.com for more information.

Check out Rebecca Rode's
inspirational book for mothers

What's the hardest part about being a mother? Almost every woman will say the same thing—stress. *How to Have Peace When You're Falling to Pieces* examines a mother's life from a new perspective and helps scattered moms to love motherhood again.

With humor, wit, and helpful insights, award-winning author Rebecca Rode brings a fresh perspective on the demands of everyday moms. Filled with uplifting stories, poems, quotes, and scriptures, *How to Have Peace* explores seven aspects of motherhood and teaches you how to find peace in the turmoil. The quick-fix wisdom in this helpful mother's guide will have even the busiest moms feeling peaceful in no time.

"A charming book full of wit, humor, and great ideas to help readers enjoy and renew their dedication and commitment as mothers."
–Sandra Covey, wife of the late Stephen R. Covey,
Seven Habits of Highly Effective Families